PRAISE FOR DEBRA WEBB

Gone Too Far

"An intriguing, fast-paced combination of police procedural and thriller."

—*Kirkus Reviews*

"Those who like a lot of family drama in their police procedurals will be satisfied."

—*Publishers Weekly*

Trust No One

"*Trust No One* is Debra Webb at her finest. Political intrigue and dark family secrets will keep readers feverishly turning pages to uncover all the twists in this stunning thriller."

—Melinda Leigh, #1 *Wall Street Journal* bestselling author of *Cross Her Heart*

"A wild, twisting crime thriller filled with secrets, betrayals, and complex characters that will keep you up until you reach the last darkly satisfying page. A five-star beginning to Debra Webb's explosive series!"

—Allison Brennan, *New York Times* bestselling author

"Debra Webb once again delivers with *Trust No One*, a twisty and gritty page-turning procedural with a cast of complex characters and a compelling cop heroine in Detective Kerri Devlin. I look forward to seeing more of Detectives Devlin and Falco."

—Loreth Anne White, *Washington Post* bestselling author of *In the Deep*

"*Trust No One* is a gritty and exciting ride. Webb skillfully weaves together a mystery filled with twists and turns. I was riveted as each layer of the past peeled away, revealing dark secrets. An intriguing cast of complicated characters, led by the compelling Detective Kerri Devlin, had me holding my breath until the last page."

—Brianna Labuskes, *Washington Post* bestselling author of *Girls of Glass*

"Debra Webb's name says it all."

—Karen Rose, *New York Times* bestselling author

CAN'T
GO
BACK

OTHER TITLES BY DEBRA WEBB

Gone Too Far

Trust No One

CAN'T GO BACK

DEBRA WEBB

THOMAS & MERCER

Published by Thomas & Mercer, Seattle

www.apub.com

Amazon, the Amazon logo, and Thomas & Mercer are trademarks of Amazon.com, Inc., or its affiliates.

ISBN-13: 9781542032315
ISBN-10: 1542032318

Cover design by Shasti O'Leary Soudant

Printed in the United States of America

My grandmother on my mother's side was one of the most patient and most resilient women I have ever known. There was a strength about her that wasn't readily visible, but strong she was. She never owned a television, and there were no toys or books at her house, but I loved going to visit her as a child. Mary B. Proctor was an incredible storyteller. How could I not be a writer with her as my inspiration? Though she has been gone for decades now, my memories of her and her stories are as vivid as ever. This one is for you, Mamaw. Love and kisses!

There are no facts, only interpretations.
—Friedrich Nietzsche

1

The Day Before

Sunday, November 21

11:45 p.m.

Boothe Residence
Chablis Way
Birmingham

There were words that could not be unsaid.

Actions that could not be undone.

The harsh glare of the present was never a good place for the well-hidden secrets of the past.

All those things were known, understood . . . committed to memory. And still things never changed.

To prompt change, an impetus was required.

Flashes of light slashed across the dark window as the fire grew in strength, flames licking at the interior of the house. The soft roar of its fury rose and hissed in warning. Thick, choking smoke would steal into every room, seeking its victims. Each breath drawing the danger closer and deeper until it extinguished all in its path.

The appropriate next step was to disappear into the darkness. Watching only permitted a vague measure of regret for delivering the necessary impetus.

The naked fact was, this terrible thing hadn't needed to happen.

No one had had to die. The decision had always been a matter of choice.

Glass shattered. A shout pierced the night. Senses surged to a higher state of alert. Lights switched on in a neighboring home. Help would almost certainly be summoned. No doubt a team was already on the way.

Didn't matter.

The ending of this unfortunate choice had already been decided.

2

Today

Monday, November 22

6:05 a.m.

Devlin Residence
Twenty-First Avenue South
Birmingham

Cradling her mug of coffee, Kerri Devlin mentally reviewed her calendar for the next few days. It was Monday, and she had about a dozen things besides work she wanted to get done this week. Reconciling her personal life with her work as a detective in the Birmingham Police Department's Major Investigations Division was at times difficult. The holidays were no exception.

Cop life.

This holiday in particular felt a bit off even before it began. Her daughter, Tori, had left Saturday morning for New York to spend the Thanksgiving break with her father. This was the first holiday that Kerri and Tori would be apart. The divorce had changed everything, leaving their lives in emotional turmoil for far too long. It felt good to finally be able to plan their lives without battle lines being drawn. Kerri and her ex had struggled for nearly a year to find their footing in this new separate-lives territory while still sharing their precious daughter. Almost as important was finding someone other than her ex and her daughter with whom Kerri could share her innermost, utterly honest feelings about starting over. As much as she loved her family, sometimes she yearned for someone not related by blood with whom to celebrate the good and to commiserate about the bad.

Someone who got her and backed her up.

The shower shut off upstairs, making her smile. Funny, the person she'd found was the last one she had expected, and yet now she couldn't imagine her life, personal or professional, without him. She was glad he had come into her life and that he was *here*—with her.

Last night wasn't the first time fellow detective Luke Falco had stayed overnight at her house, but this was a bigger step than a mere sleepover. With Tori gone for the week, they had decided to give living together a test drive. Their personal relationship had deepened far more quickly than either of them had expected over the past six or so months, but they had so far opted to keep their off-duty relationship quiet at work. After all, they were partners on the job. When the powers that be learned of their personal relationship, their working one would have to change.

Kerri wasn't ready for such a career-altering step. Luke was a great partner.

Another smile tugged at her lips. It still felt a little off calling him by his first name. She'd called him Falco until quite recently.

They'd both crossed lines during their first case together—lines that couldn't be avoided. From that point forward they had been able to keep their personal lives and work separate. The moment they landed at a crime scene or stood before the case board in their cubicle, it was all about work. The investigation took priority over all else. But if

Lieutenant Dontrelle Brooks learned about their developing relationship, he would see things differently.

At some point they would need to fess up.

Kerri marveled at how quickly time slipped away. It seemed impossible that a mere year and a half ago Luke Falco had been assigned as her new partner. She had been certain it would never work. He was too unconventional . . . too cocky . . . too *everything*. But he was a damned good detective and the best friend she'd ever had. Equally important, her daughter adored him.

Forever wasn't on the table just now, but the foreseeable future was a definite go.

On the counter her cell phone vibrated. She set her mug aside and reached for it. *Chief* flashed on the screen. Anticipation seeped into her blood, and a frown marred her brow as she accepted the call. Receiving a call directly from the chief of police was hardly routine. Her first thought was that Lieutenant Brooks might have been in an accident of some sort or might be ill. Though they butted heads often enough, she respected and admired the LT.

"Detective Devlin," she said in greeting, though the chief was no doubt aware of exactly whom he had called. And no matter that Kerri had no clue why he was calling, she instinctively understood that his call would unquestionably change the course of her day. Luke's too.

"Devlin." The chief hesitated, took a breath. "Whatever case you and Falco are working at present, I need you to pass it off. I want both of you on a new homicide investigation. In fact, I would have preferred to have you here an hour ago."

Here? Why was the chief at a crime scene before the rollout of detectives?

He provided an address on Chablis Way in Birmingham's Wine Ridge community. His voice was unnaturally strained, raspy. She couldn't recall ever having heard Birmingham's top cop sound so . . .

overwhelmed, exhausted. Maybe both. Another surge of anticipation trickled into her veins.

"I'll notify Detective Falco," Kerri assured him, "and we'll head that way now, sir."

The call ended without additional discussion or even an acknowledgment of her response, much less a goodbye. She tucked her cell into her back pocket and picked through the cabinets in search of to-go mugs. When she'd found the insulated ones she wanted, she poured the coffee. She and Luke could grab breakfast later.

On cue, the man himself swaggered into the kitchen. Despite the uneasiness sparked by the chief's call, Kerri had to smile. He was dressed in worn-out jeans and a button-down cotton shirt that matched the blue of his eyes. His equally shabby leather bomber jacket waited on a hook near the door. Once he pulled it on, the classic Falco look would be complete.

Luke Falco's shaggy brown hair and ever-present five-o'clock shadow definitely set him apart from the other detectives in Birmingham's Major Investigations Division. In fact, he looked far more like an undercover narcotics detective—which he used to be. Then there was the way he carried himself and even the way he talked. He was brash, irreverent, and all too often as cocky as hell.

And she wouldn't change a thing about him.

She pitched him the keys to his sporty Dodge Charger and then passed him one of the two mugs she had prepared. "Good morning, partner. We'll have to finish up our reports on the Atkins case later."

One eyebrow raised above the other, he hummed a note of question. "Oh yeah?"

"Yeah. We have a command performance with the chief at a homicide scene in the Wine Ridge community. I don't have any details, but he sounded . . ." She considered the best way to describe what she'd heard in the chief's voice. "Distressed."

Luke's chin came up in one of those male nods that weren't really nods, just subtle gestures of acknowledgment. He knocked back a slug of coffee and announced, "What's a Monday morning without a homicide?"

Truer words had never been spoken.

Kerri grabbed her own mug and wondered how many of her plans for the week would go by the wayside. Thanksgiving at her sister's might end up a no-go as well.

Murder had a way of thrusting all else to the back burner.

———

Boothe Residence
Chablis Way
Birmingham, 7:30 a.m.

The Wine Ridge community of Birmingham was made up of older, lower-priced *Brady Bunch*–style homes, many of which were surprisingly well maintained. The neighborhood was quieter than most, pet and walking friendly. Not much in the way of criminal activity happened in the area. No matter—the address on Chablis Way was hopping with official activity. Fire department ladder trucks and two police cruisers dominated the street in front of the home. A fire had occurred, but that aspect of the situation appeared to be well under control at this point. The home's roof looked to be intact, as did the siding, which was wood or something on that order atop partial brick. The backyard was heavily wooded. It was a miracle all the fallen leaves hadn't provided a path for the fire into those woods and across neighboring property lines.

Two more police cruisers monitored the street on either side of the scene, holding back any traffic that might attempt a drive-by. Luke held his badge up to a uniformed officer as they rolled past the blockade. The home's yard had been cordoned off with yellow tape, designating the area as a crime scene. The department's crime scene unit had arrived, but the two techs lingered around their van. Kerri decided the fire department hadn't turned over control of the scene just yet, or the scene was not safe for the techs to enter.

Beyond the collage of official vehicles, Luke pulled to the curb. He downed one last slug of his coffee and placed the mug in the console cup holder before reaching for the door. "Looks like the gang's all here."

From this vantage point Kerri spotted a swing set in the backyard, tightening another knot in her gut. She steeled herself for the possibility that one or more children had been lost to whatever had happened inside the house. Damn. As Kerri emerged from the Charger, the cold morning air heavy with the acrid smell of smoke and charred wood filled her lungs. She clenched her jaw and started toward the yellow tape hanging in the unseasonably chilly air.

The Major Investigations Division typically focused on high-profile homicides that clearly crossed the usual jurisdictional lines. Since the chief hadn't given Kerri the reason she and Luke had been called out, she had done some research into the address on the drive over. The property was listed to a Jana and Raymond Scott. Raymond Scott was the former assistant chief of the department's administrative bureau. He'd died of a sudden heart attack last year. The wife, Jana, also had another address, which led Kerri to believe this house might be a rental property. It was possible the connection between the property and the late assistant chief was the reason MID had been called to the scene, but it didn't seem particularly likely. Luke had agreed with her conclusion.

Whatever the case, they would know soon enough.

"Whoever started the fire," Kerri said as she ducked under the crime scene tape, "must have left a clear message that it wasn't an accident."

"Seems a little early to say so otherwise," Luke agreed as he followed the path she had taken.

In a fire involving a house or other type of structure, the first responders to the scene had the enormous task of determining if anyone was inside and getting them out while simultaneously working to control the fire. Victims and bodies were removed as quickly as possible, but the investigation for the cause of the fire was generally not tackled until after the flames were extinguished and the structure—or what was left of it—had been deemed safe to enter for further analysis. Kerri couldn't be sure when the fire had started, but obviously the victims or bodies had been removed already, since there were no ambulances present to transport injured victims and no sign of the Jefferson County medical examiner's personnel or the meat wagon.

When fires occurred during the overnight hours, whoever was inside seldom survived.

"There's the chief," Luke said, drawing her attention back to him.

Kerri followed his gaze, spotting the chief speaking with a member of the fire department, judging by his uniform. When the chief noticed their approach, he broke away from the other man and headed in their direction. His expression was nothing short of hollow, bleak. Had to be a strong personal connection beyond the professional one.

Chief of Police Patrick Dubose was in his late fifties with the white hair to prove he'd spent most of his adult life working hard and taking the necessary risks to earn the respect of the community as well as the department. Tall and fit, he was nothing less than distinguished in his bearing. Kerri had learned over the years to never doubt the man's integrity, no matter how certain aspects of a high-profile case might suggest otherwise. Though a decade as Birmingham's top cop had shifted him from detective to politician, his ability to assess people and situations remained as keen as ever.

"Detectives." He nodded at Kerri, then Luke, before his attention came back to rest fully on her. "I've spoken to Lieutenant Brooks, and he is aware that the two of you will be investigating this case. Brooks indicated your schedule is open."

They still had wrap-up reports to complete on their most recent case, and Thanksgiving was scarcely more than seventy-two hours away, but those details were irrelevant. Neither murder nor its investigation waited for holidays or the completion of paperwork. The fact that she and Luke had only just finished an investigation would generally slip them to the back of the queue, but the chief had the power to override protocol. Depending on how this investigation went down, the other detectives would be either jealous or thankful. Typically the latter.

"Yes, sir," Kerri confirmed.

Dubose glanced back at the damaged house, the grim lines around his mouth and eyes deepening. "This home belongs to a friend of mine. Her husband was my first partner when I became a detective. We had a long history together." A faint smile briefly lifted the corners of his mouth. "They asked me to be the godfather when their first and only child, a daughter—Allison—was born." His voice shook on the last.

Kerri understood then. "Is this Allison's home?"

The chief nodded. "She and her five-year-old daughter, Leah, didn't make it out of the fire. They were found in their beds." He pulled in a deep breath. "Her husband is at the hospital. His condition is guarded at the moment."

The news caused a crack in Kerri's chest. No matter how many homicide investigations she had under her belt, the ones involving children never got easier. *Never.*

"Has the fire marshal found evidence suggesting arson?" Luke asked.

Dubose stared back at the house once more. "The consensus is an accelerant was used, but we don't have more than that at this point. Based on a neighbor's statement," he went on, "the fire started before midnight. This neighbor, a Phileas Crandall, was just going to bed and noticed the flames flickering in a downstairs window. He called 911 as he rushed over to see if he could help. Allison's husband, Logan, was"—another big breath—"was found facedown in the front yard. Crandall stated that he appeared to be unconscious. When Crandall roused him, he ran into the house screaming his wife's and daughter's names. He was rescued by firefighters and taken to the hospital." Dubose took a moment to steady his voice. "At this time, we don't know why he was outside when the neighbor arrived."

"He wasn't able to communicate at all?" Kerri asked.

Dubose shook his head. "He was unconscious when he was found in the house, and the last time I checked, he has not regained consciousness. I have uniforms canvassing more of the neighbors. Hopefully someone else will have heard or seen something. If we're really lucky, maybe one or more have security cameras or at least a video doorbell."

Luke looked from Kerri to the chief. "Are you aware of any reason this family might have been targeted? Or if there were issues between the husband and his wife?"

"Boothe is a former cop." Dubose rubbed his hand over his jaw. "He spent several years working undercover narcotics before deciding he wasn't cut out for that life. About ten months ago he left the department."

"Has he been employed since?" Kerri asked. They would need to interview anyone close to him—the more recent, the better.

The chief shook his head. "Not unless he found something in the past week or so."

"Boothe," Luke repeated. "Logan Boothe?"

"That's right," the chief confirmed. "Logan Boothe, early thirties."

Kerri glanced at her partner. Luke had spent most of his early law enforcement career under deep cover with the Narcotics Division. "You know him?"

Luke nodded in answer to Kerri's question. "I knew him briefly. A few years back. We were assigned to different ops, but we shared an LT for a while."

"Then you probably know he's a bit of a hothead." The chief closed his eyes a moment. "He and Allison separated for a time before he left the department, but then Leah got sick, and they rallied together for her. The way I understand it, things have been a little rocky since."

"Allison confided these details to you?" Kerri asked.

How seriously did he take his godfather duties? Maybe more so than ever, since the woman's father had died only last year. Or had someone else passed along these details? Full disclosure—even from the chief of police—was vital.

"Her mother, Jana," Dubose explained. "We've been friends for a long time. She and my wife are very close. Jana was more than a little concerned with her son-in-law's behavior over the past few months. Allison is—was—her only child. Jana is . . ." He looked away for a moment. "She's devastated."

Kerri understood the loss all too well. Barely eighteen months had passed since she'd lost her niece. It still hurt to think about her. She couldn't even imagine losing a child.

"Is Mrs. Scott aware of Boothe's friends? Anyone who might have been privy to whatever was going on between him and his wife—from his perspective?"

"I have no idea, but I'll arrange a meeting with Jana as quickly as possible. Allison probably shared those sorts of details with her."

"The sooner we can speak with her, the better." Kerri pointed out what she felt certain the chief already understood. But he was distressed at the moment, maybe not thinking as clearly as he should be. When a case was personal, perspective was often slanted. *Been there, done that.*

"I'll call her." Dubose stared at the house for a moment. "She wanted to go to the hospital and wait for Boothe to regain consciousness, but I urged her to go home and wait for my call. There's nothing she can do at the hospital, and Boothe's mother, Rebecca, is holding vigil there."

"Is there a problem between Mrs. Scott and Mrs. Boothe?" Luke said, then shrugged. "Maybe the two don't get along."

If this was the case, the potential for an ongoing feud of some sort existed, which could provide motive. Considering the grandchild was one of the victims, the idea of the grandmothers being involved wasn't at the top of Kerri's list. Still, it was an option that had to be explored.

Dubose hesitated for a moment, then nodded. "Allison was estranged from the mother-in-law. She wouldn't allow her daughter to be around the woman at all, as far as I'm aware. Jana believes Boothe secretly took the little girl to see his mother on occasion." Dubose shook his head. "Whatever happened, Allison refused to give on the subject. Jana didn't completely agree with the decision, but she did, of course, respect her daughter's wishes."

Which also signaled to Kerri that whatever information was gleaned from Jana Scott could at the very least be prejudiced or incomplete. "Chief," Kerri said, drawing his attention back to her. "You said the little girl was ill."

He nodded. "Leukemia."

Damn. Kerri could only imagine the fear the child's parents had suffered at such a terrifying diagnosis. "We should have a look around and then speak to the neighbor, Mr. Crandall. We can meet with Mrs. Scott at whatever time is convenient for her. We'll need to interview Mrs. Boothe as well. We can try and catch her at the hospital when we check in on Boothe."

"I'll make the call." The chief frowned, reached into his pocket, and pulled out his cell to check the screen. "You learn anything, I want to know," he ordered before turning his attention to an incoming call.

Kerri and Luke moved toward the house, skirted the northern end, and headed for the backyard. Her attention settled on the swing set once more, and that crack in her chest widened a bit. Five years old. The thought made her sick to her stomach. She could not fathom what Scott—the grandmother—was going through. She'd lost her only child and her only grandchild in one fell swoop. Logan Boothe and his mother were no doubt equally devastated.

The grieving father and grandmothers would be counting on Kerri and Luke to find answers—answers that would somehow explain why this tragedy had occurred.

There wasn't always a clear-cut answer, but there would be a story. Whatever the case, it wouldn't bring back the dead. It might not even provide justice. If they were lucky, it would at least give closure.

Kerri surveyed the backyard, which looked like any other in the neighborhood. The house, from where they stood, appeared unremarkable and sedate. If not for the stench of smoke and the convergence of official vehicles, one would never know anything untoward had happened.

Except two people had died here.

In addition to the family, the chief expected Kerri and Luke to find the necessary evidence to ferret out the person or persons responsible for those deaths.

No pressure.

3

8:15 a.m.

The lingering, choking odor of smoke and toxic fumes from the fabrics and household goods that had charred beneath the flames was nearly overwhelming to Kerri. The house was a typical trilevel split. A garage and den downstairs and the main living areas on the middle level. All bedrooms were on the upper level.

Fire Marshal Dane Robinson provided the coveralls, gloves, face masks, and safety boots necessary for Kerri and Luke to enter the crime scene. The usual latex gloves and shoe covers weren't sufficient to protect the scene or the two of them. The main living area had suffered the most readily visible damage. The walls were blackened. Framed family photos had burned and shattered. Plastic decor pieces had started to drip down the walls and tables like candles left unattended too long. The fire had scorched through fabric and stuffing to the bones of upholstered metal and wood furniture pieces.

A mostly charred doll with a melted face had somehow survived total destruction. Kerri's gut tightened at the reminder that a little girl had been lost in this tragedy. She thought of her own daughter so far from home and shuddered.

"I'll take the bedrooms," Luke offered, his voice slightly muffled behind the mask.

Kerri nodded, grateful not to have to tackle the child's room. She would take staring down an armed, violent criminal three times her size any day over picking through the pieces left behind by the loss of a child. She shifted her attention to the kitchen and dining area. She opened doors and any remaining functional drawers. Picked through the contents. Most of her movements had already been made by the fire investigators, but a second look never hurt. Even a third could often uncover missed evidence.

A peek in the dishwasher revealed a few random items, including cups and glasses, but nothing else.

Kerri pushed to her feet and moved to the refrigerator. Inside were the usual suspects. Milk, eggs, et cetera. No wine or beer. The plastic trash can that had once stood at the end of the peninsula had partially dissolved into a wad over whatever it contained. The contents would need to be gone through at the lab. Room by room and item by item, she progressed through the main living space without finding anything that stood out.

Things she hadn't seen were computers, cell phones, or other electronic devices. There was a television but nothing one might use for social media or internet purposes. Maybe the victim's phone had been left in the bedroom.

These days most people had cell phones even if they avoided computers and other devices.

Luke appeared, saving her a trip upstairs to ask.

"Did you find a cell phone or computer in any of the bedrooms?" She suppressed the urge to remove her mask, flashbacks from the recent pandemic and the mandatory mask order yet another stone-cold reminder of the fragility of life.

He shook his head. "Nothing electronic except the television in the main bedroom."

Maybe the husband was the only one with a cell phone. Could have been on his person when he'd been taken to the ER. Allison's not having one was unusual.

"The killer may have taken the vic's phone." A line furrowed Kerri's brow. Obtaining the cell phone records would give them the calls and text messages sent and received. But it would take some time to get the information via that route.

Time was never an ally in cases like this one.

Luke said, "It's probably on the side of the road somewhere by now. Or in the nearest lake." He surveyed the damaged living area as he spoke.

Kerri assessed her partner. He seemed preoccupied with something more than a potentially missing cell phone.

"Anything here that doesn't look right to you?" she asked. Sometimes it was the little things nagging at you that pulled an investigation together or in a different direction.

"I'm not sure yet. Let's have a look at the lower level."

A dozen steps down led to a spacious den and another bathroom that included the laundry. Beyond that was the two-car garage. There was barely any indication of the fire here. Heat and smoke rose. The actual physical damage was primarily concentrated on the first level, but the smoke had risen to the upper-level rooms with equally deadly consequences.

Luke stood in the middle of the garage, hands on hips. "It's too clean. No overturned furniture anywhere upstairs. Nothing broken other than the few windows the firefighters most likely shattered. The scene feels more like this should have been a simple electrical fire." He shrugged. "Something unintentional . . . accidental."

"Except for the accelerant," she suggested.

"Except for that," he agreed.

How had someone entered the home, dispersed an accelerant, and then set the place on fire with the occupants inside without disturbing anyone or anything? Unless the family was either out cold or dead already?

Excluding the husband, of course. Logan Boothe had been first discovered outside the house. As a former cop he would certainly understand why he was a suspect—assuming he survived his injuries. Further, with his training and experience, he would possess the knowledge to pull off a double murder disguised as an accident.

Only, the fire marshal had confirmed the use of an as-yet-unidentified accelerant, which didn't exactly flow with the idea of making the fire look accidental. A smart or well-trained perp wouldn't be so careless.

But a desperate one might, Kerri considered. "You ready to talk to the neighbor?"

Luke surveyed the room once more. "Yeah. We can come back for another look around the house later."

The evidence techs would pick through the rubble, hopefully finding anything overlooked so far. Any evidence of the perp had likely gone up in smoke. Finding him or her would require digging deep into the lives of anyone close to the victims.

Starting with neighbors who might have seen or heard something in the hours prior to or during the fire.

As soon as they were out the front door, Kerri removed the annoying but necessary mask and drew in a deep chestful of air, expelled it, then sucked in another. Luke did the same. The air outside was still heavy with smoke but not nearly as bad as inside.

"Did you know him very well?" Kerri asked as they removed their protective gear.

Luke pulled on his trademark jacket. "Not really. He was young back then. Too young to be doing the work he was doing, in my opinion."

There was a lot Kerri didn't know about the undercover part of Luke's life. The dark years, he called them. He didn't like talking about it, and she respected his wishes. Despite how little she knew, she understood it was a truly demanding and difficult time for him. Like he said, dark. The kind of dark that forever changed a person.

"You said the two of you shared an LT. Maybe he has useful information about Boothe. We should talk to him."

Luke shrugged. "Guess so."

Her partner fixed his attention on the house next door. No matter that he didn't meet Kerri's gaze, it was more than clear he didn't want to talk about that aspect of the case. At least not yet.

As much as she regretted the idea—for his sake—at some point going down that unpleasant path would be necessary.

For now, there were plenty of other avenues to investigate.

To the north of the Boothe home was the neighbor who had first spotted the fire. Phileas Crandall. The house was from a similar era as the Boothe home and was also surrounded by large, old-growth trees. The older man had been waiting on the front porch, watching the evolving events next door. As soon as they identified themselves, he invited them into his home, away from the ongoing commotion. They settled in the living room.

Crandall looked exhausted and visibly shaken. His hair was mussed; his robe and pajamas were rumpled. An older man—seventy-four, he stated—Crandall had lived in this same house for many years. He was widowed and still struggled with living alone. Allison and her family had been like his own.

"It's just terrible," Crandall said with a shake of his head. "I can't even believe it. Allison . . ." He heaved a troubled breath. "Poor Allison and that sweet child." He pressed his hands to his face, swiped at his eyes. "It's the most horrible thing. Just think if I hadn't glanced out the window before I went to bed . . . I don't know what else might have happened. How many other lives might have been lost if the fire had spread?"

"It's good that you looked out your window," Kerri agreed. "What happened next, after you spotted the fire?"

"I called 911 as I rushed downstairs. The fire department as well as the police were here in just minutes. I've never been so thankful for our city's much-lauded rapid response time. I voted for this mayor, you know. The city appears to be faring far better since we got rid of the last one." His face crumpled again. "I just can't believe this has happened."

"Mr. Crandall," Luke said, "did something in particular wake you? A noise or maybe a shout or scream?"

Crandall opened his mouth to answer, then frowned as his lips pressed together once more. After a moment of deliberation, he said, "You know, I think there was something. I wasn't asleep, though," he clarified, "just on my way to bed. But . . ." His frown deepened.

"Take your time," Luke urged. "Think on it for as long as you need to before you answer."

Crandall squeezed his eyes shut and appeared to do just that. Finally, he blinked, then looked directly at Luke. "I believe there actually was a sound. Something loud. Not a gunshot or some form of fireworks, more like a thump or thud."

Since he didn't wear hearing aids, Kerri assumed he had no notable hearing issues. "Maybe a car door closing?" she suggested.

The driveway to the Boothe home was on this side of the property, closer to Crandall than to the other neighbor, who was actually a good distance away because of the creek that ran along that side of the property.

Crandall nodded. "Yes, yes. Exactly like that. Perhaps more like a slam. Like the door was shut with more force than necessary."

"But you're not certain," Luke reiterated.

Crandall's forehead furrowed with his effort to recall. "Well, I can't say for certain, no. But thinking back, I'm as sure as I can be."

"You went to the window," Kerri said, shifting the conversation back to the series of events he could confirm with a measure of certainty, "and looked out. Was there a reason you looked out the window?"

He nodded. "Oh yes, I always glance out the window as I'm going to bed. I suppose to make sure everything is as it should be, or maybe just out of habit." His expression clouded with sadness. "At first, I didn't notice anything out of the ordinary, but suddenly I saw a flickering in the window that faces this way. I think it's a dining room window. Anyway, I watched a moment longer just to be sure, and the flashing continued, so I called 911 as I went downstairs." He cleared his throat. "When I got outside, I could smell something burning, and I knew I was right to make that call."

"That's when you went next door," Luke offered.

"Yes. I hurried across my yard and beyond their driveway. The front door was open, and light flashed in the darkness beyond it. The house really was on fire. All I could think was that I had to get inside. I started toward the door, but before I reached it, I came upon a person lying on the ground. I knelt down and saw that it was Boothe—Logan, Allison's husband. When I rolled him onto his back, he opened his eyes. I asked him where Allison and Leah were, and he scrambled to his feet and rushed into the house. I raced after him. Got as far as the door and saw the extent of the flames. I knew better than to follow him inside." His face fell. "Perhaps I should have. I might have been able to help." He exhaled a heavy breath. "Then I heard the sirens."

When his silence went on for nearly half a minute, Kerri prompted, "The fire trucks arrived?"

He nodded. "Yes. The police arrived first. I told them Boothe had gone back into the house. One of the officers went in after him but couldn't see well enough to find him. He wasn't prepared—you know, he didn't have the necessary gear—to go any deeper into the house." Crandall shook his head. "Fortunately, the fire trucks arrived, and the first firefighter to go inside found Logan." He made a pained face, shook his head again. "He looked to be quite seriously burned. Frankly, I thought he was dead when they brought him out."

At this point, they didn't have a full accounting of Boothe's injuries, but at least he was still alive.

"Mr. Crandall, was there any indication that Boothe had been in the house before you found him?" Kerri pressed. "Were his clothes blackened, or was he already injured in some visible way?"

"I didn't notice anything like that, but honestly, it all happened so fast."

"Looking back," Kerri said, "do you think he had just arrived home? Maybe it was his vehicle door slamming that woke you." Although that scenario didn't account for Boothe being facedown on the ground.

Crandall rubbed at his forehead. "I suppose he might have just arrived home. I can't say for sure. To tell you the truth, I was in a bit of shock, I suppose. The possibility that poor Allison and her little girl were inside . . ." He shook his head. "None of it makes sense. I can't imagine why Boothe was outside. I really just don't understand how this happened. It's a tragedy." His voice broke, and he clasped his hands over his mouth.

Crandall was right about Boothe's having been outside, asleep or unconscious. It didn't quite make sense.

"Other than the police and the fire department," Luke said, "did anyone else join you in the Boothe yard?"

He was their only witness so far.

Crandall allowed a few seconds to pass before he responded. "While the firefighters were inside, the neighbor directly across the street from my house, Sam Tipton, came running over to see if he could help. Others wandered out of their homes, but the police kept them at the street."

"Did anyone in the crowd stand out to you?" Luke asked. "Maybe someone you hadn't seen in the neighborhood before?"

He shook his head, his gray hair sticking up in little tufts. "I didn't notice, but as I say, I was quite unnerved by the whole thing. When the . . . bodies were brought out, I felt incredibly ill. So very sad. I just can't believe it. It's terrible. So terrible."

"Were the Boothes good neighbors?" Kerri asked. Time to start filling in the blanks about who the Boothes were from the perspective of those who lived around them. "No fighting or partying?"

"Very good neighbors," Crandall confirmed. "If there was ever a party at their home, it was extremely quiet. Likewise, if they argued, they did so quietly. Even the little girl, Leah, was a quiet child."

"Did you have a close relationship with the family?" Luke picked at a thread from that same fabric theme. "Have them to dinner or go to dinner at their home?"

Crandall had alluded to a closeness but hadn't described the relationship.

"Allison brought me a cake for my birthday each year. Not this time, though." He smiled sadly. "With all that's been going on, I wouldn't have expected her to. Before Leah got sick, she made casseroles or soup and brought them over anytime I wasn't feeling well. But you know," he added, "despite all their own problems, she and Leah still made time to come over to check on me once in a while. We even had tea parties from time to time. Leah loved tea parties." He smoothed a hand over his pajama shirt where it buttoned as if he suddenly feared he'd missed one. "When Allison's mother and father lived next door, we dined together quite regularly. We've been friends for a long time, the Scotts and I. I've lived here for twenty years. I watched Allison grow up."

"Would you say you were equally close to Logan as well?" Kerri prompted.

"Not really. He worked strange hours. They moved in to the house two years ago. Jana, Allison's mother, had been renting the place since she and Ray moved to the lake. She mentioned that Allison and Logan were having a hard time making ends meet and she'd offered them the house in an effort to help." His eyebrows reared up. "I did get the impression that Logan wasn't so happy about the arrangement, but he never said any such thing to me. It was more my opinion than anything he said or did." He shook his head. "I'm certain he must be just devastated. Poor Jana. I can't even imagine how she feels."

Kerri pulled a business card from her jacket pocket and passed it to him. "Please call if you think of anything else that might be helpful to our investigation. Anything at all. For the family's sake, we would like to close this case as quickly as possible."

He nodded. "Of course. I want to help in any way I can."

Kerri stood, and her partner did the same. "Thank you, Mr. Crandall," Luke said. "We appreciate your time."

Outside, as they walked back to the Boothe property, Luke hesitated. "We need to talk to Boothe. Sounds like he might be the only person who knows what really happened inside that house."

"*If* he regains consciousness." This was the sticking point Kerri had with the statement Crandall had given. Boothe had been outside. Why hadn't he been in the house with his family? If he'd just come home, where had he gone at that hour? Had he finally found employment? And how had he ended up on the ground, seemingly unconscious?

"Until then," Luke agreed, "we should find out what Jana Scott thinks about her son-in-law."

"She'll be biased toward her daughter," Kerri countered. "The mere fact that he survived and her daughter didn't will make him a suspect in her mind." It certainly did in Kerri's.

Luke met her gaze. "He's the only one we've got for now."

"This is true," she admitted. "I'll check in with the chief and see if he was able to arrange a meeting with Mrs. Scott."

She started toward the huddle near the front door of the Boothe home but paused and glanced back at her partner. "Maybe you can check in with the LT you and Boothe had in common. See what he recalls about Boothe."

It was a perfectly logical step. But the look on Luke's face told her it wasn't something he looked forward to.

At all.

"I'll see if the Tipton guy is at home first," he said, hitching his thumb toward the house across the street. "I'll catch up with you after that."

Kerri watched him go. She wished there were something she could say to convince him that whatever was in the past was never going to change what she felt for him.

Maybe showing him would carry more weight.

4

11:00 a.m.

Scott Residence
River Woods Road
Hoover

Kerri was impressed with the Scott home. Though the house was perched on a rise above Lake Wilborn and was as gorgeous as any of its neighbors, inside the home was comfortable and far more relaxed than she would have expected. There was a peacefulness about it that went well beyond the serene lake view outside the broad windows. But no amount of beauty and serenity could soften the devastation visible on Jana Scott's face and in her every action.

Scott explained that she and her husband, Raymond, had bought their new home after their daughter, Allison, had gone away to college. Their first and only child was born when they were in their forties, so retirement was just around the corner by the time Allison graduated. The plan was that Allison would become a nurse, and when they were old and needy, she would be there for them, unconditionally. There would be no nursing home or assisted-living facility for the Scotts.

Except that hadn't happened.

Allison had been scarcely halfway through the nursing program when she'd met Logan Boothe, and everything had changed.

Scott sighed. "He became her entire focus. School, the career she'd planned—she couldn't see any of it after she met him. Her every waking moment was about their relationship. She was only twenty. We—my husband and I—tried to slow her down, to persuade her to step back and take a moment to catch her breath before rushing into marriage. When they announced they'd gone to the courthouse and done exactly that, I was immensely disappointed. She was my only daughter. I had planned her wedding since the day she was born. But I put the hurt and the regret behind me and focused on the future. I didn't want to lose my daughter because she didn't choose the life I had planned for her."

Scott's eyes and face were red and puffy from hours of crying. Each time she thought she had cried herself out, she had explained, more tears rose and flowed. She looked exhausted and frail. She was sixty-eight and thin. Her pale skin sank against her bones as if all beneath it had suddenly seeped out of her. Her husband was gone, and now she'd lost her only child and granddaughter. Devastation exuded from her every beleaguered breath.

"Did you and your husband have particular reservations about Boothe," Kerri asked, "or was your concern primarily about how quickly their relationship was moving?"

"My husband was very concerned about Logan's work." She pressed her hand to her chest. "Don't get me wrong: Raymond spent his entire adult life as a cop on the streets of this city before becoming a bureaucrat on the department organization chart. He understood what it took to be on the front lines. But Logan was different. Even at twenty-six he seemed fearless and perhaps lacking in mature judgment."

"You came to these conclusions in part because of the undercover narcotics work?" Luke asked.

Kerri watched him as he spoke. Her partner was well aware of the toll taken by undercover work. Like many cops, he'd been damaged by the work to some degree. Simply being a cop changed a person, but working under deep cover was a different sort of animal. Sometimes real life and the made-up one became blurred. Pulling back from the lifestyle of the cover was rarely easy and almost always dangerous.

"Yes," Scott said in answer to his question. She sighed, the effort appearing to require tremendous effort. "There were the usual problems right from the beginning, particularly those related to youth and immaturity. But the persona he adopted to do his work seemed to overlap into his personal life more and more as time went by. We worried about Allison. She lost touch with her friends. Kept to herself most of the time. When Leah came along, our worries intensified." She pressed her hand over her mouth for a moment, her eyes filling with new tears. "Allison was so thrilled. She wanted to be a mother more than anything. How could we not be happy for her? For a while, their marriage seemed to grow stronger. But I knew . . ." She cleared her throat. "I knew trouble was coming. As much joy and wonder as a child can bring, parenting also creates added pressures. Then, after the separation earlier this year, I held out little hope for the survival of their marriage."

"Did Allison share the reason for the separation with you? Any specific concerns or fears about her husband?" Kerri understood there were two things a mother would go to the ends of the earth to ensure: her child's safety and her child's happiness. Even if that child was grown.

Scott shook her head. "She only said that he had issues with his work. When they managed to pull things back together, she told me that he was willing to give up everything for her and Leah. In truth, leaving the BPD seemed to make things better for a while. I hoped it would stick. Allison talked about going back to school. I was beyond pleased." A faint smile lifted her lips. "I would keep Leah while Allison attended classes." The smile faded. "Then Leah was diagnosed, and everything . . . fell apart *again*. The financial strain on top of all the rest was more than they could bear."

"Since he'd left the department," Luke said, "there was no health insurance."

"Yes. It was a nightmare. I've drained my savings to ensure Leah received the best care possible. At this point, a mortgage on my home was going to be needed for whatever came next." Eyes shimmering with emotion, she lifted her chin. "But I was prepared to do whatever necessary. I made that very clear."

"I'm certain your support was instrumental in holding their relationship together during such a difficult time." Kerri's chest constricted at the idea of what the family had suffered.

Scott nodded, dabbed at her eyes and nose with a tissue.

"Did Logan do or say anything recently," Luke ventured, "that concerned you or Allison?"

There was a pause as the older woman considered how to answer the question. Kerri imagined that in the few short hours since losing her daughter and granddaughter, Scott had likely asked herself this very question over and over. Was there anything she might have overlooked that, in retrospect, she shouldn't have? Was there something more she could have done?

"For a while after Leah's diagnosis, they were extremely focused on her." Scott's gaze grew distant as she spoke. "I was actually a little stunned at how Logan threw himself into helping his daughter. Not that he was a bad father—just one who hadn't been there perhaps as much as he could have been. Then, a few weeks ago, something happened, and he and Allison suddenly weren't speaking. I was certain they were going to shatter completely, but then just as suddenly they seemed to rally together yet again."

She shook her head. "Really, their entire marriage had been that way—a roller coaster ride." She pressed her lips together a moment. "But this time Allison said Logan had a plan. I asked her what she meant, but she wouldn't say. She just kept telling me not to worry, that Logan was going to take care of everything. She didn't want me to take out a mortgage on the house. I tried to feel relieved, but it wasn't possible."

"You believe whatever this plan was," Kerri said, moving into more sensitive territory, "it was related to the money needed for Leah's medical care?" Logan Boothe wasn't a doctor or a miracle worker, but he might have spoken to a friend about a loan. Cops were always rallying together for fundraisers. It was possible something helpful was in the works.

Or something illegal.

"I assumed as much. I can't imagine they had anything else on their minds." Rather than look at Kerri as she spoke, Scott stared at her hands where they lay clasped in her lap.

Ten seconds turned into thirty, and Luke broke the silence. "One last question."

Scott seemed to brace herself for whatever was coming. Under the circumstances the reaction was not surprising. After a tragedy involving the loss of human life, those left behind were typically either resigned to or bracing for the dropping of the other shoe. Jana Scott was the widow of a decorated veteran cop. She was likely well versed in how these investigations were conducted. Every single thing was suspect . . . taken apart and analyzed for potential motive.

"Did your daughter have a life insurance policy? Or one on her little girl?" he asked.

"No. When a couple is so young, they don't think of these things." Her fingers twisted around each other, and once more her gaze didn't light on Luke's or Kerri's. "None of us do at that age."

"There's no chance he had a policy you don't know about?" Luke went on. "Something recent, maybe."

This time she stared at Luke for a long moment. "Are you suggesting my son-in-law murdered my daughter and granddaughter?"

Surprisingly, her tone showed no horror or shock at the idea. Then again, Kerri reminded herself, this was a woman who knew the drill.

"We have to cover all bases, ma'am," Luke said gently.

Scott seemed to pull her composure more firmly into place. "I suppose it's possible, but . . . I simply cannot believe he would do such a thing. As annoyed and disappointed as I was at Logan on so many occasions the past six years, I am certain he loved his child and my daughter."

Her voice lacked any strong conviction when she said the last. *Interesting*, Kerri decided.

"When Detective Falco and I first arrived, we touched on the idea," Kerri said, drawing the woman's attention to her, "of anyone who may have had ill feelings toward your daughter and her family. We understand there was tension between your daughter and her mother-in-law, Rebecca. Can you tell us why they were estranged?"

The older woman lowered her gaze, stared again at her entangled fingers, before meeting Kerri's eyes. "My daughter is dead. Why poke at that painful part of her life? What does it matter now?"

"Mrs. Scott," Kerri offered, "we do understand how incredibly painful this time is for you. Please know that every avenue we explore is essential to understanding why and how this tragedy happened."

Scott cleared her throat of the emotion no doubt clogged there. "Detective, I was married to a cop for forty-five years. I'm familiar with how these things go. If I thought the question was relevant, I wouldn't have hesitated a second to answer it."

Luke exchanged a glance with Kerri before saying, "We mean no disrespect, ma'am, but we're looking at this from outside the hurricane of emotions you're dealing with."

Scott closed her eyes and seemed to brace herself. "You're right. I'm sorry."

Kerri ached for her. "Take your time," she said. "I'm certain you're well aware of what we need to know."

"Logan is an only child too. I don't think Rebecca ever moved past the part where he became an adult and chose his own journey.

She wanted to make all the decisions. I think, perhaps, she was the reason he chose undercover work in the first place. He could escape his life and become someone else." She looked directly at Kerri then. "This was my husband's instinct about the situation. I agreed with him. Still do. Rebecca is a *difficult* woman. She was immensely disappointed when Logan married Allison. By the time Leah was born, my daughter couldn't tolerate her anymore. It was a painful, difficult situation, made worse by a woman who eats, sleeps, and breathes discord."

No love lost between this grandmother and the other. "Do you," Kerri began, "believe anyone in your daughter's life might have wished her or her husband harm?" In all likelihood the child was collateral damage.

"Absolutely not." Scott shook her head. "My daughter had no enemies."

"You mentioned earlier that she lost touch with her friends," Luke pointed out.

"That was because of Logan. He consumed her life for so long her friends all drifted away. I was her only real friend, I suppose."

Kerri waited for her to go on. Whatever the woman said next, it needed to come from her own feelings, with no prodding or leading.

"Logan had friends but not the sort with whom you want your daughter and granddaughter socializing. Talk to his associates. I am confident this nightmare came from someone in *his* life." A tear trailed down her pale cheek.

Kerri passed a business card across the table. "Call if you think of anything else." The lady accepted the card. "We appreciate your help, Mrs. Scott. We know this is a terrible time for you. Be assured we'll do all we can to determine how this happened and who is responsible."

Scott nodded. "When you find who did this," she said, her voice thick with emotion, "I want you to lock him away where I can't get to him."

Kerri understood. If someone harmed her own daughter, she would be the first in line to take off his head. What mother wouldn't?

When they were out the door and walking away, Luke asked, "You think she's being completely open with us?"

"For the most part." Kerri paused, her hand on the car's door handle. "After she mentioned Logan's plan for taking care of their financial situation, she avoided eye contact. It felt like she possibly regretted mentioning it. As close as she seemed to be to her daughter, why wouldn't they discuss this plan? And if they had, why wouldn't she share the details with us?"

When they'd settled into their seats and pulled on safety belts, Luke proposed, "You think the daughter told her something she doesn't want to share."

"I do." Kerri relaxed into the seat as Luke started the engine. "She may not realize the detail could be important to the investigation. It could be something totally irrelevant. Either way, she's holding something back."

"I think you should pay her a visit, alone. Have one of those mother-to-mother chats."

"I can do that." Her cell vibrated, and Kerri reached into her pocket.

"If she's aware of my undercover background," Luke commented, "she may see me as untrustworthy."

Kerri looked from the cell screen to her partner. She grinned. "You do kind of exude that dangerous vibe."

His lips twitched with the grin he held back as he lifted an eyebrow at her. "Is that right?"

"Definitely." She stared at the text from the medical examiner. "Moore says we should come by and have a look at the bodies. There's a message for us."

Luke flipped on his left blinker. "A message can be a good thing."

Kerri grunted her concurrence.

"It might be advisable to do lunch first," her partner suggested.

Or not. Kerri's stomach roiled.

———

Jefferson County Morgue
Sixth Avenue South
Birmingham, 1:00 p.m.

"Does this say anything to you?" Dr. Jeffrey Moore asked.

Kerri considered the young woman lying on the table. There were no visible burns or other wounds. Same for the little girl, Leah. The absence of external injuries was consistent with the lack of damage in the upstairs bedrooms at the scene.

Both victims had likely died in their sleep. If there was any relief to be found in all this for the family, that conclusion was probably it.

But the part that had given Dr. Moore pause and had him calling the detectives on the case was the black *X*, possibly made with a Sharpie, on the foreheads of the victims. The first responders might have noticed the marks except that both Allison and her daughter had black hair with very thick bangs.

"It does." Luke gave a slow shake of his head that spoke volumes about what the markings symbolized. "It means they were canceled." He looked to Kerri. "Whoever left these marks believed Boothe or his wife—my money's on Boothe—had crossed the line, and doing so cost him the things he cared about most."

Leaving this sort of message behind—particularly if drugs were involved—wasn't so unusual. Kerri had seen it before. Not this particular symbol, but numerous others. The killer wanted this lethal lesson known.

"Unless someone only wants us to believe that's what happened," she countered, playing devil's advocate. Until after they had interviewed Boothe, she opted not to allow any sort of judgment. Just being the victims' husband and father made Boothe their primary suspect. Still, he deserved their objective consideration just as much as anyone else.

"Nothing else so far?" Luke asked the medical examiner.

Moore shook his head. "The toxicology may give us something more. As for cause of death, I suspect the autopsies will confirm smoke inhalation."

"Thanks, Dr. Moore." Kerri flashed him a dim smile. "The minute you have more, let us know. The survivor is a former cop."

Moore understood the implications. By tonight's late-breaking news, the entire community would be aware. Was the tragedy another attempt on a cop's life? Or was it related to the misdeeds of just another dirty cop?

It wasn't until she and Luke were across the parking lot and Kerri had taken several deep breaths that the scent of chilled flesh evacuated her lungs. She'd thought in time she would learn to ignore the scent, but more than a decade hadn't done the trick. There were some things about the job that would never be so easily dismissed.

"It would be really nice," she grumbled, "if we caught a break that actually led to someone who knew something."

The neighbor Sam Tipton had been no help at all when Luke had interviewed him. By the time Tipton had crossed to the Boothe property, Boothe had gone back inside, and the police and firefighters had already arrived. What they'd just learned from Jana Scott was basically nothing they didn't already know. Crandall had provided some info, but it only went so far. He had no idea where Boothe had come from, only that he'd been in the yard at the time of the fire.

Luke checked his cell. "Someone I knew *before* shared a name with me—Josh Carr. He and Boothe were buddies. Maybe he can give us some insight into what caused Boothe to leave the department and what he was up to for the past ten months."

Before. When he'd been a different person. How many times had she heard Luke say this?

"You don't want to go straight to his LT?"

He stared at her across the top of the car for a moment. "Not yet. My source says the rumor is Boothe was dabbling in some dark places."

"Are you saying he may have started working for some of the people he previously worked to bring down?"

"Maybe."

Luke ducked into the car without further explanation. Kerri did the same. Surely talking to Boothe's former superior was the most direct strategy. She wanted to ask Luke what was up with the guy who'd once been his LT. Did he have some personal reason for not wanting to talk to him? Or was his reluctance nothing more than dread regarding going down that uncomfortable path?

Either way, it was a path one or both of them were going to have to take—sooner or later.

5

11:35 a.m.

Jana stood at the front window and watched the detectives drive away. Her heart pounded so hard she could scarcely breathe.

Dear God, she prayed she had done the right thing.

Perhaps if she could claim ignorance, she wouldn't feel so guilty. But she could not. She had purposely withheld information in a homicide investigation.

A *murder* investigation.

Hurt suffocated her, twisted her insides.

Allison and Leah were dead. Murdered.

A new emotion rushed through her. *Fury.* Hot and fierce, the rage overrode the pain for a single moment of reprieve. She would do whatever necessary to ensure the bastard responsible paid. And paid dearly. There was only one way to ensure that happened.

She had to see personally that it was done.

She searched for her cell phone and placed the call. A ring sounded in her ear, then another.

Answer the phone!

The third ring echoed across the line before the call was accepted.

Thank God!

"The detectives were here, which means they will likely be coming to you next," she stated as calmly as possible and without waiting for a hello. The sob knotting in her throat gagged her, but she bit it back. She would be strong. For Allison and for Leah.

"You have my word. I'm ready."

"Good." *Good?* Had she really just said that? What kind of mother could discuss this horror so calmly? Jana shook her head violently, tears streaming down her cheeks. The urge to vomit was nearly overwhelming. She would not be weak. She had to be strong for her girls. Raymond was not here to do this, which meant she had to.

Deep inside, that voice of doubt she'd exiled still ranted at her. Why hadn't she seen this coming? Why couldn't she have done something to stop it? Was she doing the right thing?

She closed her eyes and silently howled her agony, certain her heart would rip right in two.

"You're worried I won't hold up my end."

A moment and then two were required for Jana to recover her wits. She could not allow the other woman to hear the doubt and pain haunting her. "I'm certain you will do exactly as we agreed." Jana scrubbed her free hand over her wet cheeks. As much as she loathed this entire plan, she was well aware it had to be done.

They had planned the steps days ago. It was the first time she and Rebecca Boothe had ever agreed on anything, much less made any sort of plan.

If only they had known . . .

But they hadn't. Now, everything was different, and what they had to do was even more important.

Her lips tightened with renewed fury. She had to do this.

Had to.

Jana cleared her throat. "I am certain we will both do what's necessary and proceed as planned."

She ended the call and placed her phone on the table next to the sofa. She could do this . . . it would be difficult.

But there was no other option.

It was the least she could do for her precious Allison and Leah.

6

2:30 p.m.

The Garage
Terrace South
Birmingham

Boothe's friend, Josh Carr, had insisted on using one of the outdoor tables in the courtyard of the Garage café. The air still had a chill, but the sun kept Kerri from shivering as they waited for Carr to finish his beer. It was his first in months, he'd said. He wanted to savor it for a moment.

Kerri and Luke had opted for coffee. She sipped hers, relishing the warmth of the stoneware in her hands. Mostly she wished Carr would stop beating around the bush so they could get on with it.

"His kid was sick," Carr said finally. "Like, dying sick." He turned up the bottle and finished off the beer.

Rather than say *we know this already*, Luke nodded as if this were news to him. Kerri felt no need to respond in any way, since the guy had basically acted as if she weren't at the table. Not that his acknowledgment of her presence was necessary or even relevant. She recognized his type. Too much ego and not enough manners. Or smarts. Maybe both.

"Yeah." Carr thumped the bottle down on the metal tabletop. "He was barely keeping it together. It was a bad situation. Really bad. I had my doubts about his ability to cope. Guess I was right."

The man was thirty-one, maybe thirty-two, around the same age as Logan Boothe. A black hoodie and battered jeans along with scuffed sneakers appeared to be his go-to fashion statement. His hair was buzzed short, and the whites of his eyes were more red than white, maybe from lack of sleep, maybe from too much alcohol or whatever elixir helped him through the days.

"He confided this to you," Luke stated for confirmation.

Kerri stayed quiet and allowed her partner to do most of the talking. The fact was, Luke was familiar with Carr's world. She had heard her share of trauma stories about undercover narcotics cops, but only someone who had been there, done that, identified with the whole story.

Carr shrugged. "He and his old lady were under a lot of stress to begin with. You know how it is." He lifted one shoulder in another careless shrug. "The girl was out of his league. If they hadn't had a kid, she would probably have written Boothe off a long time ago. I told him this. The 'fairy tale'"—he made air quotes—"was doomed from the beginning."

"Are you saying," Kerri said, unable to restrain herself, "that Boothe's financial status didn't match hers? Or maybe it was a religious thing?" She understood exactly what he was implying, and it was oh so cliché. She waited for Mr. Ego to respond, since he appeared content to stare at her while saying nothing at all. Maybe he was trying to remember exactly who she was. She had no confidence whatsoever in this guy.

Carr snickered. "It was more than just money, and it damned sure wasn't about religion. Boothe doesn't do religion. You know what I mean." He looked from Kerri to Luke and back. "It's like the two of you. Obviously, you don't belong together. You're like opposites. I'll bet you don't get along at all." He shot a grin at Luke. "Maybe she calls all the shots, and you do whatever she says."

Kerri wanted to punch him. "Looks can be deceiving, *Detective* Carr."

He did one of those half grunts, half laughs. "Yeah, sure. I had you figured out before you said one word. Uptight, by the book, never broke a rule in your life."

Some of what he'd said was true. Kerri had that Miss Goody Two-Shoes comportment. She had no tattoos. Wore dress slacks and jackets to work most every day. Her brown hair was kept in a sleek ponytail. But this man did not know her at all. He had no idea what she had done or was capable of doing.

Rather than argue or bother stating as much, she simply smiled. "I suppose you would think that."

"What's the real story," Luke cut in, drawing the man's attention back to him, "with his leaving the department? He had nearly ten years under his belt. That's a lot of investment to throw away. What went wrong?"

"Boothe screwed up." Carr stared at his empty bottle as if he could make more beer appear simply by wishing hard enough. "You know, he cracked. Stumbled and couldn't catch himself. The usual. Some guys just can't hack it. He should've gotten out long before he did. It's hard to say what he was thinking."

Luke's eyes narrowed. Kerri's senses went on alert. Why the sudden evasiveness? Carr had seemed all too ready to talk when Luke had contacted him for the meet. So far he'd been reasonably open, but he'd told them basically nothing.

"He let himself be made?"

Carr glanced up, his gaze snagging on Luke's.

For two beats, Carr hesitated, trapped in the heat of Luke's glare. "No one *officially* said what he did was intentional, but you know. I mean, he let down the whole op. Screwed up big time."

"He was reprimanded?" Luke kept that laser focus on the guy.

"You'll have to talk to the LT about that. I figure he was, but Boothe never told me about it. The next thing I knew, he'd quit."

"The op was compromised," Luke said, "but there was no postmortem to discuss what went wrong?"

Carr licked his lips. Shifted in his chair. He was nervous now. "It was more like the situation took him out of play and the rest of the op continued. It was just, you know, up in the air for a while. The LT came up with a work-around."

Luke gave a curt nod. "I get it. But the LT didn't talk about what happened? Didn't clue you in?"

"No point." Another of those listless shrugs from Carr. "Boothe quit."

"Did his decision to walk away surprise you?" Luke asked the question on the tip of Kerri's tongue.

"Guess so. He had a wife and kid to take care of. It was after that when the kid got sick, and they had no insurance. LT had everybody donating to help. He's like that, you know. Even though Boothe stepped in his own shit and then quit, he was still one of us."

"Rumor is," Luke said, "Boothe found some other source of income."

Carr glanced around like he was worried someone might be listening. "I heard he got desperate, yeah. But it's like you say, a rumor. We pretty much lost touch after he quit. There's not a lot I can tell you beyond that point."

The conversation lapsed, and silence hung on for half a minute too long. Kerri waited for Luke to ask the next logical question, but he didn't.

"Tell me about Lieutenant O'Grady," she spoke up. "Does he have detectives walk away often?"

Lieutenant Patrick O'Grady was part of the past Luke didn't like to talk about. Kerri knew nothing about the man. She was aware of who he was, but his personnel jacket was kept in those files that required a higher clearance than hers to access.

"Paddy doesn't have trouble with his crew." The statement came out as defensively as Kerri had anticipated. "We know what he expects," Carr went on, "and we make it happen. You do your job, and there's no trouble. Boothe is the one who screwed up, not Paddy." Carr hitched his head toward Luke. "See, if you talked to your partner—really talked to him—you'd know Patrick O'Grady is the best. He doesn't let his people down, and they don't let him down."

"Except," Kerri argued, "Logan Boothe let him down."

"Boothe let us all down." Carr spat these words at Kerri, his anger flashing briefly.

"You didn't talk to Boothe again," Luke interceded, "after he walked away?"

"Not really," Carr said as noncommittally as a man wrestling with the concept of invoking the Fifth from this point forward.

Luke pressed on. "Did he ever talk about what happened?"

"Nah. He was just telling me about his kid being sick." Carr grabbed his bottle with both hands and glanced toward the window separating the courtyard from the busy interior.

"If you think of anything else," Luke said, terminating the discussion, "give me a call." He pushed a business card across the table. "Anything at all," he emphasized.

"Yeah, sure." Carr tucked the card into the kangaroo pocket of his hoodie.

They left Carr seated at the table. He kept his face turned down. Made no move to leave or to wave down a server. At the gate that led to the parking area, Kerri glanced back one last time. Carr was watching them—or, more specifically, her. She looked away first.

Detective Carr didn't like her. Or maybe it was only about trust.

Kerri held her comments until they were in the Charger and driving away. "I got the impression he's not sharing the whole story."

In truth she could see Carr's motive for holding back. Cops didn't like spilling the dirt on their fellow cops. But this was a homicide case; having a potentially relevant source holding back was something they couldn't afford.

"He won't give us anything beyond the necessary unless we find something to negotiate with," Luke said, effectively confirming her conclusion.

Leverage.

"Why barter with this guy? We can go straight to the source— Lieutenant O'Grady."

Tension tightened Luke's jaw. His undivided attention remained fixed on the street.

Kerri dropped her head back against the seat. "Look, I get that you don't like visiting the past—"

He did look at her then, a pained glance that said it all. "You can stop waiting for me to drop the ball. I'm not about to compromise this investigation because I don't want to, as you say, 'visit' the past."

Damn. She hadn't meant to make him feel as if she didn't trust him to hold up his end of the investigation. "Sorry. I guess I let Carr get under my skin."

"He's in deep." Luke's hesitation before going on punctuated the words. "When you're in that deep, you don't see the rest of the world clearly. You can't afford to risk your focus that way."

"I can interview O'Grady if you'd prefer." She had made the offer already.

"He won't talk to you." Luke braked for a traffic light. He turned to look her directly in the eyes. "He'll give you the practiced pitch, not the real story. We need the real story. He understands that I'll know the difference." The light changed, and he set the car in motion once more. "I know how he plays the game."

This concept was another difference between the detectives Kerri worked with and the undercover ones. Nothing about homicide was a game. The undercovers were like actors in a tense action movie, only the danger was real. The acting, however, was much the same, except that the endgame wasn't winning an award; it was staying alive. Play the part well, or lose the game and potentially everything.

"I should pick up my Wagoneer and check in on Boothe," she suggested. The chief would have called if he'd regained consciousness, but she wanted to speak with his nurse. Get the details of his injuries. A head injury or drugs could explain why he'd been discovered lying facedown in the yard while his family had suffocated in their sleep.

"I'll talk to O'Grady," Luke offered. "Like I said, he's more likely to speak freely if it's just me and him."

He was right. No question. The real issue for her at the moment was Carr's comment. A part of her wanted so desperately to protect what she and Luke had that his visiting any part of his past without her felt wrong.

But this wasn't about them—this was about the case.

7

4:50 p.m.

Mulligan's Pub
Five Points South
Birmingham

Luke didn't recall the last time he'd been in this place. It was O'Grady's favorite hangout. His Irish heritage had been his claim to fame back in the day when he'd been a beat cop. If given the chance, he'd go on all day about how he'd spent most of his off-duty time in Mulligan's. They even had a booth with his name on it where he'd once held mini conferences with his crew.

The original owner of Mulligan's had died years back, but O'Grady still dropped in occasionally and talked about old times with the son. O'Grady had no kids of his own. Could never keep a wife long enough to get the job done, he'd say. Luke understood his reasoning. Undercover work and family life didn't go well together. He thought of his own son, Liam. He'd turned nine this year, and though Luke hadn't gone to his party, his ex-wife had sent pics.

He reached for his beer and drowned the images that came instantly to mind. Liam wasn't his son anymore. Hadn't been since he was only a few hours old. Luke had given up his parental rights to protect his child.

The boy knew nothing about Luke. Liam believed his father was the man married to Shelly, his mother. At the time Luke had made the decision, it had been the right thing to do. Didn't feel that way sometimes, but his life was different now. Didn't matter. Once the choice had been made and Shelly had moved on, there was no going back. He'd stayed out of Liam's life so the kid could have a normal one. He could have a real father who hadn't done the things Luke had done.

Another deep drink of the beer, and he pushed aside the thoughts. This—the reason he was here—was not about *his* past.

As if fate wanted to show him differently, Lieutenant Patrick O'Grady waltzed through the entrance. He gave a shout to the owner and signaled for his usual before heading to the table in the back corner where Luke waited. Using O'Grady's honorary booth would have given him home field advantage. Luke had allowed him to pick the place, but he'd purposely arrived ahead of schedule to select where they would sit face to face.

It was still early, so the pub was like a ghost town, which was why Luke had gone for something before seven. He didn't want to do this in front of a crowd. If he could have avoided doing it at all, he would have.

"Falco." The LT held out his hand as he reached the table. Reflexively, Luke stood and took the outstretched offer. The older man immediately pulled him in for a quick hug.

Every nerve ending in Luke's body fired with tension. He drew back and gave a nod. "How you doing, man? Long time no see."

They both settled at the table, and the bartender delivered the LT's shot of tequila and bottle of Corona. He thanked the man and downed the tequila, then chased it with a slug of beer.

"Better now." A deep laugh rumbled from his gut.

O'Grady had barely changed at all. A little thicker in the middle. His hairline had receded a bit more, and he'd grayed considerably. Luke hadn't laid eyes on the guy in eight years. Not since he'd moved on to a new assignment. One far enough away and so damned deep he'd been able to forget who he had been.

That person didn't exist anymore. He was gone for good.

Luke sipped his beer. It was warm now, but he wasn't ordering another. He needed his head crystal clear for this meeting.

"I heard a rumor," Luke said, kicking off the conversation, "you were thinking of retiring."

O'Grady made a face. "Who told you that lie?" Another swig of beer went down the hatch. "Hell, man, I'm a lifer. The day I retire is the day they plant my ass in the cemetery. You know my deal. It's been the same for most of my career. My last old lady said I wasn't good for anything else, so what am I gonna do? The job. That's my life." He shrugged. "I've got no complaints. Happy as the proverbial pig in the sunshine."

Luke noticed he'd left out the "dead" part of the old saying. He nodded. "Yeah, I figured as much. Patrick O'Grady ain't the retiring kind."

He stared at Luke for a long moment. "I hear you're on the straight and narrow now. Playing by all the rules with a cute little partner." He moved his eyebrows up and down. "Word is you two do some playing after hours too."

Irritation fired deep inside Luke. He would not talk with this man about what he and Kerri had. "We get along," he said, trying his level best to prevent the words from sounding tight and clipped.

How could it be that nearly a decade had passed and yet just being in the same room with the guy made him want to disappear? Made him want to run for his life—for the one he'd clawed his way toward for those eight fucking long years?

Patrick O'Grady represented all that once was—all that Luke had fought so hard to leave behind. He forced Luke to look back, to remember . . . and he didn't want to do either of those. He only looked forward now. Always. Forward.

O'Grady finished off his beer, plopped the bottle on the table. "I imagine you called me about Boothe." He harrumphed. "When you don't hear from a man in more than seven years—wait, eight years—you sort of figure you're done. But I guess this is different. It's lawman business."

Luke had wondered how long it would take for him to mention the elephant in the room. "I was a little busy down in Mobile."

"Yeah." Another beer appeared in front of O'Grady. "I heard about that. Big coup for you, huh?"

Luke held a hand over his mug to indicate he was good. "Big enough." To get him out of the life. To propel him forward.

The bartender disappeared, and O'Grady asked, "Boothe is still hanging on, I hear."

Kerri had called the hospital for an update before Luke had dropped her off at home to pick up her ride.

"He's still unconscious, but I think that's how the docs want him right now. Apparently, the emotional trauma would be too overwhelming for his body to focus on healing. Sometimes it's better not to be aware of what's happening."

Luke knew that strategy firsthand.

"It's a real shame." O'Grady sipped his second beer. "Especially about his wife and kid. I was really worried about them when he walked away from the department." He shook his head slowly. "Just threw everything away because I gave him a much-deserved kick in the ass."

"What'd he do?" Luke kept both hands in his lap now. Kept his posture and face relaxed. Keeping the bitterness from the past out of his tone wasn't easy, but it was necessary. This wasn't about him.

"He was deep in an ongoing op, so I can't spell it out"—O'Grady flared his hands—"for reasons you know all too well, but suffice it to say the dumb fucker showed his hand and almost got his ass killed. Just about blew the op."

Same story Carr had given. "Showed his hand how?"

"Do we really need to do this?" O'Grady searched Luke's face as if looking for some ulterior motive. "The man has lost his wife and his child. I don't see any need to bring up his past mistakes—mistakes that could send him to jail. I took care of the situation, all right? It's done. Over."

"So he allowed himself to be made and then cut a deal with the bad guys." The LT's evasiveness told the story. The tension in Luke's gut tightened.

"He was in trouble financially," O'Grady said. "Even then his kid was sick a lot, and that was before the leukemia diagnosis. His wife had left him. He was desperate. You know the story. We've all been there. Get in too deep and lose everything else. Can't swim, so you just sink."

The memory of waking up next to a cold, dead body pierced Luke's brain like a bullet fired at close range. The air stalled in his lungs. He blinked the image away. "I need a name."

O'Grady leaned forward. "What difference does it make? It's over. In the past. I took care of it."

Oh yeah, O'Grady always *took care* of things. Took care of his people. Wasn't that what a good LT did?

Luke kicked the thoughts aside. "There's a strong possibility that Boothe was working with someone and made a costly mistake. Maybe someone on the other side. If that's what got his family killed, I need to know."

O'Grady sat back, his expression arranged into one of certainty. "No way. I would have known. Boothe made that particular stupid move in the past, but he wouldn't do that again."

"The wife and kid were marked." Luke glanced around to ensure no one had moved within hearing range. A few patrons had filtered into the establishment, but none chose a table or booth nearby.

Shock pushed aside the certainty on the other man's face. "You're sure about this?"

"Positive." Luke wasn't sharing details. O'Grady was aware of what this meant and the possibilities for how Luke had picked up on it.

O'Grady held Luke's gaze longer than necessary. "If I give you names, you have to let me into the investigation," he said, caving but tossing out his own caveat. Before Luke could shut down whatever he intended to say next, he went on. "This could overlap a major op. I can't risk you screwing it up, Falco. No offense, but you've been out of this world for a long time."

"Homicide trumps all else," he reminded his former mentor. "We both know you won't win that battle, so let's not even get into the pissing contest."

O'Grady held up both hands in surrender. "You're right. Yes. But you have to let me be your adviser. Otherwise, you could end up dead. Or that sweet little partner of yours could end up marked. You know how this game is played. It's never pretty."

It was impossible to contain the anger this time. Luke leaned forward, looked the other man dead in the eyes. "Anyone touches her, and I will take it all apart, from the top down."

A beat of silence, then two, shuddered in the air between them.

O'Grady smirked. "I guess I was right, after all. Falco's on the straight and narrow, no looking back. Got it."

"You have my word I'll keep you in the loop," Luke lied. "Any step I take that feels iffy, we'll talk about it first." Whatever it took to get the information he needed.

O'Grady nodded. "If what you're saying has any merit whatsoever, the man you want to talk to is an up-and-comer. He wants the moon and the stars and everything below. If he stays on course, he'll be getting just that. If Boothe was into something, Clinton Sawyer will know."

Luke recognized the name. The piece of shit had made quite the reputation in the past couple of years. He finished off his beer. "Thanks. That's all I needed."

When he would have stood, O'Grady stopped him with a hand on his arm. "I warn you, be very, very careful, Falco. You've worked hard to get where you are—shit, man, MID—don't make a mistake now. Sawyer is one dangerous mofo."

Luke shrugged. "Aren't they all?"

———

Devlin Residence
Twenty-First Avenue South
Birmingham, 8:30 p.m.

Luke sat in his car for a minute before going inside. Kerri had sent him a text that she'd hold dinner for him. It was the old reliable, she'd said with a heart emoji. Spaghetti. Sauce from a jar and quickie noodles from a box. Tori's favorite.

His chest felt so tight he couldn't seem to draw in a good breath. How the hell had he ever gotten so lucky? Kerri and Tori cared about him. Loved him, maybe. His eyes burned, and he blinked back the emotion that threatened. He'd had a family long ago, but he'd lost them. He was grateful that Shelly kept him in the loop about Liam, but not once in eight years had he dared to consider that he might have another chance at having a family. Hell, he'd figured he didn't deserve another chance at a life like the one he was living right now.

It was more than possible that he didn't deserve any part of it. Not Tori's adoration and damned sure not Kerri's feelings for him. She hadn't said the *L* word, but he hadn't either. He'd thought it plenty of times. Fear kept him from saying it out loud.

Yeah. Fear. He was a coward. Scared to death of losing this new family that wasn't really his.

Maybe he was still playing games with himself. Pretending a life that didn't belong to him. And yet he wanted this life so badly it hurt to even think about losing it.

After the meeting with O'Grady, he'd made a few inquiries about Sawyer. Put out some feelers. Done a few drive-bys to put himself on the bastard's radar. Now he would wait for a reaction.

Doing those few things, seeing O'Grady again—it all reminded him of how much he'd hated that life. He didn't want to go back . . . didn't want that shit to leech its way into the present. He'd worked too hard to leave it behind.

Pushing aside the pile-up of emotions, he got out of the car and shut the door. Kerri waved at him from the kitchen window, and that cramping in his chest deepened. He forced a grin and waggled his fingers at her. She opened the side door in invitation, and the scent of tomatoes and garlic drifted out to him.

"Smells good." He walked into the warm house and shouldered out of his jacket.

"You say that every time," she teased.

"So do you." He hung up his jacket. "No matter what I cook when it's my turn to make dinner."

She grinned. "Sit. Let's eat. You can fill me in on what you learned from O'Grady."

"Not that much." He dropped into his chair and dug in to prevent having to say more right away.

She gave him a break for long enough to down a few bites. When her curiosity got the better of her, she shot him an expectant look. "Does he feel Boothe was on the verge of some sort of breakdown, or maybe he's involved in the drug world?"

"He seemed surprised at the idea. Like he couldn't imagine Boothe going that far."

"You told him the victims were marked." She opened her beer and had a drink.

He nodded. Took another bite of spaghetti. To occupy his hands, he opened his beer as well.

"Did he suggest anyone you might talk to?"

"He did. I put out a few feelers. We'll see if anything comes of it. How did it go at the hospital?"

She studied him for a moment, wondering, he imagined, at his abrupt shift back to her. "They have Boothe stabilized. He's scheduled for more tests tomorrow now that his condition has improved. We should know later in the afternoon if he sustained any other injuries."

There had to be an explanation for why Boothe had been outside, on the ground, and possibly unconscious. Had he jumped from a second-story window to escape the fire while leaving his family to perish? Or had he arrived home and been injured in his attempt to prevent the perpetrator from getting into the house in the first place? Luke didn't really know Boothe, had only run into him once or twice back in his undercover days with the BPD. There was far too much unknown at this point to make a reasonable assessment.

"What happened between you and O'Grady? Before, I mean."

Luke blinked, pulled his attention back to the present. "My first assignment as a detective was in his unit."

"He was your mentor, then."

Luke picked at his food; his appetite had vanished. "Guess so. He taught me a lot. But I had better teachers, better examples, later on."

Even as he worked at keeping his voice even and his tension tamped down, he heard the strain in his own voice.

Luke hated the man he'd been when he'd worked with O'Grady. There it was. The whole truth. Seeing the bastard, hearing his voice, made him sick with regret and other things he didn't want to feel.

"I get the sense we need to talk more about your relationship with him."

Luke placed his fork next to his plate. No point in pretending he could swallow another bite. His throat wouldn't relax enough to manage the feat. "There is no relationship. I haven't seen him in years until today. He's nothing more than a source of information for this case."

Kerri placed her fork next to her plate almost as carefully as he had. She searched his eyes, and he prayed she wouldn't see the fear there. "I won't let you shut me out."

"I'm not shutting you out." He was. He knew this. It was necessary. There were things . . . things she didn't know. Couldn't know.

She nodded. "Good."

Stacking their plates, she pushed back her chair and walked to the sink. He wanted to go upstairs and take a shower. Wash the day off him and pretend it had never happened. Some part of him recognized that would be a mistake. Instead, he got up and joined Kerri at the sink to help with the dishes.

They worked in silence for a bit. Her rinsing, him loading the dishwasher. Her silence told him she planned to wait him out. She was well aware he wasn't being honest with her.

"Stuff happened," he said at last, the words like knives carving out his insides, "when I worked with O'Grady and his crew. Stuff I don't like to talk about. I was different then. It was a different life. I don't even like to think about it." He waited until she looked at him before saying more. "I don't want that life to damage this one."

She carefully dried her hands, then placed them against his chest. Her touch instantly soothed him, made him less frantic. How the hell had he gotten so lucky?

"We've all done things we wish we could take back or edit in some way." She let him see the painful truth in her words. "No one is perfect, Luke. We are who we are, and who we once were shaped us to some degree, but the past doesn't rule us unless we allow it to."

He liked when she called him Luke. It didn't happen on the job. Just when they were alone, like now.

"I don't want any part of that life to poke its way into this one," he reiterated.

She smiled up at him. "Then we won't let it."

If only it could be that simple.

8

Eight Years Ago

December 1

10:30 p.m.

"Trust me," the LT says. "I've seen it a thousand times."

I want to trust him. He helped me get into the department. Pulled me into his crew, ensuring I reached the rank of detective early despite some really stupid mistakes I've made. Over the past five years he's helped me learn the ropes of undercover work. Took me under his wing. Guided me.

I know him well.

That's why I'm worried.

"She hasn't failed me yet," I counter. "Why would she turn on me now?"

O'Grady laughs like he's never going to stop. "Tell me you're kidding, man. This shit happens all the time. CIs are loyal to the highest bidder. Someone got to her. It's the only answer. You know it, but you don't want to see it. Tell me I'm wrong."

When I say nothing, he laughs. "See?" he accuses.

As many times as I have argued the subject, he keeps repeating what he believes, but I don't believe it. I know this CI. She has never failed me. Not in more than a year. I get that not all confidential informants can be trusted, but she's different.

"She's got a kid. She wouldn't take that kind of risk."

LT looks at me like he did the first time I screwed up as a rookie narcotics cop. "You're serious, aren't you? You're involved with this woman." He rolls his eyes. "Shit, Falco, what did I tell you right from the start?"

I blink. Don't want to answer.

"If you lead with your dick, you'll always get fucked."

"I'm not that stupid." I'm pissed now. Really pissed. "She wants to keep her shit together for the kid. She wouldn't screw it all up now. She's come too far."

"She's a junkie whore, you dumbass. If she's using again—and she probably is—she will do whatever is necessary to get that next hit." He shook his head. "God damn it, Falco. Listen to me. I have seen this over and over in my career."

I hold up my hands to stop him before I really do go stupid. "You made your point."

"Good. Now take care of this rapidly sinking mess before it pulls you under with it. Got it?"

I nod even as I tell myself I'm right. I know I am. Lieutenant Patrick O'Grady is wrong. And I'm going to prove it.

9

Tuesday, November 23

7:30 a.m.

University of Alabama Hospital
Sixth Avenue South
Birmingham

The call that Logan Boothe had regained consciousness came at 5:15 a.m.

Kerri hadn't slept for more than a couple of hours at that point. Luke had tossed and turned and alternately whispered and shouted unintelligibly for a good portion of that time. They'd worked homicide cases before that involved the most vulnerable victims, and he'd never had nightmares. It wasn't necessary to be a psychologist to conclude it was about revisiting his past.

She stole a glance at him. He sat in the chair next to her, eyes closed, the collar of his leather jacket riding up around his ears. His long jean-clad legs stretched out in front of him, booted feet crossed at the ankles. Once they'd arrived at the hospital, they had been sequestered in a private lobby. The nurse had explained that another doctor was in with Boothe at the time. As soon as he finished, they would be allowed to see him. With burn victims the risk of infection was extremely high.

She and Falco would need to scrub and don the necessary protective gear before entering Boothe's room.

"I'm not asleep," Luke said, "just resting my eyes."

A smile tugged at her lips. He'd sensed her watching him. "I'd understand if you needed to catch a few extra z's."

He opened his eyes now and sent her a sideways look. "Something you want to say, Devlin?"

Following her lead, he didn't generally use her first name when they were on the job. On the rare occasion he did, it always startled her. She supposed that reaction would eventually fade.

"You had nightmares." She kept her head turned toward him so she could assess his reaction. "You don't usually have nightmares."

His eyebrows reared up. "Did I say or do something that made you uncomfortable?"

The answer wasn't a straightforward yes or no. "Not really. But you seemed very uncomfortable. Your words were unintelligible. I'm guessing the meeting with O'Grady prompted old issues?"

Enough time passed before he answered that she began to think maybe he wouldn't—which would be a first. Their ability to be open with each other was one of the aspects she appreciated most about their relationship.

Except they never talked about his past life as an undercover cop. She'd been okay with that until now.

He hesitated for one too many beats. The idea that he was having difficulty finding a way to share those feelings with her made her chest feel heavy.

"He reminds me of things I'd rather forget."

Before she could come up with a way to articulate her concerns, the sound of rubber-soled shoes on tile drew her attention to the corridor beyond the open door. The nurse who'd brought them to this room appeared in the doorway.

Kerri pushed to her feet. Falco did the same.

"It's time to scrub in."

This was the first time Kerri had gone through the ritual for seeing a patient. The gowns, gloves, and face masks came on, and then they were led to the burn unit. A BPD uniform was stationed in the corridor outside Boothe's room.

"Don't overtax him," the nurse instructed. "The doctor would like you to keep the interview short."

"We will," Kerri assured her.

The nurse opened the door and entered the room. Kerri and Falco followed. A rhythm of beeps and sighs from the machines sounded. Boothe's arms were covered in bandages, as was one side of his neck.

Rather than approach the bed from both sides, Kerri moved forward while Falco stayed in the background. Boothe's condition remained guarded. It was essential to keep the mood calm, relaxed. Their movements had Boothe's lids fluttering open.

"Mr. Boothe, I'm Detective Kerri Devlin, and this is my partner, Detective Luke Falco."

Boothe stared at her, his eyes red from his time inside the burning house.

"I'm sorry for your loss, Mr. Boothe, and I'm even sorrier we have to be here asking you questions. But I'm certain you're familiar with the routine."

He swallowed, the movement of his throat momentarily drawing her attention.

"Would you like something to drink?" Kerri glanced at the cup and straw on the side table. "Water?"

Boothe nodded. Kerri carefully held the cup close enough for the straw to reach his parched lips. When he'd had a drink and pulled away, she returned the cup to the table.

"Mr. Boothe, can you tell us what happened at your home the night before last?" she asked, officially beginning the interview.

He stared at Kerri without speaking, hardly even blinking.

"Do you know how the fire started?" she asked, narrowing the scope of her inquiry.

Still, he said nothing. His gaze remained glued to hers.

"Were you awakened by intruders?"

"No." The single syllable whispered roughly from his mouth.

"According to the fire marshal," Kerri pushed on, "an accelerant was likely used to spread and intensify the fire."

His eyes closed, and the agony he clearly felt both mentally and physically strained his expression.

"If you heard or saw anyone who might have been involved with what happened, it would be very helpful if you could share that information." Kerri watched as his lids slowly opened just enough to look directly at her once more. "I'm sure," she prompted, "you want to help us learn what happened and to find the persons responsible for this tragedy. Every hour we lose lessens the likelihood that we can accomplish that goal."

"I saw nothing. Heard nothing." Boothe shifted his attention to the ceiling.

"Were you at home when the fire started?" Kerri asked.

There was a hesitation, and then, "I was just coming home."

"You have a new job?" Kerri asked. "No one seems to know anything about you having started a new job since leaving the department."

"No new job."

Luke moved up beside Kerri. "Hey, Boothe, remember me? We bumped into each other a couple of times when we were both assigned to O'Grady's crew."

Boothe continued to stare at the ceiling, painfully dry lips pressed together like ancient parchment paper that might crumble if touched.

"Your neighbor," Kerri said, "stated he found you facedown on the lawn, and when you roused, you rushed into the house to save your family." She opted not to say *wife and daughter*. He'd lost both. No need to remind him.

Another half minute of silence.

"Why were you outside, Boothe?" Luke asked. "Did someone force you out of the house or stop you on the way inside before the fire started?"

"No."

The harsh sound was louder this time. Boothe flinched with the noise of it.

"All right, then," Luke said. "Why were you outside?"

No answer.

"Mr. Boothe," Kerri urged, "we can't properly investigate this case without your cooperation. I'm confident you want to help."

Nothing.

"Anything you remember," Luke pushed, "could make the difference."

"It was me."

Unlike his last response, the words were scarcely a whisper.

Kerri frowned. "What are you saying, Mr. Boothe?"

"I did this."

She exchanged a look with Luke.

"Maybe you'd like a lawyer present," Luke suggested. "You know the deal, man, anything you say—"

"I did it."

Kerri went for a different angle. "We're going to assume, Mr. Boothe, that the pain medication is fogging your memory. We can come back later and talk about this again."

"No," Boothe growled with his too-rusty voice. "I did it."

"The marks on their foreheads say otherwise," Luke countered. "You can save us a lot of wasted time and effort by just telling the truth. That little girl of yours—who died in that fire—deserves the truth."

A single tear slid down the side of the man's face. "It was me."

"Boothe," Kerri reminded him, "if you're confessing to a premeditated double homicide, then I strongly advise you to seek legal representation."

"I don't need a lawyer. You can arrest me now. I did it."

"We'll let you rest now," Kerri said. "You should think about what you're doing, and we'll be back to take your official statement."

He said nothing more.

Once she and Luke were in the corridor, they located the nurse at her station.

"Do you have the results on his various scans and x-rays?" Kerri had learned yesterday that more tests were being run now that he was relatively stable. The last thing they wanted to do was be accused of coercion. If Boothe was on heavy pain medication or there were other injuries that could affect his state of mind, he might not be fit to give his statement.

"Let me check his chart."

Kerri turned to her partner. "Why would he be covering for the killer or killers? Does he blame himself? Maybe he was involved with the bad guys, and he screwed up. This was his payback, and he's feeling the guilt."

"It's possible," Luke agreed. "But I have to tell you, I'm wondering what kind of guy would let the people who did this to his family get away with it regardless?"

"I was wondering the same thing."

The nurse came back to where they waited. "In addition to the second-degree burn on the left side of his neck and the third-degree burns on both forearms and hands, his left tibia is shattered, and there's a fracture to his right fibula. Two fractured ribs and a concussion."

Kerri thanked the nurse and waited until she had returned to the other end of the station to answer the phone before saying to her partner, "Boothe either jumped out a window—"

"With some assistance, maybe," Luke suggested.

"With some assistance," Kerri agreed, "or he was on the losing end of a violent struggle."

"My money's on the latter."

"Mine too." Kerri paused at the bank of elevators and pressed the call button. "I guess his mother must have taken a break."

Luke glanced back toward Boothe's room. "Maybe Boothe didn't want her around while he confessed."

The elevator dinged, and the doors slid open. A woman stood face to face with them, ready to step out of the car. Kerri and Luke sidestepped, moving out of her way. Kerri watched as she walked away, wondering if the sixtyish woman was Boothe's mother. She had the same dark hair, only hers was run through with gray. Same beefy build.

As if Kerri had said her thoughts aloud, the woman paused and turned around. "Have you talked to my son?" Her accusing tone warned she'd already surmised as much. "I told him not to talk to you without a lawyer."

As the elevator doors slid closed behind them, Kerri said, "I'm Detective Devlin, and this is my partner, Detective Falco. We have spoken with your son, and we have questions for you as well, ma'am. May we have a few minutes of your time?"

"Absolutely not," she declared. "If you want to know what happened to my precious granddaughter and my son, talk to Jana Scott. That daughter of hers caused this." With that she promptly whirled around and strode toward her son's room.

"That went well," Luke commented.

Kerri pressed the call button once more. "I'll give her this one. She just lost her grandchild. Next time I'm taking her downtown."

"Snap," Luke teased, "the lady done got on your bad side."

As they left the hospital, the chief called for an update. His silence after Kerri had filled him in warned that as much as he, too, wanted to blame Boothe for the deaths of his wife and child, he understood it was far more complicated.

Kerri tucked her phone away as Luke drove out of the lot. "The chief wants us to dig deeper into Boothe's friends and work relationships."

"If I was Boothe," Luke said, "I would keep my mouth shut and wait to get well enough to be released; then I would hunt down the bastard who did this and take them apart one piece at a time."

"But he didn't do that," Kerri said, thinking aloud. "Instead, he's protecting the real killer and is basically assuring he won't be leaving police custody."

Luke sent her a pointed look. "I have a feeling our boy Boothe has an alternate plan. We just haven't figured out what it is yet."

10

10:00 a.m.

Boothe Residence
Chablis Way
Birmingham

Crime scene tape swung in the chilly breeze. The house that had once been a home to a small family stood alone, some of the windows shattered, soon to be boarded up. Dry grass was crisscrossed with lines where heavy vehicles had crushed it against the hard ground. Kerri couldn't remember the last time it had rained, which was the only reason those lines weren't muddy ruts.

While Luke walked around the yard, Kerri passed through the house again. Between the flames and the water, finding prints or genetic material from an intruder was unlikely—assuming there had been an intruder. If anything was discovered, the folks in forensics would let her or her partner know.

The main living level would require a good deal of demo and new construction. Upstairs Kerri lingered at the door of Leah's room for a time. The invading smoke had left its mark on the walls. The odor would linger until a professional cleaning and restoration company had eradicated it, assuming there was insurance to take care of the damage.

Beyond the smell and the soot that had settled on surfaces, the child's room was hardly touched by the tragedy. She surveyed the rumpled bedcovers. Except the little girl would never return to this home. She would never again play with her dolls or the little pink cottage on the table in the corner.

Her ability to breathe stuttered as Kerri moved to the primary bedroom. The covers there were tousled just as they had been when the mother's body had been removed. The room was neat. The closet well organized. Kerri started to turn away but then hesitated. She stepped deeper into the closet and inspected more thoroughly the wardrobe hanging on the rods and folded on the shelves. All appeared to be female apparel and obviously too small for a man the size of Logan Boothe.

Where was the husband's clothing? There was nothing in this closet that belonged to him. Same with the dresser and bureau drawers. Not one article of male attire or accessories.

Had Boothe and his wife been sleeping in separate rooms?

Kerri made her way to the third and final bedroom. The bedcovers were tidy. No tousled linens here. She went to the closet and opened the door.

"Voilà."

A not-so-neat row of shirts hung on the single rod. Trousers, mostly blue jeans, were stacked on a shelf. One pair of boots and a well-worn pair of sneakers sat on the floor. Kerri went to the single dresser and checked the top drawer.

"Socks." Men's socks, the white tube type. The next drawer revealed boxers.

Kerri surveyed the room slowly. Lots of couples used the closet in an extra bedroom for overflow. But the socks and boxers in the drawers suggested more than just storage issues. She checked the single drawer in the bedside table. Antacid tablets and toenail clippers.

If Logan Boothe slept in this room—she surveyed the bed once more—why had everyone else been in bed when the fire had started . . . except him?

Back downstairs, Kerri walked across the living area and then through the family room and garage on the lowest level. Nothing more caught her eye. All appearances would suggest just another tragic house fire.

But that wasn't the case.

She caught up with Luke outside. He'd walked the entire property, scanning for anything that had been missed. During the initial flurry of activity after an event, it was easy to overlook the small things. The BPD's crime scene investigators were good; they rarely missed much, but no one was perfect.

"Nothing new out here." He glanced around. "You find anything?"

"The husband's clothes are in the third bedroom."

Luke's eyebrows drew together. "I noticed clothes in there, but I figured the wife's clothes took precedence in the other closet. Not unusual."

"Socks, boxers in the drawers, along with antacids and toenail clippers in the bedside table. I don't think it was just the need for more storage space."

"Good point." He hitched his head toward the neighbor's house. "I see our one witness is enjoying the cool morning air."

Kerri spotted Mr. Crandall on his front porch. "Saves us from having to knock on his door and hoping he's home."

The walk across the driveway and the narrow strip of grass between the two properties took less than a minute. Crandall waved as soon as he noticed their approach and called out an invitation for them to join him.

"I just brewed a fresh pot of coffee." He held up his mug as they climbed the steps. "If you're interested."

Luke deferred to Kerri. "Coffee would be great," she agreed.

"Cream? Sugar?" their host asked.

"Black," Kerri and her partner echoed simultaneously.

Crandall sat his mug on the table next to his rocker and pushed to his feet. "Have a seat, and I'll be right back."

Kerri settled into one of the four available rocking chairs. Falco checked his cell as he leaned against the railing. "I nudged our friends in forensics," he said. "Just got a text from the lead CSI, who had a briefing with the fire marshal. Gasoline was the accelerant used in the fire."

Not exactly a creative way to get the job done. "Evidently our fire starter wasn't a signature kind of arsonist."

"Generic choice," Luke granted. "But easy to access, impossible to trace back to who and when."

"*Arson for Dummies*," Kerri muttered. Not that she'd really expected to glean any useful information from the type of accelerant used, but it was disappointing. Any clue was better than no clue, she supposed.

"Exactly."

The front door opened, and Mr. Crandall appeared with a steaming mug in each hand. Luke took the mugs and passed one to Kerri.

"Anything new on how this awful thing happened?" Crandall looked from Kerri to Luke and back. "I'm still in a sort of daze. I keep expecting to look over and see the girls in the yard."

"Not enough," Luke admitted. "We're still hopeful another witness will come forward."

"Mr. Crandall," Kerri said, drawing his attention to her, "we'd like to ask you a few more questions about the fire and the Boothe family."

He set his rocking chair in motion. "If I have the answers, I'll be glad to share them."

"Did you notice any trouble between Allison and her husband? Maybe you overheard arguments? You mentioned something about the two arguing quietly." Kerri allowed the statement to hang in the brief silence that followed. Crandall had known Allison and her mother for a very long time. Speaking ill of the family wouldn't likely be his first choice.

"Well, I may or may not have said before that, like most young couples, Allison and her husband had their share of difficulties. But they were very quiet and considerate."

"No serious shouting or pushing around by one or the other?" Luke asked.

"None that I'm aware of. I did see Allison sitting on the back steps crying a couple of times," he said. "I took her a glass of lemonade once, but she didn't want to discuss why she was crying, so I let it go. In retrospect I should have realized she was crying for her child. Leah's illness was more than enough to have her in tears every day. It was a tremendous burden. An incredible pain. For her and for poor Jana."

"Have you thought of any other details from the night of the fire?" Luke asked.

"No." Crandall shook his head. "I've played those moments over and over, and I can't recall anything beyond what I've already told you. It seemed to happen so fast, and yet I felt as if I was in slow motion."

"Mr. Crandall," Kerri said, "did you notice if Logan's car was home before you went up to bed that night?"

Kerri had asked this before, and he had stated that he didn't recall seeing the car. Sometimes glimpses of memory occurred days after an event, particularly a traumatic event. The downside to human recall was that sometimes it was reliable and sometimes it was not. People often recalled what they were accustomed to or expected to see rather than what was actually there.

"I've been thinking about that, and I believe it was," he said thoughtfully. "But I still can't say for sure. It's one of those everyday things that you don't pay attention to. Some part of you notes all those little things, but they aren't necessarily committed to memory, because they're expected."

Kerri was surprised Crandall recognized this. Most people didn't. For cops, particularly detectives, intense training was required to consciously note those small things.

"When you recognized there was a fire," Luke said next, "and you hurried over to the house, you stated that you found Mr. Boothe facedown in the front yard."

Crandall nodded. "That's right." He shuddered. "My heart was already pounding, but when I realized it was him, the most awful feeling overtook me. All I could think was, Where were Allison and Leah?"

"When you turned him over and he came to," Kerri asked, "did he appear to be injured?"

"Not that I observed," he admitted, "but I was greatly out of sorts. I may not have recognized his injuries. In any event, nothing like that sank in."

"When he got up," Kerri continued, "did he appear to have any trouble walking?" When and how he'd broken not one but both legs could certainly prove relevant to the events that had occurred that night.

"Walking?" Crandall frowned. "My word, the man literally ran into the house. He was calling his wife's and daughter's names. It was a moment I will never forget." Another visible shudder shivered through him.

"Did he say anything else?"

Crandall shook his head in response to her question.

"He didn't stumble?" Luke asked.

Crandall opened his mouth to answer but then closed it. "Actually," he began again, "now that I think about it, he did stumble. Twice, I believe." His frown deepened. "He cried out as if he was in pain. My word, how did I forget that? He . . . he sort of howled like a wounded animal. It all seems like a very bad dream now."

Kerri glanced at Luke before suggesting, "He may have been injured after all, then?"

"Yes. You're right. I'm certain of it." Crandall nodded slowly. "He fell not once but twice while trying to reach his . . . *family*." He drew in a harsh, ragged breath. "My God."

"And you saw no one else in the yard or on the street?" Kerri restated.

"I didn't. I'm sorry. I have racked my brain trying to remember. But I just didn't see anyone until the one neighbor I told you about, Sam Tipton, rushed over. The police arrived and then the fire department. It seemed to happen immediately, but I do believe it was about twenty minutes. I truly can't say with any measure of certainty."

"I understand," Kerri assured him. It was possible there had been no one else nearby. The rest of the neighbors could all have been asleep. "But if you recall otherwise, please let us know."

When the mugs were emptied, Kerri thanked Crandall, and she and Luke headed back to where they'd left his car in the driveway next door.

"We got nothing from any of the other neighbors," he pointed out. "At least from none we've been able to catch at home. But we know something happened to Boothe before he rushed into the house to save his family."

"The family he says he murdered," Kerri reminded him.

"Who the hell is he covering for?"

That was the million-dollar question.

Kerri spotted movement in the yard across the street and to the left of the Boothe home. A woman, younger than her, maybe the same age as Allison, was walking to the mailbox with a child who looked to be about the same age as Leah.

"Check in with Moore and see if he has anything on toxicology for Allison Boothe and her daughter. I want to say hello to this neighbor."

Luke followed her gaze, then hitched his head in acknowledgment and dug in his pocket for his phone. Kerri walked to the street, checked for traffic, then crossed to the yard, where the mother was sorting through a handful of envelopes.

"Good morning," she called to the woman, who had stopped sorting and pulled her child close. "Detective Kerri Devlin." Kerri showed her credentials to the lady. "I wondered if I might ask you a few questions about the Boothe family."

"It's just awful," the neighbor said, her hand moving to her chest. "Rosie and I are devastated."

The little girl buried her face in her mother's leg.

"Rosie and Leah were friends?" Kerri inquired.

The woman nodded, her eyes filling with tears. "I'm sorry, I'm Candace Oden. My daughter and I were in Huntsville visiting family. We only got back this morning." She shook her head. "The news is simply horrifying." She glanced across the street. "I still can't believe it."

"Did you know Allison well?"

This was the moment when the neighbor's expression shifted from grief and regret to something like wariness. "Rosie, why don't you go inside and find the marshmallows? Mommy will be right in, and we'll make hot chocolate."

Hot chocolate would be a good thing on a cold morning like this one. The little girl shot one final look at Kerri before darting inside.

When the door closed behind her, Oden said, "Allison and I didn't really know each other that well. I only moved to the neighborhood last year. But our daughters are"—she blinked—"the only small children on the street, so we got acquainted. Allison was really a nice person."

"Did you know her husband, Logan?" Kerri asked.

"Not very well." She stared at her stack of mail once more.

"He's having a hard time," Kerri ventured. "His recovery is going to be long and difficult."

Oden glanced up, then away once more. "I'm sorry to hear that."

The husband was a sticking point for Oden. She didn't like talking about him.

"The other neighbor I interviewed was quick to say what a good relationship Allison and Logan had. The perfect couple."

"Leah was very ill," Oden announced, almost pointedly. "Of course they had trouble. Their lives were far from perfect. But they were very private people."

"Are you suggesting there was trouble in the marriage?" Kerri pressed.

Oden blinked, irritation abruptly overtaking the deer-caught-in-the-headlights look in her eyes. "There were problems, yes. How could there not be? Allison and Logan had a rocky relationship to begin with. When Leah got sick, the pressure became nearly unbearable. There were times when I think the only reason they stayed together was for Leah." She pinched her lips together as if she'd said too much and only just realized it.

"Allison shared this with you?" Kerri asked.

"We talked sometimes, yes. Two mothers watching their children play." She shrugged. "Of course we talked. We all have problems. Allison and Logan had theirs, but it's not my place to judge."

"Did you notice any recent changes in the relationship?"

"Nothing I wouldn't expect. The stress was unbelievable. They were both at their wits' end." Oden shook her head. "I don't know how they held up."

A new thought occurred to Kerri. "Sometimes when things like this happen, people blame God. Or a doctor who they feel didn't pick up on the problem early enough. Did Allison ever say anything about Leah's doctor?"

The frown on the other woman's face warned that Kerri was nowhere near the right track.

"Allison never said anything like that, and Logan sure didn't blame God." Oden shook her head. "As far as I know, he didn't go to church, and I'm not sure he even knew the name of Leah's doctor before the leukemia. He wasn't in the loop like that until her diagnosis. He was always working."

Except it appeared he had been unemployed for the past ten months. "He never mentioned blame?"

If he blames himself, this could be his reason for confessing to the murders, Kerri considered. If he'd blamed one or more of the doctors, he surely wouldn't have said he was responsible. Whatever the case, there had to be a reason he felt compelled to assume such a burden. There was always the possibility it was more about his inability to protect his family. Even so, he was a former cop. He understood the true guilt lay with the perpetrator. Why would he cover for the person or persons who'd murdered his family?

"That's the really crazy part," Oden said. "The only person Logan blamed was Allison. It was all her fault, in his opinion."

The answer wasn't one Kerri had expected.

"Do you know why he blamed his wife?"

Oden shook her head. "I can't answer that question. I'm sorry."

Kerri thanked the woman and left a business card with her before heading back across the street.

Maybe if Logan Boothe really did blame his wife for their child's illness, his confession was the real thing.

Except why would he take his child's life too?

11

1:00 p.m.

Pediatric Oncology Associates
Seventh Avenue
Birmingham

"I'm sorry, Detective, but the doctor is out of town for the holidays. He won't be back until Monday. I can try and contact him for you, if you'd like."

Kerri tamped down her exasperation. She really needed more information on Leah Boothe's illness—from an objective source. Who better than the child's pediatric oncologist? Any insights into the mother's state of mind and outlook would be useful as well, but she doubted the doctor would go down that road. According to Kerri's Google search, Dr. Wilson Smith was considered the best in the Southeast. Managing to get on his patient list was likely a feat accomplished by maternal grandmother Jana Scott.

Kerri passed the office manager her card. "It's very important that I speak with him as soon as possible."

Sheree, according to her name tag, pressed her lips together for a moment. "We were all so sad and horrified to hear about Leah and her mother. Such a sweet little girl. I'm certain Mrs. Scott is devastated. She came to every appointment with Leah and Allison."

Kerri wouldn't have expected any less. "Did Mr. Boothe come as well?"

The woman's brow lined in distaste or something along those lines before she schooled the reaction. "In the beginning he was always with the family. But the last several appointments he wasn't able to come. Allison said he was working." Sheree surveyed the corridor. "His absence was obviously painful for Allison."

If he'd remained unemployed, why wouldn't Boothe have been present at every single appointment? "Is there anyone else I might be able to speak with about Leah?" Kerri held her breath. It never hurt to ask.

"I'm afraid not. Dr. Smith is very particular about patient privacy, as you can imagine. He takes confidentiality very, very seriously. As we all do," she tacked on. "I've already said too much."

Kerri didn't bother explaining that his patient was deceased and exceptions could be made under the circumstances. Sheree assuredly understood this. Pressing her on the issue probably wouldn't generate the desired results.

"I understand." Kerri gave an acknowledging nod. "I hope you understand that I wouldn't ask, but we desperately need to find answers. The fire that took Leah's and Allison's lives was no accident, and we want to find the person responsible."

Sheree's eyes rounded in renewed horror. "I read that the fire was under investigation, but . . ." She pressed her fingers to her lips and gave her head a little shake. "How very, very awful."

"You can see why it's imperative that we learn all we can as quickly as possible."

Sheree's eyes widened again. "You don't think it was the father, do you? Surely not." She shuddered. "I can't even imagine."

Interesting that the father would be her first conclusion but not really surprising. "We're investigating every possible avenue." Kerri studied her a moment. "Is there any reason you believe he should be a suspect?"

Sheree's face instantly blanked. "Oh . . . no, no. Of course not. I just meant . . ." She shrugged. "You know, all those crime shows on television. It's almost always the spouse, isn't it?"

Kerri made a conscious choice not to answer the question. Let her stew on the idea. "Thank you, Sheree." She nodded to the card still in Sheree's hand. "Please call me if you think of anything else that might help with our investigation. We want to do this right for Leah and Allison."

Tears brimmed in the office manager's eyes. "Of course."

Kerri found Luke in the corridor outside Smith's office. The clinic was shoehorned among numerous others in a medical tower close to the UAB Hospital. Luke had taken a call just as they'd been entering the doctor's lobby. Either the call was ongoing or he'd taken another.

She waited until he'd ended the connection and looked at him expectantly. "Anything new?"

"Crime scene folks are finished with the Boothe home. Like we figured, they didn't find anything useful to our investigation." Frustration edged into his expression. "There has to be someone who saw something. Heard something. No way this went down with no notice."

"Maybe we'll get lucky and someone will come forward." In Kerri's experience, this was where the media could be useful. Oftentimes a potential witness was unaware they'd seen or heard something that needed to be reported until they spotted the resulting event on the news. The chief had held a press conference that morning; hopefully getting the word out would trigger a response. Typically, Kerri and Luke would have participated in any press conference related to their ongoing investigation, but the chief wanted them to stay focused on the case.

"I'm still getting no feedback from Sawyer or his people."

Luke was frustrated. Kerri understood. She was damned frustrated herself.

She filled him in on her conversation with the office manager as they headed for the bank of elevators at the other end of the corridor. Thirty-odd hours after the fire, the generic accelerant was basically the only piece of evidence they had. The single eyewitness account of events only confirmed the approximate time of the fire and the fact that the one survivor had been outside and, purportedly, unconscious at or around the time it had started.

"We need to find a way to get Boothe's mother to talk to us," Kerri said. "If Boothe blamed his wife for their daughter's illness, we need a reason why."

"She's not going to flip on her boy," Luke countered.

"I wouldn't expect her to flip, but she could give us her version of what went wrong in the marriage and maybe what her issue with the Scott family entails."

"*Her version* being the key words," Luke agreed.

"We'll give Scott the same opportunity. Between the two of them, we might find a common denominator. My money is on the little girl."

"You'd win that one for sure."

Her partner was right. When in-laws went to war, it was more often than not about the grandchild or grandchildren.

As they settled into the Charger, Kerri considered bringing up O'Grady again, but Luke reached for his phone to take another call before she had chosen the right words. The two of them worked so well together. Discussed everything from a dozen different angles, professionally and personally, with no problem. Except that long-ago past of his. Not until now—in this case—had she realized just how badly they needed to clear the air on the subject. Whatever haunted him, he needed to allow her to help him deal with it.

When the short call ended and Luke had driven from the medical center parking lot, she took the first stab at that hulking barrier. "Is there a chance O'Grady may have some additional insight into Boothe's personal life? Something maybe he's reluctant to share?"

Luke kept his attention on the street as he drove. "Funny that you ask."

"Funny how?"

"That call was from O'Grady. He wants to meet. Pass along some information that might be useful."

"Great." They could use some useful information.

Except Luke's rigid jaw and suddenly white knuckles on the steering wheel suggested something other than great.

What the hell had happened between those two?

As if she'd said the words out loud, he turned to her. "This time you should be there. Maybe you'll pick up on something I miss." He turned his attention back to the street. "I'm not exactly objective where he's concerned."

Kerri bit back a smile. "Two heads are better than one."

One of the things she really appreciated about her partner was that he recognized when he was wrong.

As long as they could both do that, they could deal with most anything.

Hattie's
Seventh Avenue South
Birmingham, 2:30 p.m.

Kerri picked at her fries. O'Grady had insisted on ordering lunch. She sensed he liked taking over the moment, whether it was just a conversation or a homicide investigation. He had that I'm-the-boss air about him. He also possessed that good-old-boy mentality that made her want to punch him. He was old school, no question. As annoying as she found this trait, it didn't make him a bad cop. If he could help with this one, she was happy to ignore his throwback attitude.

"This is beginning to feel like old times," O'Grady announced as he pushed aside his empty plate.

He'd devoured the burger and fries like a man who hadn't eaten in days. Luke, on the other hand, had scarcely touched his meal. Since he sat on the same side of the table as she did, Kerri could feel his right knee bouncing ever so slightly. He was anxious. Tense. Very un-Falco-like. This in turn made her tense and anxious.

"You said you had new information," Luke reminded his former LT.

He'd made them wait through the ordering and the delivering and then the consuming of the food. The man's control issues irritated her. Mostly because his presence bothered Luke, she realized. Made him think about things he clearly did not want to think about.

O'Grady leaned forward, braced his forearms on the table. "I did some asking around. I've got a CI who can confirm your theory about Boothe. I can't believe it escaped my attention, but it seems he had started playing delivery boy for Clinton Sawyer. Fairly recently, as I understand it."

"I'm surprised you've been able to get a reaction out of anyone close to Sawyer. I'm getting nowhere with that lead." Luke's voice reflected the impatience clear on his face.

"I doubt you have the kind of connections I do," O'Grady tossed back. "This is my world, Falco. You're just an outsider looking in nowadays."

The two glared at each other. Kerri figured she would be pulling them apart any second now. Clinton Sawyer maintained numerous layers of security. He wouldn't be easy to touch even for O'Grady, she suspected. Sawyer was a rising star in the Southeast's drug trade. He'd started out as a runner, and the story was he'd climbed over the bloody body of anyone who got in his way to get to the top. The rumors were hearsay, of course. No one had been able to get the goods on the guy.

But his time would come. Even if he continued to elude the law, some other thug would rise up the ranks to take him out.

It was the cycle of thug life.

"You couldn't have told me this on the phone?"

"You think"—Kerri spoke up in an attempt to move past the stalemate—"Boothe was attempting to make money for his child's medical treatments?"

Sometimes people did the wrong things for the right reasons. The Boothe family had certainly been in an optimal position for falling prey to that kind of setup. Animals like Sawyer loved using personal tragedies to lure a person—particularly a cop—over the line.

O'Grady shrugged. "I can't say for sure. Boothe has always been hard to read. I could never really tell if he just liked playing a bad guy or simply used his undercover work for revealing his true self. Either way, that's the word I'm getting. Makes sense. Desperate people do desperate things."

"How do I find this CI?" Luke asked, drawing O'Grady's attention back to himself.

He made a face. "This is where things get a little touchy. I have to be very careful. This CI is important to me. I can't afford any trouble. I'm thinking I should be the communications link. That way we keep things nice and calm. No trouble. No unnecessary risks."

Before he even spoke, Kerri knew Luke would never go for that one.

"That doesn't work for me," Luke argued. "I want the name. I can't assess the merit of what this CI says without looking him in the eye."

"*Her.* This CI is female."

This news seemed to take Luke aback. He blinked. "Whatever. I still need to look her in the eye when she answers our questions."

"I don't know," O'Grady hedged. "You remember what happened last time."

"We're done here." Luke scooted back his chair and stood; anger radiated from him like a boiler set to blow any second.

"Wait, wait, wait." O'Grady motioned for him to sit down. "Let's not get all out of sorts."

"We don't have time for these games," Luke said from behind gritted teeth as he sank back into his chair. "This is a double-homicide investigation. Either give me the name or stop vying for my attention. This is twice now you've tried to push your way into our investigation."

The stretch of silence that followed was jam packed with tension from both men. Kerri opted to ride it out.

"Carla Brown." O'Grady broke first. "She lives over on Fairfax. I'll text you the exact address."

Luke stood once more. Kerri did the same.

"You hear anything else," he said, his voice gruff, "you let me know ASAP."

Luke left money for their meals on the table and headed for the door. Kerri hesitated but thought better of what she'd started to say, then followed.

"What did he mean about last time?" Kerri asked as she slid into the passenger seat. The best thing about being the senior partner was not having to drive unless the mood struck.

"There was an incident with a CI. She ended up dead."

The muscle in his tense jaw started to flex.

Okay. "Was the CI one of yours?"

He passed his phone to her. "Read off that address for me, would you?"

Kerri recognized the nonanswer as a yes.

So, Luke had lost a CI. Wow. No wonder he didn't like to talk about it.

She gave him the address and let the quiet linger between them. What she'd learned about his past wasn't much, but it was a rather explosive beginning and spoke volumes about what haunted him. His reasons for not wanting to discuss the past were becoming clearer and far more understandable.

No wonder he didn't like going back to that place, and O'Grady, simply by virtue of being who he was, automatically took Luke back into that dark time.

The drive to Fairfax took a few minutes longer than usual with the extra traffic. This time of year people were already shopping for Christmas. Everyone wanted to get the job done before the real insanity set in. Kerri refused to consider that she had done nothing in the way of holiday shopping.

There was always Amazon.

Carla Brown opened her door on the first knock. O'Grady had obviously briefed her about their visit. The CI lived in a tiny apartment that was clean if not luxurious. Her pencil-thin body and sickly yellow complexion spoke of long-term drug abuse. The fidgeting and excessive chatter backed up that conclusion. Her willingness to speak so openly was another confirmation that O'Grady had paved the way for their visit.

"I was freaked out the first time I saw Logan with one of Clinton's men," she said, her eyes huge with possibly feigned and certainly exaggerated shock. "I recognized him as one of Paddy's, and I figured the shit was about to hit the fan." She lifted one razor-thin shoulder. "I didn't tell. Didn't see the point. In the end I figured it was part of an op. No cop had gotten so close to Clinton, and to tell you the truth, I was impressed. Then I heard about his wife and kid dying in that house fire, and I knew what I'd seen was bad, bad, bad. I was already thinking I needed to touch base when Paddy called. I told him exactly what I just told you."

"When did you first spot Boothe with Sawyer?" Luke asked.

"About two months ago. I can't say exactly when. The days run together sometimes."

"But you're certain," Kerri pressed, "of what you saw?"

"Oh yeah. It was the two of them in a dark corner over at the Peppered Pig. After what happened the other night, I asked one of my contacts. He said Boothe had started facilitating deliveries. You know, making sure the mules don't run into any trouble. He knows the other cops. Still friends with some of them. It was a big coup for Clinton."

"Did anyone provide you with the information to give us?" Luke asked, his tone just shy of accusing.

Carla Brown drew back from him, sinking deeper into the ratty chair that appeared to be her favorite. "Are you calling me a liar?"

Luke shook his head. "No. I'm just asking if someone might have told you what to say. Like Paddy, maybe."

Her eyes narrowed. "Why would he do that?"

"You know how he likes control. He controls you, controls his crew and their CIs. Maybe he wants to control me and my partner too."

Brown glanced at Kerri, uncertainty flashing like a neon sign on her face. "No. He wouldn't do that. Not Paddy. No way."

"You and Paddy are close?" Kerri asked.

The other woman smirked, her posture straightening. "We're close enough."

Well, that said it all, didn't it? Kerri kept the comment to herself.

"Two months is a long time to avoid telling Paddy what a former member of his crew was doing," Luke pointed out.

The CI glared at Luke. "I already explained why. No reason for me to mention it. I don't talk shit unless it's relevant. You surely remember how these things work."

"Too bad. Maybe his wife and kid would still be alive if you had," Luke tossed back.

"Right. Blame me, asshole," Brown snapped. "It's my fault the bastard got his wife and kid killed."

"I imagine you're afraid of Sawyer," Kerri offered in hopes of cooling things down. One of them needed to. Luke was obviously too close to this to be objective.

Brown nodded. "He's a piece of shit. He'd kill his own mother if the mood struck him. Anyone would be a fool not to be afraid of him."

"Was there anyone else you saw Boothe with who worked with Sawyer?" Kerri asked before Luke could stick his foot any deeper into his mouth.

"Not that I recall, but that wouldn't be likely," she explained. "Clinton has a very tight group of people around him. The ones, like Boothe, who provide an exclusive service for him but aren't part of his family are kept separate. Only he deals with them. He never allows the outsiders to mingle with each other or with the insiders. He's really strict like that."

Luke dropped his card on the coffee table. "Call me if you think of anything else."

When he stood, Brown pointed a finger at him. "I know you." Her eyes widened. "You used to be in Paddy's crew."

"You don't know me." Luke said this on his way to the door.

12

5:30 p.m.

University of Alabama Hospital
Sixth Avenue South
Birmingham

Kerri stopped at the nurses' station and checked on Boothe's condition. He was stable and steadily improving. Good news.

Better news was that Logan Boothe had been taken to a therapy treatment. His mother, however, sat in the chair next to his bed doing crossword puzzles. The son being out of the room presented the needed opportunity to get her alone.

Rebecca Boothe looked up as they entered the room. Kerri braced for what would no doubt be a rant. The lady was very outspoken.

"I have nothing to say." Rebecca turned her attention back to her book and scrawled letters into empty white boxes.

"We don't have to talk," Luke said as he propped himself against the counter that ran the length of the wall opposite the bed. "We'll just wait quietly. We're here to ask Logan a few more questions."

"He has nothing to say either." Rebecca flipped to the next page, folded over the previous one, and readied her pen.

The box of tissues in the seat next to her as well as the growing mound of crumpled ones in the trash bin between her chair and the bed warned that as indifferent as the woman wanted to appear, she was not. Her own grief had taken a toll. The anger she held on to with such a firm grip was to conceal the fear. Fear that she would lose her son as well as the granddaughter who had already been taken from her.

"Actually," Kerri said, "these are only follow-up questions. He's already given his official statement."

"That's right," Luke confirmed. "His confession is pretty cut and dried. We just want to cross our *t*'s and dot our *i*'s before turning in the official report."

The older woman's eyes shot to Luke and narrowed with suspicion. "I don't believe you. What on earth would he have to confess? He's done nothing wrong."

So, he hadn't told her he'd confessed to a double homicide. "It's true, Mrs. Boothe," Kerri insisted. "Logan took full responsibility for what happened Sunday night."

The pen the woman had been using hit the shiny tile floor, and the book followed in its path as she rose to her feet, swayed slightly. "I don't know what you're trying to do, but my son would never hurt Leah . . . or . . . or Allison."

"They weren't hurt, Mrs. Boothe," Luke corrected. "They were murdered."

She swung her attention to Luke, pointed a finger at him. "I'd like you to leave now. I have nothing to say."

"Mrs. Boothe," Kerri urged, "your son confessed. We recommended he speak with an attorney, but he refused. Unless we find evidence to suggest otherwise, he's our only suspect. If he stands by his confession, we'll have no choice but to arrest him for premeditated murder."

Her eyes growing wider with every word, the older woman took a long, ragged breath, seemed to mull over her options. "He only said that because he survived. It's . . . it's that survivor's guilt thing. He believes he should have died too." She blinked at the moisture gathering in her eyes. "I've tried to make him see that he's not thinking straight, but he won't have it. You can't believe anything he says right now. His emotions are all over the place. My God, he's likely still in shock on some level."

"Do you know of any reason he would claim responsibility?" Kerri pressed. "Besides survivor's guilt, I mean. There must be something."

She squeezed her eyes shut, but the tears slipped past her hold as she collapsed back into her chair. "He wouldn't tell me." Her eyes opened, and the pain there was convincing. She was telling the truth—at least to the best of her knowledge. "Something happened that changed everything, and he won't say what."

"Why didn't you and Allison get along?" Luke asked, his tone gentler this time.

A frown deepened the lines of her face. "It started right from the get-go. Allison hated my relationship with Logan. She thought I hovered too much. Thought he listened to me too much."

Kerri couldn't imagine where Allison would have gotten such an idea.

"She didn't like that I dropped by what she felt was too often. After Leah was born, things only got worse. She took offense at my every comment or suggestion. I couldn't say or do anything to suit her."

"She believed," Kerri ventured, "you were interfering in their lives?"

The woman's lips tightened, but she nodded in acknowledgment. "After Leah's birth, her mother got more involved too. She was jealous of how much Leah adored me, and she did all in her power to push me out of the picture as well. It really was painfully obvious. Anyone could have seen it."

Kerri thought of Jana Scott, and the image didn't quite fit with the persona she had presented in their interview. But people rarely showed what they didn't want seen. "How did Logan feel about this? Did he attempt to intervene?"

Rebecca shook her head sadly. "He said it would only make things worse. By the time Leah was three, I was banned completely. Logan still called me behind her back and sent me pictures and videos."

"But you weren't allowed to visit?" Kerri clarified.

"Never. Not birthdays, Christmas—nothing. Until she got sick. When her leukemia was discovered, Logan finally convinced Allison to let me see Leah."

Kerri could understand how humiliating the situation was to the paternal grandmother. It was too soon to tell if she'd deserved such drastic measures. There were people who just pushed all the wrong buttons. It was a true shame when children were involved.

"Did you notice any changes recently," Luke asked, "in Logan's relationship with Allison or Mrs. Scott?"

"It was obvious that Allison had been pushing him away for a while—well before Leah got sick."

"Was this because of you?" Luke asked straight out.

Rebecca stared at him for a long moment before responding. "I'm sure I was part of it. She hated me. I was in a no-win situation, as was Logan. Her feelings toward me were never going to change."

"How did that make you feel?" Kerri wondered if the lady understood the situation presented as motive . . . for *her*.

"Are you asking if it made me want to kill her?"

No point beating around the bush. Kerri said, "I am."

"No, but it did make me daydream about all the ways she might end up out of the picture. Divorce. Car crash. Slip and fall in the shower." She shrugged. "I'm human. I didn't mean it, of course." Her voice trembled on the last.

"I appreciate your candor," Kerri allowed. At times, good people had bad thoughts. Didn't mean they were bad or that they would follow through.

But there were those who did. Was Rebecca Boothe one of them? Maybe.

"I would never have hurt her." Rebecca closed her eyes and drew in another of those deep, dramatic breaths before opening them. "And I most certainly would never, ever hurt Leah. She was my angel." Her lips trembled. "I can hardly bear the thought of never seeing her again."

That was one of the worst parts of losing someone you loved. Kerri pushed the thought away. Never being able to say the things you might have left unsaid . . . or to just see them again.

"Mrs. Boothe," Luke said, "I need you to think long and hard before you answer my next question."

She looked to him, swiped at her eyes. "Okay."

"Logan is one of us. He was a cop for a lot of years, and we aren't forgetting that fact. We're not looking for an easy way to close this case. We're looking for the truth . . . whatever that is."

Rebecca nodded. Dabbed at her nose with a tissue.

"Was your son involved in anything that might have made his family a target?" Luke asked, getting down to the nitty-gritty.

Her hand went to her chest as alarm claimed her face. "Absolutely not. Logan is a good man. He would never do anything to hurt his family, or anyone else."

"There has to be a reason," Kerri countered, "that he feels responsible. We need you to think really hard. Anything you tell us might help clear your son."

The seconds ticked off so loudly in the silence, Kerri found herself waiting for an explosion.

"No. I know my son. He was not involved in any sort of wrongdoing."

If she was lying, she was damned good at it. If she was telling the truth, that would mean O'Grady and his CI were the ones lying. Or maybe she simply wasn't aware of what her son was doing. Kerri pressed harder. "How can you be so sure? He had to be desperate for money."

"He was. I know better than anyone. I mortgaged my house. I sold all my jewelry. I sold my late husband's beloved car. I'm practically bankrupt from giving Logan what he needed to help his family. To help Leah."

Wow. Both grandmothers had been bleeding cash and collateral to help. Why would Logan Boothe cross the line between good and bad when he had support like this? Why would O'Grady leap across that thin blue line to say he did if he didn't?

"Please don't tell him I told you." She glanced at the open door. "He's already humiliated and devastated; I don't want to add to his burden."

"We won't tell him," Luke assured her, "unless we have no choice."

She nodded. "Thank you."

"Thank you, Mrs. Boothe." Kerri glanced at her partner. "We'll be back another time to speak with Logan. If you think of anything else at all, please call us. The more information we have, the more quickly we can sort out what happened and find the truth."

"I will. As long as you're not trying to railroad my son, you have my word."

On the way to the elevators, Kerri waved to the nurse who'd provided the update on Logan's condition. The elevator car was open and waiting, and they stepped aboard.

Luke tapped the button for the lobby.

"You think she's the one lying?" Kerri asked as the elevator bumped into downward motion. "She's certainly giving a completely different story than O'Grady."

"She might not be telling us everything she knows," he admitted. "His momma has the most obvious motive for lying. As for O'Grady, I just don't trust him."

Halfway across the first-floor lobby, Kerri's cell vibrated. She checked the screen, putting her hand up to block the sun as they exited the building. *Chief.*

"Devlin," she said.

"I've spoken with the DA," he said, rather than *hello* or *how's it going.*

Kerri opened the car door and slid into the passenger seat. Luke dropped behind the wheel. "I'm putting you on speaker, Chief, so Falco can participate in the conversation."

She tapped the screen. "You spoke with the district attorney," Kerri said to bring her partner up to speed. She doubted the news to follow would be anything they wanted to hear or would in any way prove useful to their investigation.

"Since Boothe is a former BPD detective, and considering the connection of the victims to the BPD family, we've had several meetings regarding how to proceed with Boothe, particularly in light of his confession."

Allison's father being the chief's dear friend and first partner might have something to do with it as well, Kerri thought.

"It's a little early for that conversation, isn't it?" Luke contended. "We don't have enough evidence to build a case." He flashed Kerri a what-the-hell look.

"Boothe confessed," the chief argued. "What else do you need?"

This was the chief's personal involvement speaking. He was fully aware of what they needed to close a case. He had agreed with their conclusions only yesterday. What had changed his mind?

"All due respect, sir," Kerri spoke up, "we suspect Boothe's confession was about survivor's guilt. There are too many inconsistencies. Like the fact that he has fractures to both legs, broken ribs—all consistent with a violent struggle or a fall. The victims had no such injuries, suggesting someone else was involved."

"It's possible," the chief argued, "he set the fire and realized his only way out of the house was to jump out a window. That would explain his injuries."

The scenario wasn't impossible. Kerri couldn't deny she'd considered this as well.

"Look, boss," Luke said in his usual irreverent manner, "the confession looks bad, but my gut says there's a lot more to this. We need the chance to properly investigate before we start moving toward an arrest."

Her partner made a good point, but the chief likely wouldn't see the validity. He sounded as though he'd already made up his mind.

The chief said, "You've spoken with Lieutenant O'Grady."

This was not a question; he knew they had.

"I spoke to him only minutes ago," the chief went on before either of them could answer. "He tells me that Boothe was unstable, which is part of the reason he walked away from the department earlier this year. O'Grady believes he's unquestionably capable of cold-blooded murder. In fact, he had plenty to say about the guy. Were you aware he was thought to be cheating on his wife? The financial problems were overwhelming. The child's prognosis was dim. The motive is there, Detectives. Find the evidence."

"We need time to plug the holes, sir," Kerri said before Luke could respond. He looked ready to blast the chief. Not a good idea. "Any decent lawyer could take apart what little we have so far."

"Take the rest of the week," the chief said, his own voice as taut as Luke's jaw. "Show me evidence to refute his confession by close of business on Friday, or he will be charged."

The call ended.

"Did O'Grady mention Boothe's cheating to you?" she asked. He certainly hadn't let Kerri in on it if that was the case. Boothe had been cheating? Where the hell had that come from?

The glare that arrowed in her direction was not pleasant and answered her question even before he asked, "Do you think he did?"

"No. You would have told me." She knew this. She shouldn't have asked.

"The son of a bitch lied to us."

Her partner was right. Omissions were lies, too, and O'Grady had left out a bombshell. But why lie? What was the point?

"We should confront him," she suggested, her own anger mounting. What kind of cop was O'Grady that he'd play it this way when another cop's life—ex-cop or not—hung in the balance? "It's possible this was something new he discovered since we spoke earlier." Even she doubted that one. Either way, the confrontation needed to happen.

"I'll take care of O'Grady."

The way Luke said the words made her uneasy. It was the first time he'd ever made a statement that sounded like a veiled threat. "What does that mean? You going to take him out? Beat the hell out of him? Bust his kneecaps?"

"I would love to beat the hell out of him," he bit off. "But I don't do that kind of shit anymore. You know this, right?"

"Okay." She held up her hands. "You need to tell me. Now. What is the deal between you and O'Grady? I know you don't like to talk about that part of your past, but this . . ." She motioned to him and then to herself. "This is affecting us personally, and it's affecting the case. That's unacceptable."

Fingers tight on the steering wheel, steely gaze straight ahead, he took a moment, then said, "You're right. It's affecting everything."

Relief chased away some of her own tension. It was about time.

"O'Grady has this way of making people do things they don't want to do." He dropped his head as if ashamed. "The things I did—the life I lived—are on me." He lifted his face to Kerri's. "But he made me what I was. He's not a good guy, Kerri. I don't trust him at all."

Damn. "I don't trust him either," she confirmed. She covered his right hand with her own. "But I do trust you."

"That means more than you can possibly know."

"Good." She smiled, gave his hand a squeeze. "Let's go back to the house and look for a window on the upper floor that's broken or open."

"I hate to tell you this, Devlin." He backed out of the parking slot. "But there are a lot of broken windows in that house."

The firefighters had broken a number of them. Whatever necessary to clear the smoke. "We're not looking for one that's been broken from the outside. We're looking for one that was opened or broken from the inside so Boothe could jump to escape the smoke and flames."

"*If*," Luke countered, "he started the fire."

"We don't have a lot of time to prove whether he did or not."

He shot her a grin. "We've been against the clock before."

They definitely had. Kerri relaxed into the seat as Luke navigated to their destination. She suddenly realized that she hadn't had the time in more than twenty-four hours to miss her daughter. The thought unsettled Kerri. How had she gone that long without thinking of Tori?

She crossed her arms over her chest and fought a shiver as she considered that Jana Scott would never again see her daughter or her granddaughter.

But did her love for both make her any more innocent than the other grandmother? Or the husband?

No one close to the family could be exempt from scrutiny.

13

6:15 p.m.

Rebecca waited patiently while Logan was wheeled back into the room. She watched as the nurse and attendant moved him back to his bed. It wasn't so easy.

Her poor, poor son.

Tears rose on her lashes, and she batted them back. He needed her to be strong. He was under tremendous pressure. Everything she said and did had to reaffirm how completely she stood behind him. Whatever happened, she would always be on his side. Until she drew her last breath, she would love and support him.

No matter what.

Deep inside she shuddered at the accusations those detectives had made.

Their words sickened her. There were things they didn't know. But they would in time. When justice had been served.

Until then, she would not waver. This was her responsibility.

Pain twisted inside her. She forced it away. Nothing could change what had been done. Nothing. Her sweet Leah was gone.

She would not lose her son too.

When the nurse and attendant had gone, closing the door behind them, she placed her crossword puzzle book aside and pushed up from her chair. To some the distraction of the puzzles might seem foolish, but if not for being able to escape in some way, she would surely lose her mind.

She couldn't permit the thoughts to consume her. Not now. Not until this was finished.

The ache tore at her chest as if a great fist had burst through and grabbed hold of her heart.

She paused at the tray table to pump sanitizer into her palm. She rubbed it over her hands and moved to his bedside. He could not know the battle she fought. His eyes were closed, but he wasn't asleep. He didn't want to talk to anyone. Not even the mother who loved him more than life.

"Logan, sweetheart," she said softly. "I know you're in terrible pain, and your heart is hurting so badly from what's happened." She took a moment to steady her voice. "But you need to think beyond this moment, beyond the horrendous pain. Your life depends on what you do and say now."

His eyes opened, and he stared at her as if he didn't even recognize her. His precious brown eyes were empty. His heart shattered.

"I don't care what happens to me now."

His voice sounded too coarse from the smoke inhalation. Her chest squeezed at the idea that he had barely survived the horror of that night. Memories twisted inside her. She fought them back.

"Please, son," she pleaded. "I need you to care. I cannot lose you too."

He said nothing. Closed his eyes once more.

She moistened her lips and chose her words carefully. Caution was very, very important. Especially now. "All you have to do is take back your confession. Tell the detectives you didn't really mean it, that you were distraught. Emotional. They'll understand. The woman—Devlin—has a child. She'll understand for sure."

Still, he said nothing.

"Think about it," she urged softly. "You have my word this is going to be taken care of. There will be justice."

She would not fail.

Her son was innocent. She would see that those responsible paid for what they had done.

For her own part, she would pay as well.

14

7:50 p.m.

The Cabin
Oak Mountain State Park
Birmingham

Luke shut off the headlights and rolled the last few yards to the cabin. He recognized the location even in the dark. A lot of years had passed since he was here last, and his showing up now might not be welcome, but he was pretty much out of options.

On Tuesday nights, sometimes on Sunday mornings, members of O'Grady's crew met here to talk shop. They didn't actually own the place, but O'Grady knew someone who knew someone, so they had a sort of permanent unwritten lease on the place. It stayed locked up like a fortress, with all sorts of cameras and alarms to make them aware if anyone messed around the place when they were gone. It was the one getaway where they could come and talk openly. Drink themselves unconscious and shit like that. In all the years they had used this place, no one had ever dared to leak the location.

Before Luke made it ten paces from his car, the muzzle of a barrel jammed into the back of his head. "Who the hell are you, and what're you doing here?"

He put his hands up. "Detective Luke Falco. I used to be in Paddy's crew."

"Well, you aren't now," the man who remained behind Luke said. "And that's a problem. *For you.*"

For about three seconds Luke considered that he might have misjudged his ability to talk his way into the good graces of the current members of this club.

"Bachman, let him in."

Luke recognized the voice that called out from the darkness. Relief trickled through him. Maybe this wouldn't get him killed after all. Kerri would be seriously pissed if he allowed that to happen.

The pressure on the back of his skull relaxed, and Luke moved forward, toward the light coming from the windows of the rustic cabin. Toward the voice that had the hair on the back of his neck standing on end.

"I was just doing my job," the man—Bachman—said.

"No problem." Luke was intimately familiar with the drill. Coming here unannounced was at his own risk. This he knew as well.

As they approached the door, a figure moved out of the shadows. "If it ain't Luke fucking Falco."

Douglas Durham, a.k.a. Dog. Luke was surprised the bastard was still alive, much less still working undercover. "What's up, Dog."

A brief hesitation and then a quick clasp of hands before Durham said, "Looks like you're what's up. What're you doing here?"

Dog gave Bachman a nod, and the younger man disappeared inside the cabin.

"I need some advice from the crew," Luke said, getting straight to the point.

Dog grunted. "Man, you aren't part of this crew anymore. You looking to get a cap popped into that thick skull of yours?"

Luke shrugged. "I thought the crew was like the marines. You know, semper fi."

Durham hesitated again, a little longer this time, then reached for the door. After opening it, he gestured for Luke to go in. Four other men, none that Luke recognized, were gathered around the pool table. The main room in the cabin was outfitted with an extensively stocked bar, a pool table, and a pair of worn, comfortable sofas. There were two bedrooms filled with bunk beds down a narrow hall and a single bathroom shared between them.

If a crew member needed to chill off the grid, this was the place.

"Luke Falco," Durham said to the others. "He used to be part of Paddy's crew."

Greetings were mumbled; heads gave vague nods. Funny thing was, they all looked about the same as Luke except younger. Grungy jeans, black tees covered with sweatshirts or hoodies. Biker boots. Most hadn't seen a shaving razor in days. Hair was long and could stand a good wash.

Memories slammed into him like a punch to the gut. This was the life he'd worked so hard—sacrificed everything—to dig so deep into. Then he'd run hard and fast to escape it. Just another one of those dreams that looked and sounded far better than it was. The grass-was-always-greener shit.

Durham called off the men's nicknames, going left to right. "Chop." Chop glanced at Luke as Durham pointed him out. "Don't ask how he got that name."

Luke forced himself to laugh despite not feeling the slightest bit amused. Chop was kind of short. His head was shaved clean, the ceiling lights reflecting off it like a newly waxed floor.

"Bachman," Dog went on. "Slater and Riker."

Nods were exchanged.

"I'm not trying to crash your chill time," Luke assured them. "I just need a little help with the case I'm investigating."

The one called Riker turned to face Luke, propped a hip against the pool table. "You working the Boothe case?"

Logical conclusion. "I am. Me and my partner."

Riker made a face and wagged his head. His hair was buzzed short, but he made up for the lack on his head with a long beard and mustache. "Man, that's a tragedy. Boothe is a good guy. It sucks he got hit so hard."

"It's fucked up." This from trigger-happy Bachman, who sat on a sofa, watching the others as if he feared being tagged at any second.

Luke pegged Bachman as a rookie. New to the crew. Too damned scared to join in the game unless he was told to. His shaggy hair was mussed, like he hadn't bothered with a comb in a while.

"How is it you think we can help?" Dog asked.

"You want a beer, man?" The offer came from Slater. His long hair was tied back in a ponytail, and every inch of flesh Luke could see was covered in tats.

"Sure." Declining would be seen as an insult or as a signal that he suspected one or more of the crew of some wrongdoing.

Slater grabbed a beer from the fridge and tossed it to Luke. He twisted off the cap and took a long swallow, drawing in the foam from the shaken brew.

They all watched and waited. If Luke hadn't once been one of them, he would have been totally creeped out. This was how the flesh eaters stared at potential victims in horror flicks.

The idea that he'd ever been like this made him feel sick. Not because of the way they dressed or the tats but because he knew the rest of the story. The parts that never made it onto the page in official reports.

"I'm trying to figure out how Boothe got himself into such deep shit. The guy had ten years' experience under his belt. Why walk away?"

Chop and Dog exchanged a glance.

"Paddy was extra hard on Boothe," Dog said. "They had a beef of some sort. I guess it was personal, 'cause he didn't share the details. You know Paddy—if he thinks you're not living up to your potential, he pushes and pushes to try and get you there. I think Boothe just cracked. Fell apart. Couldn't take the pressure. He was having trouble at home, and it just all got to be too much."

"Was he cheating on his wife?" Luke downed another swallow of beer.

Another shared glance, this time between Chop and Riker.

Luke waited. Chop turned to the pool table and took his shot; apparently it was his turn. Then he shifted his attention back to Luke. "The rumor was he had himself a little something on the side."

Unfortunately, in this life the little something on the side was not unusual. "Was this something serious or just a hobby to pass the time?" Luke ventured.

Chop shrugged. "You'd have to ask Boothe about that."

"You remember her name?"

Riker shook his head. "Nope."

Luke turned to Dog. "You have any idea who she was?"

"Not a clue."

Well, hell. "But you believe there was someone?"

"Isn't there always? Whether by accident or design, shit happens."

Luke ignored the jab. "Boothe and Paddy didn't get along?"

"Not really," Dog confirmed. "Boothe never learned his manners. Paddy takes care of his crew. Keeps the wives—if there are wives— informed. Checks on the kiddies. Makes sure everyone has what they need. You understand. He always takes care of things. Boothe apparently didn't appreciate all Paddy did for him and his family. He was too busy bucking for a promotion or better assignment. Whatever."

"He didn't fit in," Slater said. "Never really tried."

"This is why Paddy was hard on him?" Luke looked to Dog for an answer. "Kind of seems like Paddy wasn't taking care of Boothe."

Dog shrugged. "You'll have to ask Paddy about that."

He hadn't really expected these guys to spill anything big. But he would take what he could get. "Word on the street is," Luke said,

"Boothe was working for Clinton Sawyer. You know anything about that?"

"He's about that stupid," Slater said. "I swear the man couldn't see past his emotions. He had no business in this world."

No one really fit in this world, Luke realized. They were recruited, broken, and molded back into something that fit. He pushed away the voices that echoed through his head.

"You haven't heard any rumors like that?" Luke prodded.

Shoulders hitched up and down with little or no interest.

Luke tried another avenue. Fishing. He'd throw out a possibility like bait and see if he got any bites. "I hear he had anger issues. A real hothead."

Heads shook. "I never saw anything like that," Riker said.

"He'd get pissed, sure," Slater added. "No different than any of us."

"I got nothing," Bachman tossed out. "He seemed as normal as any of us."

Which isn't saying much.

"But you said"—Luke directed his words at the one called Slater—"he had a problem controlling his emotions."

Slater shrugged. "He was a whiny ass. Always whining about something."

"Things aren't the way they used to be, Falco," Dog said. "We have different rules now. After what happened . . . we watch each other more closely. Call it like we see it before it's too late."

A combination of regret and anger fired through Luke's blood. He hadn't needed the reminder. "I should go. Thanks for talking to me." He nodded to the men gathered around the pool table, then headed to the door. The chatter and laughter resumed behind him.

Dog put his hand on the door before Luke could open it. "We go back," he said.

Luke met his gaze.

"Way back," Dog added. "I respect the decision you made, man, but that's as far as it goes. Don't ever come back here. This isn't your world anymore. You're treading on thin ice. Next time I won't say a word, and that bullet will plow straight through your brain."

Luke walked out. As he reached his Charger, he stalled. With nothing but the light of the moon trickling through the treetops, he made out the figure leaning against the driver's side door.

"Did you get what you came for?"

O'Grady.

Either the bastard had a tracking device on him, Luke decided, or someone had informed the boss about a stranger's arrival.

"You trained them too well for that," Luke tossed back. What the hell had he been thinking? That some member of the crew would say what he wanted to hear? Not in a million fucking years. Maybe he'd just wanted this bastard to know he dared to ask.

"I get where you're coming from, Falco," O'Grady said. "You hate me; you hate the life you had in this crew. It's a free country. You're entitled to feel whatever it is you want to feel. But don't confuse what you want to feel with what's real. I'm a good cop. Always have been. If you have some misguided idea that I had something to do with what happened to Boothe's family, you're fucking crazy. You, of all people, should know I protect my own."

"Seems to me you didn't protect Boothe," Luke pointed out. "I'd say you fell down big time on the job with him. Did telling the chief," he demanded, his anger flaring, "that Boothe was cheating on his wife protect him?" Before he could respond, Luke held up his hands. "Why would you keep that from me and Devlin and then go spill it to the chief?"

"Maybe the chief misinterpreted what I said," O'Grady offered. "He's the one all tied up personally with this one."

This was pointless.

Luke reached for the door handle and waited for him to move. Even with Luke standing right next to his former LT, face to face, the bastard didn't move. "We're done here," Luke clarified.

"You need to hear me, old friend," O'Grady said. "Get your head together. You're barking up all the wrong trees on this one."

When O'Grady walked away, Luke was finally able to drag in a breath and force his coiled muscles to relax. He wanted to go after him. To beat the hell out of him for things he couldn't even name.

No.

The one thing he really wanted right now more than anything else was to see Kerri. She'd agreed to try to catch Jana Scott while Luke came here. If she'd come with him, these guys wouldn't have talked to him at all.

He hadn't wanted her to come.

He didn't want her exposed to any more of this than absolutely necessary. More than anything he wanted to protect her from this place. These people.

This life.

———

Devlin Residence
Twenty-First Avenue South
Birmingham, 9:05 p.m.

Relief swarmed through Luke at the sight of Kerri's vintage Wagoneer parked in the driveway. Whenever they worked apart, he was always glad when he could confirm that she was okay. Being a cop was not for the faint of heart. It was more dangerous now than ever. That said, if anyone could take care of herself, it was Kerri. The realization did not prevent him from worrying about her.

Particularly after spending even a few minutes in the past he'd worked so hard to leave behind. He hated looking back.

He only wanted to move forward. Toward Kerri and the life they were building together.

She and her daughter were over-the-moon important to him.

Kerri waved from the kitchen window. He smiled and waved back. No matter how often it happened, that simple gesture never ceased to make him happy. Even on a chilly night like this, watching her through the kitchen window backlit by the glow of overhead lights made him feel like he belonged.

Like he was home.

He opened the door, and the smell of pizza filled his nostrils. "Mmm. Smells good."

She laughed at their inside joke. "Straight from the delivery guy's warming bag."

He hung his jacket by the door, washed his hands, and grabbed two beers from the fridge. They settled on the stools around the kitchen island and opened the box. Steam rose from the cheesy, meaty concoction.

"You catch up with Jana Scott?"

"I left a message on her cell, but she wasn't home. I drove to the Chablis house to see if maybe she was there. She wasn't. But"—she flashed a big smile—"Mr. Crandall invited me for tea."

"I think he likes you." Luke tore a slice of pizza from the pie. "Did he have anything new to relay?"

"Sadly not. He mostly wanted to talk. He's lonely." Kerri ate for half a minute before firing her first question at him. "Did you find your former colleagues?"

"I did." He opted to leave out the part about the gun pointed at the back of his head and the departing warnings. "The guys who last worked with Boothe confirmed the rumor about an affair but couldn't or wouldn't give me a name. They all agreed on one thing—O'Grady was hard on Boothe."

"Why?" She grabbed a napkin and dabbed at the sauce on her chin.

Luke couldn't stop his smile as he reached over and swiped away the spot she'd missed. "The consensus was that Boothe had a respect problem."

"Anything about him having a temper?"

"They all agreed he was more whiny than hotheaded."

Kerri watched him closely. "You okay?"

She read him all too well. "I'll live." He bit off a chunk of pizza to prevent having to say more.

"If there was an affair, we need to locate the woman. Find out what Boothe was saying to her. If he dumped her, she's likely willing to talk. She could even be a suspect. Get rid of the wife and kid and maybe win back her lover."

Luke agreed. It was the getting it done that presented the problem. Maybe he could strong-arm the name from Boothe.

Thankfully, before he could mention the plan to Kerri, his cell vibrated, and he dragged it from his hip pocket. The name on the screen was his ex-wife's. His heart instantly kicking into a higher gear, he showed it to Kerri and then answered. "Hey, Shelly. What's up?"

Shelly didn't call him often. Mostly she sent text messages. Let him know about upcoming events involving Liam. Gave doctor updates. Sent pics. Stuff like that. Worry nudged him harder. Kids got sick and injured. So far Liam hadn't suffered anything serious, but there was always the potential.

"We have a big problem, Luke."

Worry started to gnaw harder at his gut. "Okay." His gaze met Kerri's. She smiled, and he felt a little better. Her smiles had that kind of power.

"Liam had an orthodontist appointment yesterday, and he's going to need braces."

Luke groaned. "I remember those days." He frowned then. Seemed awful early for braces. Liam was only nine. But what did he know? Everything seemed to happen earlier with kids these days. "What can I do to help?"

The sigh echoed loudly across the line. "Merilee—you know, Brad's mom—and I were discussing the braces."

Luke had met Brad's mom. Maybe *met* was the wrong word; he'd seen her from a distance. But yeah, he understood who Shelly meant. And Brad . . . well, Brad was the new husband. Not new, really. He and Shelly had married not long after she and Luke had divorced. When Liam was just a baby.

"You can't blame him for not wanting braces." What kid did? Luke had hated them.

"It isn't that, Luke."

Her tone caused his tension to escalate to the next level.

"I thought Liam was in his room, but I was wrong. Merilee was saying that Brad and his sisters never needed braces. She asked me if I did, and I told her no, but that you had."

Luke's gut clenched. "He overheard you."

"Yes. What's worse, he kept quiet and listened to the rest of the discussion. Merilee suggested I make a list of any other things his *biological* father had that we might need to know in the future—in case I wasn't around to tell them. She meant well, but the timing was unfortunate. Now we have a serious situation."

Luke's gaze collided once more with Kerri's. On a scale of one to ten for bad, this was a forty. "What happened when he got tired of eavesdropping?" Luke's heart thundered in his chest, threatening to fracture his sternum.

"He demanded to know what I was talking about. You know he's really smart and perceptive for a nine-year-old."

The kid was for sure. His progress reports from school said it all. Liam was way smart. Smarter than Luke, without question.

Damn.

"You told him, then." Of course she had. What else could she have done?

"I did. After Brad got home, we talked more. In the end, Liam wanted only one thing."

Luke held his breath. "I'm listening."

"To talk to you in person."

Luke had only spoken to Liam a few times when Shelly had introduced him at games. She had called Luke an old friend. Allowing him to come to the games to see Liam was a fairly new arrangement in his and Shelly's tenuous relationship. Two years ago, after Luke had moved back to Birmingham, she had approached him with the idea that he get to know Liam—from a distance, of course. She was glad he'd turned his life around and said as much.

He hadn't deserved the opportunity, but he was tremendously grateful.

"He wants to talk to me?"

"Yes."

Okay. He could do that. Holy shit. "When?"

"I tried to persuade him to wait until the weekend. With Thanksgiving and everything, we're all a little overwhelmed, as I'm sure you are."

"When, Shelly?"

"He wants to see you now. Like, right now. Would you mind coming over?"

"Okay." A kind of numbness took over as Luke said the word. "What do you want me to say?"

"Brad and I talked about that before I called you. We believe it's best to just tell the truth. If we don't, we'll be in this position all over again at some later date. The truth is best, don't you think?"

"Yeah, yeah. The truth. So . . . I'll be right over."

"We'll get through this," Shelly assured him. "It's time."

Luke nodded. "We will." He ended the call and stood. "Liam knows about me." He walked to the door and grabbed his jacket from the row of hooks there. "He wants to talk to me tonight."

If his heart didn't stop pounding, it was going to pop right out of his chest.

"I'll go with you." Kerri reached for her own coat. "I'll wait in the car. I have some calls to catch up on."

"Thanks."

Just knowing she would be there made what he had to do a little easier.

Tell the truth . . . to his son. The one he'd given up parental rights to when he was only a few hours old.

Martin Residence
Oak Crest Cove
Hoover, 10:05 p.m.

The brick house where his ex-wife lived was nice. Four bedrooms, five baths. Highly sought-after neighborhood. The works. Luke had driven past it plenty of times. Shelly and her second husband, Bradley "Brad" Martin, had purchased it when Liam was just a toddler. He'd grown up here. Believed Brad was his father.

At least until now.

As much as Luke had wanted to hate Brad all these years, he couldn't. The man had done what Luke could not, and he was grateful. He and Shelly had agreed at the time that it was best that way.

Had the decision been a mistake?

Jesus Christ, he did not know.

"If you need me," Kerri said as she placed her hand on his forearm and gave it a squeeze, "I'm right here."

Unable to stop himself, he took her face in his hands and kissed her, then pressed his forehead to hers. "You know I don't deserve you."

"Go," she ordered. "You're getting all mushy."

Mushy. That was Tori's word for whenever she caught him and Kerri being lovey dovey.

Time to do what had to be done.

Getting out of the car was easy. Walking to the door, simple. But knocking on the door was as hard as hell. He managed, then remembered there was a doorbell. He rolled his eyes and pressed it.

"Keep it together, man."

The door opened, and Shelly stood there looking worried and frazzled. "Thanks for coming on short notice."

"Course." He stepped inside out of the cold night air. He hadn't even noticed how cold it was until he was blasted by the warm air inside the house.

In the living room the television was tuned to the local news. From the sofa, Brad nodded. Luke did the same. It was a man thing. Brad's mother, Merilee, lived in the house, too, but Luke saw no sign of her tonight.

"He's waiting in the family room."

Luke's attention swung back to Shelly. He steeled himself. "Okay. Show me the way."

Brad didn't follow. Probably best if Luke did this alone.

The family room was on the other side of the kitchen. The room was way too quiet, and Liam sat on the sofa staring at the muted television. Some kind of alien flick played on the screen.

"Liam," Shelly announced. "Luke is here."

The kid looked up then. The anger on his small face tore at Luke. He had done this. He'd been the one to walk away. Shelly had tried to make things work—to make him see he had to change.

But Luke had taken the easy way out. He knew this now.

"I want to talk to him alone," the kid said.

He sounded so mature. How could this be Liam? He was just a little kid.

A very angry one. The kind of angry Luke had gotten at his old man when he was that age.

Luke felt sick.

"I'll be in the kitchen," Shelly said with obvious reluctance.

When she'd gone, Luke walked deeper into the room and sat in the nearest chair. How the hell did he do this? Where did he start?

"You're my real dad, then," Liam said, his furious gaze nailing Luke.

On the drive over here, Luke had silently talked himself through this moment. He needed to stay calm and logical. Not overly emotional. Kerri had basically suggested the same. He had to do this right for Liam. This was a major moment in both their lives. Part of him wanted to be excited about the future possibilities, but mostly, he was terrified.

"I am your biological father, yes. But Brad is your *real* father."

The kid's lower lip stuck out even farther. "That's a lie. You're a liar."

Luke nodded. "I've told more than my share of lies when I had to. But a dad is more than just the person who . . ." Shit. How did he say that? Maybe he'd just skip it. "A real dad is the person who takes care of you. The one who is there when you need him. Like Brad is for you."

"Why did you not want me?" That poked-out lip trembled a little then.

Oh, Jesus Christ. Luke rubbed a hand over his jaw. "It's complicated, but it was not because I didn't want you, Liam."

"Am I named Liam because your name is Luke?"

He nodded. "Yes."

The kid looked away.

"When you were born, I was an undercover cop. A deep, deep-cover cop. I was involved with a lot of really bad people. And for my job, I had to do a lot of bad things." He hesitated a moment to rein in his emotions. There were so many: anger, fear, anticipation. His head was spinning. "I didn't think I was good enough to be a real dad for

you. I couldn't take care of you and your mom the way I should have."
He hesitated. "The truth is, I wasn't . . . I was a bad guy in those days.
I decided it would be better if someone who could do the job right was
your real dad."

Oh hell. Why had he called it a job? He was doing this all wrong.
Damn it!

"If you're a bad guy, why has my mom let you come to my games?"

He had to hand it to the kid—that was a very good question. One
he was thankful for the opportunity to answer. "Eventually I stopped
working undercover, and I stopped doing bad things. I got my life
and career together, and now I'm a good detective and a good person.
It took a long time, but I left the bad life behind. Your mom and dad
agreed to let me see you now and then because I'm doing really good.
I am very grateful they allowed me to see you. I'm very proud of you,
Liam. You're a great kid."

Liam stared at him as if waiting for him to continue speaking. Luke
had no idea what to say next.

Okay, maybe he did. "I'm sorry I couldn't be a good father for you.
Letting someone else be your father was the hardest thing I've ever done,
but I still believe it was the right thing to do for you and for your mom."

"I'm changing my name."

Luke blinked. Slowly nodded his understanding. "Okay."

"You're right." Liam looked at him then. "Brad is my real dad. And
you're nobody. I hate you."

The kid bounced up and ran out of the room.

Luke sat for a moment, too stunned to move. He heard Shelly
calling the kid's name, but he couldn't seem to find the wherewithal
to stand.

"What happened?"

She was suddenly hovering over Luke. He managed to push to his
feet. "He wants to change his name."

Shelly made a face. "What?"

"He said he hates me."

Her hands went to her face. "Oh my God. I am so sorry. I'm certain he doesn't mean that. He's upset, that's all. This has been a big shock for him. It'll take time for him to come to terms with all that it means. I think I'm in a sort of shock myself considering I'm as calm as I am. I keep expecting to fall apart."

"You're doing great, Shelly. You always have." Luke struggled to recapture his bearings. "It's okay—what he said, I mean. He has every right to hate me." He drew in a lungful of air. "I should go."

Shelly followed him to the door. She kept talking, but her words didn't register.

His son hated him.

No surprise.

The rock in his gut seemed to swell bigger and bigger.

"Luke."

On the stoop, he turned back to her. "Yeah?"

"Are you and"—she glanced at his car—"*her* a thing? I mean, a real thing?"

He nodded. Kerri was the realest thing in his world.

Shelly smiled. "Good. I'm glad. You deserve someone nice. She seems really nice."

He managed another nod, then headed for the car.

Shelly was right. Kerri was really nice.

But he didn't deserve her.

He could pretend he did, but he knew. He knew the things he had done . . . the people he had hurt.

15

Eight Years Ago

December 2

8:00 p.m.

"What's wrong, baby?"

I turn my head and stare at the naked woman snuggling up next to me. I force my lips into a smile before taking another drag from my cigarette. The amount of bourbon I've consumed has me in a pretty good place in spite of the world collapsing around me. It has all gone to hell.

"It's all good," I lie. "Don't worry about me."

My answer doesn't satisfy her. I read her like a book. If only this smoke were something stronger. What I need is a hit of coke to take me on over the top and lose myself in the haze. I don't want to face reality right now.

Maybe I never will again.

I think of the baby—my baby—at home with Shelly. *My wife*. What a joke. I'm no father. No husband. I'm nothing. No one. I, Luke Falco, am the biggest mistake of her life. The kid's too.

What a fuckup.

I shake off the troubling thoughts and focus on the hot body rubbing harder against mine. This dump is her place. A shitty little one-room studio in the worst part of town. But it feels more like home than home.

How pathetic is that?

The story of my life. Like father, like son. I don't want to do to my son what my father did to me.

"Tell me," she murmurs. "I know something is wrong."

In one swift move, I roll her over and hold my cigarette close to her face as if I would dare scar that smooth perfection. She really is attractive, almost beautiful. Smart too. She could have done so much more with her life. "Why do you keep nagging at me? Does it feel like something is wrong?" I press my lower body into hers, let her feel how hard I am. Which proves nothing, but what does she know?

Nothing.

She's like me. Nothing. No one.

Anger flares in her green eyes. She's pissed now. Good. No need for me to be pissed all by myself.

"What the hell is wrong with you, Falco?"

Oh yeah. She's pissed. She never calls me Falco.

I stare at her, try to see beyond the mask she wears. We all wear masks. It's how we hide the bad . . . the ugly. The truth. "A little birdie told me you were cheating on me. Using me." I burrow between her legs, force my way into her. She gasps. "Any truth to that?"

"No." She shakes her head to make sure I understand, since the word comes out all high pitched.

"You're a liar. Why should I trust you?" I grind my hips deeper into hers.

"I would never lie to you. Never!" She bites her bottom lip, liking what I'm doing to her in spite of the slightest hint of fear in her eyes.

"You're a junkie," I remind her.

"Ex-junkie," she snarls like a cat whose tail was just yanked.

I take a final draw off the smoke and drop it into this morning's coffee cup, which still sits on the bedside table. "There's no such thing, doll. Once a junkie, always a junkie."

She tries to wiggle out from under me. I press my chest into hers, flatten her luscious tits into my hard flesh, effectively pinning her to the mattress.

"Apparently, I'm a whore too," she retorts. "You plan on paying me after you take what you want?"

This hits me where it hurts. I'm a total asshole. I relax. Withdraw and flop onto my back. "You're not a whore."

She sits up. Pulls the tousled sheet around her body. "What was that all about?"

I tangle my fingers in her hair and pull her down to me. "Don't ever double-cross me," I warn.

"Never," she promises as her lips start a path down my chest.

I close my eyes as she takes what she wants from me.

I hate this. Hate myself.

This is not how my big chance was supposed to go. I was going to make a difference . . . make something of myself. Be better than my old man was.

Never happened. I'm nothing. No one that matters.

If my LT is right, I've even screwed this up.

Instead of allowing the stark reality to swallow me, I let myself drown in the physical desire she rouses so easily. The best thing that could happen to me would be if I woke up dead.

Then I could never ruin anyone else the way I've ruined myself and everyone close to me.

16

Wednesday, November 24

9:45 a.m.

Birmingham Police Department
First Avenue North
Major Investigations Division

Kerri flipped to the next page of the fire marshal's report. So far, they hadn't learned anything new from any of the forensics reports beyond the accelerant used to fuel the fire. The few usable prints lifted matched those of persons living in the home. Jana Scott had provided her prints. The long-awaited phone records for Allison and Logan Boothe had arrived, and they had skimmed those as well.

"I need more coffee," Luke announced as he pushed back from his desk in preparation to stand.

"That's all I get?" she demanded.

They had gotten up at the usual time this morning: five thirty. Had a quick breakfast. Drove to the compound where Clinton Sawyer lived but got no response at the gate. Made some calls to contacts in an attempt to nudge Sawyer or one of his close associates. It was like the guy was a myth or an illusion. He could not be found. People, like Carla Brown, would talk about seeing him, but otherwise he was a ghost.

Then they had come to the office. Reviewed messages and sat in on the daily briefing, which they didn't do nearly as often as they should. Now they were going through reports. And he was going for his third cup of coffee.

All without mentioning last night.

He frowned. "What did I miss?"

"You don't want to talk about last night?"

Confusion deepened his frown. "We did talk about last night."

They had. Yes. They'd talked about Liam and what had happened during Luke's visit with the boy. It would take time for this shock to stop rumbling and for things to settle down and work out. Kerri believed this wholeheartedly. Liam was a child. He needed time to come to terms with this new and unexpected reality. He felt betrayed and angry.

"I don't mean the part about Liam. I mean the nightmares."

The nightmares had been far worse last night. He'd tossed and turned and mumbled loudly. Grabbed at her more than once. Finally, she'd gotten out of bed and sat on the window bench and watched the fight with his demons.

He made a face. "We talked about that too."

"No," she argued, "I asked you about the nightmares, and you said that meeting up with the crew had stirred up the past. Had you dreaming about the CI—Mina—who died. But that's all you said."

"What else do you want to know?"

He asked this with the same blank expression he wore when he begged off talking about the past. So, they had graduated from *I don't want to talk about it* to *What else do you want to know?* Was that progress?

She could hope.

"Get your coffee," she said, giving him a brief reprieve. "We'll talk then."

"You want more coffee?" He stood.

"No thanks."

He grabbed his mug and swaggered out of the cubicle. All this time, she hadn't worried about his past. In fact, she'd insisted that it was who he was now that mattered. Frankly, that part of his life hadn't come into play. At all. She was okay with that.

But now somehow this case and that life had collided.

Luke strolled back into the cubicle and reclaimed his seat. He knocked back a slug of coffee, then said, "Hit me. I'm ready. Whatever you want to know."

She leaned forward in her chair, braced her elbows on the desk. "You were close to this CI, Mina?"

He nodded. Gone was any hint of the usual cavalier Falco attitude. Gone was the blank expression that hid whatever he felt. His face revealed a sadness that came from deep inside. "We were. I let things get personal. It was a mistake. My life with Shelly was falling apart. I knew it was my fault. Mina was an easy target for making me forget. I was selfish. What's happening with Boothe is like déjà vu."

"Because Mina died?" Kerri's heart kicked into a faster rhythm.

"Yeah." He nodded. "Liam and Shelly didn't die, but I still lost them. What happened to me isn't the same, obviously. But it feels too close. Boothe and I both lost what we cared about most."

"I'm sorry you had to go through that." There were other questions she wanted to ask, things she wanted to say, but she had pushed enough. After what had happened with Liam last night, he needed a break.

"I made a lot of mistakes. I don't want to make any more."

"We've got this," she assured him, wanting him to understand that he was not in this alone.

His gaze held hers. He didn't need to say anything. She understood.

"So," she said finally, "let's take a look at all these phone records." She turned her computer monitor so they could both see the screen. "The rest of the reports we ordered popped up in my inbox a few minutes ago."

"We didn't find what we were looking for at the house," Luke noted. "No open or broken window—from the inside. However Boothe got his injuries, it doesn't appear to have been in an attempt to escape the fire he may have allegedly started."

Kerri moved to the case board and added this beneath Boothe's name. "Which means he struggled with someone. Maybe was tossed out of a moving vehicle."

Luke nodded. "Oh yeah. That would do it. He may have crawled from the ditch into the yard, where Crandall found him."

The fire lit in Kerri's belly. "We found nothing on social media that suggested anything other than the need for prayers for Leah. Allison's cell phone hasn't been found, but the records we requested gave us calls and text messages to her mom, her husband, and her child's doctor. No contact with unknown numbers. She hasn't socialized with friends in years. Hasn't worked outside the home in the same. Basically, other than her mother and daughter, Allison was isolated."

As much as Kerri loved her own daughter, she couldn't imagine being so totally isolated from the rest of the world. According to Scott, Logan Boothe had taken Allison from all her friends and associates. On the other hand, it was possible that Allison had been in over her head and isolated herself. She'd married very young and had a child almost immediately. Could she have been suffering from depression? Surely her mother would have noticed. Then again, maybe not. Mothers more often than not only wanted to see the best in their children. Anything else was difficult to acknowledge.

"But," Luke said, drawing Kerri back to the here and now, "there is that one call to a burner phone on the husband's call log." He stood and walked to the case board, opened a marker, and added the word *call* and a question mark beneath Boothe's name. "He made this call at seven p.m. on Sunday night."

"Suspicious much?" Kerri said as she scanned the bank statement she'd just opened. They had hoped to run down the owner of the number before confronting Boothe with the information, but when she'd run the digits, the number had come back as belonging to a phone purchased a week ago at a local big-box store by a One Smith at an address that didn't exist. "Wait, wait, wait. What's this?"

Luke leaned down to see the screen. "Five thousand dollars was collected by PayPal from his and Allison's joint bank account five days before the fire."

Kerri opened the folder on her desk and ruffled through the notes until she found the list of the Boothe family's monthly expenses. "There's no mortgage payment. No credit cards with balances of more than a couple thousand dollars. One car payment collected automatically from the account. The medical expenses are all paid via check. I don't see anything he pays using PayPal."

"If the five K wasn't for bills," Luke pointed out, "then what?"

"Maybe he bought something." The car Boothe drove was financed at a local bank. His wife's van had been a gift from her mother.

Luke stood. "We should pay Boothe a visit this morning and ask him. Who knows, maybe he'll even tell us who the owner of the burner phone is."

"Why not?" Kerri agreed. Her cell vibrated against the desk. Jana Scott's number appeared. "Hang on," she said to Luke as she snatched up the phone and accepted the call. "Devlin."

"Detective Devlin, this is Jana Scott. I got your message. Has there been a development on the case?"

"No, ma'am, unfortunately not. I had a few follow-up questions."

"Do I need to come to your office?"

"That's not necessary. I can ask you now if you don't mind." Kerri searched her desktop for her pen and a pad to make notes. Luke settled back into his chair and waited.

"I want to help any way I can," Scott assured her.

Kerri understood. The devastated woman wanted the person responsible for her loss to be found. "Did Allison ever mention that she believed her husband was having an affair?"

There was a hesitation, but only a short one.

"Just before Leah's illness," Scott said, her voice morose, "Allison worried that Logan was involved with someone or in something that had him completely distracted. They argued constantly. There was a brief separation, as I told you before. But she never said that she discovered or that he admitted to an affair. She was very private like that. I worked hard to respect her privacy even in the more troubling times."

"What about Allison? At any time did she feel the need to seek comfort elsewhere?"

Kerri braced for the mother's reaction.

"Did Rebecca Boothe say something like that to you?" Scott demanded, anger flaring in her voice. "That woman—"

"Mrs. Scott," Kerri said, interrupting her, "these are the same questions we've asked about Logan as well. It's not an accusation. It's just another question we have to ask. Sometimes we ask more than once. Standard protocol. I'm sure you heard your husband speak of this," Kerri reminded her.

Scott took a moment before speaking again. "My daughter was a very good girl, Detective. She always was. Played by the rules. Always kind. I'm her mother, and of course I'm biased, but I feel confident in saying that she would never do such a thing."

"You and Allison would have spoken about something this deeply personal?"

"We talked about most things, Detective. Openly and with love. Allison did, however, closely guard her relationship with her husband. Her vows to him came first, as they should have."

Allison had been hiding at least one truth: what her husband had been up to the last week of her life. Scott had said as much in a previous interview.

"Mrs. Scott," Kerri asked, "you mentioned that Allison had lost touch with all her friends. Do you think she may have been suffering from depression? Particularly after Leah's diagnosis?"

"We talked about that possibility," Scott said. "I worried that she was spending too much time alone or with just Leah. But she always denied the suggestion. As I said, she was very private regarding personal matters. But she always assured me she was fine. I honestly did not get the impression she was depressed more than anyone would be under the circumstances. Her child was seriously ill. Some amount of anxiety and depression goes with the territory."

No question. Kerri thanked her and promised to call with any news. As she ended the call, Luke said, "I take it she knew nothing of an affair."

"Allison never mentioned an affair. She also can't say if her daughter was suffering from depression. As close as she insists they were, it seems there was a lot her daughter didn't share."

"Funny how that is sometimes," Luke agreed. "We want to believe we know everything there is to know, but do we ever?"

Before Kerri could ask if he was speaking from personal experience, her cell started to vibrate once more. This time it was the mother-in-law, Rebecca Boothe.

"You are one popular lady this morning." Even as he said the words, his own cell lit with an incoming text. He chuckled at the irony. "Maybe I'm popular too."

Cop life.

Kerri accepted the call, and Rebecca Boothe said, "I need to talk to you," before Kerri could say a word.

"Are you all right, Mrs. Boothe?"

"Yes." Her tone belied her response and relayed the depth of her misery.

Something was up.

"Where would you like to meet?"

"The hospital lobby. When can you come?"

"I can come right now," Kerri assured her. "If that's convenient for you."

"I'll be waiting."

The call dropped off, and Kerri frowned at the screen. Why the sudden urgency to talk? This was the same lady who hadn't wanted to say a word beyond the fact that whatever had happened was not her son's fault.

"The mother-in-law wants to meet." Kerri stood and reached for her jacket.

"You must have pushed all the right buttons with that one," Luke said as he dragged on his own coat. "She probably stewed over your comments all night last night." He paused to check his phone again.

When he frowned, she asked, "Is everything okay?"

"One of the guys from last night wants to meet privately." His gaze moved up to hers. "It might be nothing, but if he can give me the woman's name who was involved with Boothe, we might gain some ground."

"Allegedly involved," she reminded him.

"Allegedly," he agreed.

"Where are you meeting?" Kerri asked.

"At a cabin where we used to hang out."

"Same place as last night?"

"Yeah." He gave her a wink. "Don't worry. It's all good."

She didn't like him going there alone again. Whatever was happening with the people from his past, it was giving him nightmares and taking a visible toll. With this case and what was happening with Liam, he had more than enough on his plate.

"Be careful," she cautioned. "I don't want to have to break in a new partner."

"Same goes," he tossed back with a one-sided grin. "You'll be at the hospital?"

"I will. Maybe Mrs. Boothe can tell me what her son paid five K for."

Whenever she and Luke went in different directions, she always had the urge to blow him a kiss the same way she had done to Tori each morning at school drop-off until she'd hit thirteen. Not a good idea in the office.

"I'll drop you by the house for your car."

Taking a department vehicle was always an option, but she hated doing so. She preferred her own vehicle.

"Thanks."

The ride to her house would give them a few minutes to toss around possible explanations for the 5K Boothe had paid out. Could be a perfectly logical explanation. It didn't make a lot of sense otherwise. Boothe was a seasoned detective. Leaving a paper trail was a rookie mistake.

Or maybe he'd been subconsciously leaving bread crumbs.

———

University of Alabama Hospital
Sixth Avenue South
Birmingham, 11:55 a.m.

Driving the short distance to the UAB Hospital took forever. Construction was an endless cycle in Birmingham. Generally, Kerri was able to avoid the most congested areas. This time she was caught in a situation where there was no going around.

As promised, Rebecca Boothe was waiting in the lobby when Kerri finally did arrive. They moved to the cafeteria. Grabbed drinks and a sandwich and sat as far away from other people as possible. Not difficult, since most people took their food with them back to rooms or workstations.

Rebecca stared at her pimento cheese sandwich for a minute, maybe a little more, before she picked it up and took a bite.

Kerri opened her water and washed down a bite of roast beef on rye. More often than not during an investigation, she had to remind herself to eat. Not lately. Her appetite was constantly vying for her attention. Her sister, Diana, teased her that her renewed appetite was about being in love. Kerri, of course, adamantly denied this accusation.

But there was a strong possibility she was lying to herself. Her feelings for Luke were deep. Deeper than she'd expected to feel again.

When Rebecca continued to eat in silence, Kerri asked, "How is Logan today?"

She already knew the answer, of course. She called for updates every morning and every evening.

"He's gaining strength." Boothe sipped her sweet tea. "We're very lucky that there is no sign of infection so far. I've had everyone I know praying for him." She searched Kerri's eyes then. "I truly do believe in the power of prayer, Detective. Don't you?"

Kerri wasn't the best person to ask about prayer. "Prayer is always good," she agreed without answering the question specifically.

"He's despondent, of course. He won't talk about Leah or Allison. He really doesn't talk at all. He just lies there and stares at the television."

"He's suffered a tremendous loss." Kerri decided the bread was a little stale and focused on her water. "You said you needed to talk. You've had a change of heart about talking to us?"

Boothe pushed aside her plate. "It seems like you and your partner have been focused on Logan and the idea that he may have had an affair or had some reason to hurt his wife and child. But have you looked into what Allison was doing behind his back?"

Mothers typically wanted to protect their children. Pointing out other possibilities beyond her son's potential guilt was to be expected.

"We have. Yes. We've reviewed financial statements and social media accounts. We haven't found anything unusual or problematic. In fact, Allison rarely did anything that didn't include Logan or her mother—and Leah, of course."

"She had an affair. It was years ago." Boothe traced a bead of water down her sweating glass with the tip of her finger. "Logan wouldn't talk about it, but I know he was devastated. It had to be an affair."

In other words, she wasn't certain there was an affair. "He shared this information with you?"

She shook her head. "He would never do that. But I know. I was aware something was going on, and then there was this long standoff between them after he found out."

She wasn't making complete sense. "When did this occur?"

"Since Leah got sicker and needed new treatments." Boothe closed her eyes and winced as if merely saying her granddaughter's name thrust a dagger through her chest. "At least, that's when he found out."

"Are you certain it wasn't related to an affair Logan was having? We've had others suggest there was someone else during his final weeks of work with the department."

The other woman shook her head adamantly. "I am telling you he would not do that. Ever."

"I understand you're his mother and you love him. Think the best of him. I have a daughter. I know how much you want to believe that everything they do is good. But how can you be so certain it was Allison and not Logan—beyond your motherly instincts?"

Rebecca Boothe looked Kerri square in the eye then. "Because if Logan had been having an affair, I would have heard about it from Jana Scott."

Was she saying the two of them were friends? If that was the case, it would be a total one-eighty based on the dislike she'd shown for the other woman so far.

"How so?" Kerri asked.

"Because that . . ." She caught herself. Moistened her lips and started over. "Because she would have gloated in telling me. She had people watching him, you know."

"What people?"

She shrugged. "I don't know, but that neighbor, Crandall, was always watching and reporting back to Jana. If you ask me, the two of them are thick as thieves. Neither one of them likes Logan. They're constantly finding fault in everything he does. Allison told him so."

"What sorts of things?" Getting to the point was like pulling teeth with this lady.

"When he left the department is a perfect example." She seemed to brace for battle as she spoke. "When he first quit, he tried to find something else before telling Allison so she wouldn't worry. But Crandall saw him at home two days in a row and called up Jana and told her. She took it upon herself to call someone in the department and found out what had happened. Rather than going to Logan and asking him what caused him to walk away, she went straight to Allison and told her."

"Allison was her daughter," Kerri countered. "Is it possible she believed she was protecting Allison?"

Boothe looked away a moment. "I would, except there are so many other examples. Like the time he had to buff a place on his car where he clipped another vehicle. There wasn't any real damage, just a transfer of paint from the older vehicle onto his newer one. He didn't want Allison to worry since Leah had been with him when it happened. But Crandall saw what he was doing and told Jana. The next thing Logan knew, he was being interrogated by his own wife about his driving skills. There are so many others. It would take all day to tell you how they ganged up on him and treated him like an outsider. Like he didn't belong. Like he was trespassing in their lives."

"I will look into it," Kerri assured her. "We look into everything. Never doubt that."

"I'm telling you that something happened. It was only a few weeks ago. And whatever it was, it related to something bad that Allison had done a long time ago. I know my son. He was so hurt and so angry. It had to be something big, like cheating."

The timing didn't really fit, but what she was telling Kerri fit precisely into a particular category. Motive. "Did it make him angry enough to kill his wife?"

Horror claimed the woman's face. "How can you ask that?"

The few diners around the cafeteria looked their way at her raised voice.

"It's my job to ask."

Boothe exhaled a big breath, attempting to calm herself. "He would never, ever have hurt Leah or Allison."

"Mrs. Boothe," Kerri said, deciding to smooth over the moment. She needed this woman to keep calling with info. "You have my word that I consider your son innocent until I find evidence to prove otherwise. That's the way this works."

Boothe dabbed at the tears slipping from the corners of her eyes. "I'm counting on that, Detective Devlin. From one mother to another."

"One more question," Kerri said. "A few days before the fire, there was a large withdrawal from your son's bank account to PayPal. Do you know if he bought something?"

Boothe shook her head, but not before Kerri spotted a flare of fear in her eyes. "Not that I'm aware of. I can ask him, if you'd like. The account was Allison's too. Maybe she was the one who made the purchase."

"We do need to clear that up," Kerri said, fully aware the woman was probably lying.

Didn't matter, really. A warrant would get the answer eventually. It would just be easier and a hell of a lot faster if people simply told the truth.

Before leaving, Kerri accompanied Mrs. Boothe to her son's room. Unfortunately, he was in therapy, so Kerri decided to come back later rather than wait.

Outside, the sky had turned gray and the temperature had dropped. She should touch base with her sister, Diana, and warn her that tomorrow's family Thanksgiving dinner might or might not happen given the way this case was going. Holidays took a back seat to murder.

Her cell vibrated, and she pulled it from her pocket. *Dispatch.*

"Detective Devlin."

Kerri stood in the middle of the parking lot and listened to the words that shook her to the very core of her being.

Luke was injured.

He was in the ER.

Her gaze flew across the parking lot.

Here.

17

12:59 p.m.

Kerri burst through the ER doors, badge and weapon displayed for security to see. She rushed to the registration desk and took a breath, ordered herself to remain calm as she waited for the nurse behind the counter to finish her phone call.

The instant the handset headed toward its cradle, Kerri blurted, "I'm Detective Devlin. My partner, Detective Falco, was brought in a short time ago."

Her heart pulsed in her throat as the endless possibilities of how badly hurt he could be ticked off in her brain. *Please, please let him be okay.*

After clicking a few keys on her computer, the nurse said, "He's at x-ray now. I'll let his nurse know to call you as soon as he's brought back to his room."

Rather than insist on being taken to radiology, Kerri managed, "Thank you."

She found an empty seat near the double doors that separated the waiting area from the emergency department where triage and treatment took place. She closed her eyes and focused on slowing her respiration. He'd told her he was going back to that cabin and meeting up with one of the guys from last night. She tried to think if he'd mentioned a name. She couldn't recall. She'd been focused on the meeting with Rebecca Boothe. She should have paid better attention.

Forcing away the troubling thoughts, she distracted herself by checking her messages. Tori's name made her smile. It was a miracle. What teenage girl spending the holiday in New York City had time to think of Mom, much less send her a text message?

Miss u!

Miss you too! How's it going?

Kerri had not attempted to master the text messaging shorthand. It drove her nuts.

Shopping!

"Of course." Kerri chuckled.

Spend big!

She deleted the message before tapping send.

Have fun! Love you! 💕

This time she sent the message.

Ditto! 😊

Her good deed for the season. She hadn't urged her daughter to spend lots of her father's money. She tucked her cell back into her jacket pocket.

She glanced around the crowded waiting room and spotted the refreshment center. Her mouth was parched. She needed water. Hoping no one would snag her seat, she walked over to the machine and poked in the necessary cash for a bottle of ridiculously expensive water.

A check of the nurses' station and the double doors showed that nothing had changed. People were still crowded around the counter, and the doors remained closed. Thankfully her chair was still vacant, so she dropped into it and chugged half the bottle of water. What was taking so long? She checked the time on her cell. Stared at the double doors as if she could mentally will them to open.

She should call the LT. Scratch that. She should wait until she knew Luke's condition and then make the call.

Diana would want to know. No need to tell Tori. She would just worry, and she was too far away to do anything about it. Sadie Cross? Kerri would call her later. Over the past year and a half, the former detective turned PI had become a good friend. *Good* might be a stretch, but reliable for sure. Definitely a call to Shelly. Later. The thought that Liam had said he hated Luke ripped at Kerri's chest.

"Detective Devlin."

Her gaze shot to the woman in scrubs standing in the open double doors. She hadn't even heard them open.

"Yes." Kerri pushed to her feet and followed the nurse beyond the doors, which closed with a slow-motion whoosh behind them. "How is he?"

"The doctor will give you more details," she said as she led the way along the corridor. "I can tell you he has two fractured ribs. A concussion and a whopper of a swollen and bruised eye."

Deep breath. Could have been a lot worse.

At the door to an exam room, the nurse paused. "The doctor will be around soon."

"Thank you." Kerri steadied herself and pushed through the door.

Luke lay on the exam table in his boxers and a hospital gown open in the front.

Her heart took a plunge, hit her stomach, and had her choking back the water she'd guzzled. He was alive. He wasn't bleeding.

"What the hell happened?" she demanded, fury igniting.

"I got the shit kicked out of me." He grinned and winced.

In addition to the swollen and rapidly darkening black eye, he had a split lip.

"Who did this?" Her voice was brittle with that mixture of anger and fear roaring through her like a hurricane.

"I can't be sure because he got me from behind." He reached up to touch the back of his head. "While I was down trying to shake it off, he kicked me in the gut a few times." He held up a hand with one finger extended. "I did manage to get a swing in, but I missed. He kicked me in the face, and then he was gone."

"You didn't see his face or anything else that could ID him?"

He growled a sigh. "Boots, ragged jeans. Black hoodie. One of the guys from last night, I'm figuring. Slater, the guy I was supposed to meet, showed up and brought me to the ER."

"So someone—possibly one of the guys in the crew you once worked undercover with—ambushed you."

"Slater didn't think so, but it looks that way to me. Technically, I only worked with one of the guys; the others I didn't know. They all came on board since I left."

Her outrage consumed the last of her fear. "I need all the names, Falco."

His bleary gaze collided with hers. She grimaced at his swollen and bruised jaw and eye. "You know I can't do that, *Devlin*."

"At least tell me about these guys so I can see them coming if one comes after me."

She didn't really expect that to happen, but it was a valid point that might even get her what she wanted from him.

"They look like me." He stared at the ceiling. "You know the type. Grunge on steroids." He reached out, took her hand in his. "I'll be fine."

Every ounce of willpower she possessed was required to prevent her from sobbing like a child. "You could have been killed."

"Trust me—if they wanted me dead, I'd be dead."

Why hadn't she thought of that? She blinked back the damned emotion and stepped back into cop mode. "Are we just going to let them get away with this?"

"For now." He groaned and reached up again to touch his head. "But I'm like an elephant—I don't forget."

A knock on the door just before it opened signaled the doctor had arrived. Like the nurse had said, two fractured ribs and a concussion. No work for a few days. No driving. They wanted to keep him a couple more hours until all the blood work was in and to ensure all else was as it should be, like his spleen.

Kerri thanked the doctor and guaranteed she would see that Luke followed orders. By God, she intended to do exactly that. He wasn't going anywhere without her.

When the doctor was gone, her partner argued, "You know I have to work."

"We'll see," she groused. She should have the doctor put him on bed rest. It would serve him right for doing something so entirely stupid.

Her cell vibrated. Damn it. "It's the LT."

"I'm asleep." Luke closed his eyes and feigned sleep.

"Devlin," she said in a crisp, professional voice as she accepted the call.

How had he found out about Luke?

"I need to see you in my office ASAP."

His demand without preamble or even a hello surprised her.

"I'll be right there, sir. Falco—"

"I'm not ready to speak to him just yet."

The call ended.

Kerri stared at the screen for a second. "I don't know what we did," she said to her partner, "but the LT is not happy."

Damn. She did not want to leave Luke here like this. "I have to go to his office. I'll be back as soon as he's finished chewing me out or whatever. You going to be okay?"

"I'll be fine. I'm hoping for a sponge bath." He tangled his fingers with hers. "I'll be here when you get back."

She glanced down at his torso. "By the way, I love the gown."

He tugged at the sides, drawing the flaps over his boxers. "The nurses like it too."

Kerri laughed in spite of herself. "Behave."

If she was lucky, he would. At least until she figured out what kind of bug the LT had up his backside.

Birmingham Police Department
First Avenue North
Major Investigations Division, 2:40 p.m.

She'd driven straight here and rushed up the stairs, only to be left waiting in the LT's office for twenty-three minutes.

During every single one of those *twenty-three* minutes, she had considered how easily Luke could have ended up dead today. The idea sent a fresh wave of fear roaring through her. To fend off the feeling of helplessness, Kerri had called and left Sadie Cross a message to call her. Sadie had all sorts of contacts. It was time to nudge some of those sources.

"Sorry to keep you waiting, Devlin."

Lieutenant Dontrelle Brooks closed the door behind him and skirted his desk. He removed his suit jacket, hung it carefully on the coat-tree in the corner, then sat down. When he'd adjusted his chair just as he wanted it, he settled his attention on her.

She waited, every nerve ending in her body pulsing with irritation. It was always best to hear what the trouble was before launching an excuse or an explanation. Oftentimes the trouble wasn't exactly what you'd anticipated. This was a good guide for those skirting the rules on a regular basis.

Not that she did.

Often.

Very often, anyway.

But she wanted to do something to get him started, since the sooner they got this over with, the sooner she could get back to the hospital.

The pressure inside her mounted.

"A complaint has been filed against Detective Falco."

If he'd said Santa was running nude along the corridor behind her, she wouldn't have been more startled. "What?"

Brooks picked up the folder lying on top of a dozen call messages and removed the document there. "A Carla Brown claims Detective Falco questioned her regarding Logan Boothe."

"That's right. We interviewed her yesterday."

"You were with him?"

"I was."

"She says in her complaint that Falco was alone and very aggressive. That he threatened to 'hurt' her if she didn't tell his version of the truth."

Kerri shook her head. "Absolutely not. He was not threatening, in word or action, at any time. I was right there. I heard every word, watched the entire interaction, and then we left together."

"It's come to my attention that Falco has a history of trouble with witnesses and CIs," Brooks said as he picked up what appeared to be a personnel jacket. "According to Lieutenant Patrick O'Grady, there were numerous issues back when Falco was assigned to his unit. Most were undocumented out of consideration for Falco's future in the department. This recent complaint has raised concerns as to whether overlooking those issues was misguided."

Kerri held up her hands. "I've met and spoken with O'Grady. Frankly, it's my opinion that he is overly concerned with protecting his crew and not entirely objective."

The LT studied her for a long moment. "I'll bear that in mind," he finally said. "However, I'm sure you recall when Falco was first assigned to MID, to be your partner?"

"Of course. I was skeptical of him in the beginning." Clearly that was where he was going with this. "But I was wrong. Falco has proved to be an outstanding detective and a great partner."

Brooks considered her once more—for long enough to make her antsy—as if weighing what he wanted to say next. "I've known you for years, Devlin. You're one of our best. The chief says the same thing. We're very proud of you and the work you've done."

Now she was really worried. "What's going on here, sir?"

Again, he picked up the document presumably submitted by Brown. "The department takes these sorts of allegations very seriously. Particularly when there is a history of this kind of behavior. I thought Falco was doing well. I need to be sure about this. I need," he reiterated, "to be certain *your* assessment is completely objective."

Fury whipped through her, but she managed to keep it in check. "I don't understand. Falco is the most easygoing detective I know. And you backed him completely from the get-go. Why the sudden uncertainty about him?"

"You asked me once why so much of the information in his personnel file was redacted, and I told you there was nothing we could do about that. For security purposes, the backgrounds on detectives like Falco must be protected."

"I fully understand that necessity." What she didn't understand at all was Carla Brown filing a false statement. How did it tie to Luke's past or this case? There was just one common denominator: O'Grady.

"O'Grady went over the redacted information with me, item by item," Brooks explained. "Suffice it to say that violence with witnesses and CIs is just the tip of the iceberg."

Kerri shook her head. This was beyond ridiculous. "Sir, I have no idea what O'Grady's motive is for making these statements, but I don't believe him. Based on what you've just said, it would appear Lieutenant O'Grady has some grudge against Detective Falco and is attempting to frame him in some way."

The entire scenario was ridiculous. Completely. Utterly. Her anger was beyond restraining now. There was no denying one glaringly obvious fact: O'Grady was up to something.

"A woman died, Devlin."

The CI. Mina. Kerri knew this. Before she could respond, Brooks went on, "The circumstances are unclear, but most who were involved with the situation at the time believe Falco was responsible for her death."

Kerri's heart dropped into her stomach. "If this is true," she countered, incredibly calmly considering the emotions rising inside her, "it was either an accident or self-defense."

This had to be wrong.

The need to breathe propelled her heart back into an unsteady rhythm.

"I appreciate your loyalty, Devlin, and no one is more surprised about this than me. That said, we will need to investigate this complaint and determine if Falco is a liability. This division is far too important, too high profile, to allow someone who can't control his impulses to be part of the team."

Kerri silently counted to five before daring to speak. "Sir, I've worked with Detective Falco for a year and a half. He has no trouble controlling his impulses. This is obviously some sort of witch hunt that O'Grady has set in motion for reasons I can't even fathom."

Brooks held her gaze for several beats before reacting to her statement. "Bottom line, Devlin, eight years ago, just before Falco transferred down to Mobile, a CI named Mina Kozlov died. If Falco had anything whatsoever to do with that or if there is any merit whatsoever in this Carla Brown incident, I need to know."

Kerri took a breath, chose her words carefully. "I am confident an investigation will reveal nothing of the sort. I stand by my partner."

"Because I trust your judgment," Brooks said, "I won't suspend him until we've fully investigated this complaint. Do not make me regret that decision, Devlin."

Then and there she decided not to mention the fact that Luke was in the ER right now after having been ambushed—most likely by a member of O'Grady's unit. O'Grady could claim Luke had started it. A new wave of outrage rushed over her.

"Yes, sir."

"I will keep you informed of the progress," he said. "Until this is done, I do not want Detective Falco taking a single step without you at his side."

"I understand." Kerri stood. "For the record, this is bullshit."

Brooks gave a nod. "I hope you're right. That said, I'm aware something more than your professional partnership is happening with you and Falco. Do not let whatever that is color your objectivity."

Of course he knew. Brooks knew everything.

18

3:30 p.m.

Kerri collapsed behind the wheel of her Wagoneer and closed her eyes in an attempt to regain her balance.

A maddening mix of fear and anger rushed through her veins. What the hell had happened eight years ago? What did O'Grady hope to accomplish with this ridiculous story he'd thrown at Brooks?

She forced her eyes open. No way had Luke killed anyone. Not possible. Not unless there was no other choice or it was an accident. She would not believe this story without irrefutable evidence.

Maybe not even then. She was all too aware that evidence could be manipulated. O'Grady was the sort of person capable of all manner of theatrics and manipulation. The type who got the job done whatever the cost and who always found a way to cover his tracks.

Exactly the kind who gave cops a bad name.

Kerri started the engine and forced her mind onto the process of driving. When she and Luke got home, they would figure this out.

He deserved the benefit of the doubt, especially from her. She was his partner. His lover. She trusted him completely.

At the street, she waited for an opportunity to merge into traffic. Another vehicle rolled up behind her. Black car. Sporty. Reminded her of Luke's Charger. The traffic cleared, and she eased out of the parking lot. In the city there was always traffic. She could be rolling down Sixth Avenue at midnight, and there would be traffic.

The upcoming traffic light flashed yellow to red. She braked, rolled to the white line, and instinctively glanced in her rearview mirror.

The black car wasn't stopping.

She braced for impact.

Didn't happen.

Somehow the driver managed to stop.

Kerri released a breath. "What the hell?"

The asshole in the black car couldn't be more than a couple of inches from her rear bumper. His aviators hid most of his face. If he recognized she was shooting daggers at him with her eyes, he showed no reaction.

Like her, he appeared to be alone in the vehicle. Probably had his cell in his hand and hadn't been paying attention. "Idiot."

The light changed and she lunged forward, determined to put some distance between them.

Deep breath. First, she should call Diana and explain about Luke. Depending on how he was feeling, they might have to cancel and stay home tomorrow. Without Tori it wouldn't feel like Thanksgiving anyway. Diana wouldn't be happy, of course.

The sound of an engine being gunned blasted the air. She glanced in the rearview mirror again. The hood and windshield of the black car were all that was visible.

He was tailgating her.

"What is your problem?"

She pushed on her right blinker and prepared to turn onto a side street. When she'd made the turn, she pressed harder on the gas to lunge away from the intersection.

The black car stayed on Sixth.

As much as she would like to believe the driver was just some jerk showing off his muscle car, she had been a cop for far too long to ignore the potential. She pulled her cell from her pocket and prepared to call for backup.

She passed through the next intersection. There was hardly any traffic along this street. Many of the old businesses were closed. Traffic was practically nonexistent. If the car showed up again, his intent would be undeniable.

The black car reappeared in her rearview mirror.

"And there he is."

She slammed on her brakes, coming to a dead stop in the middle of the road.

The black car darted left to avoid hitting her. Skidded to a sideways stop.

She put her cell on speaker and placed it on the dash, then drew her weapon. Holding it steady with her right hand, she put her window down with her left.

The man emerged from his car, and Kerri took a bead on his head.

A dispatcher came on the line.

"This is Detective Kerri Devlin."

The man's hands went up; in one he held what appeared to be a badge.

"Detective?" the dispatcher said.

Kerri gave her location to the dispatcher as the man came closer. Ragged jeans, black tee. Biker boots. When he jammed his shield directly in front of her, she said, "Never mind, dispatch, I have the situation under control." She repeated the last, and the dispatcher confirmed before the call ended.

"Detective Douglas Durham. I meant no harm, Detective Devlin. I just needed to be sure I had your attention."

Kerri opened her door with her left hand, keeping her bead steady on the man in the aviators, and got out. "Oh, you've got my attention, asshole."

He grinned, his beard-shadowed cheeks sliding back to reveal straight white teeth. His brown hair was military short. "No need to get excited, Devlin. You can lower your weapon."

She ignored the suggestion. "I'm good. Where's your weapon, Detective?" He wasn't wearing a shoulder or waist holster.

"I have a message for you."

"Turn around."

"I just need a moment of your time."

"Turn around!" she repeated with a look along the barrel of her weapon and to his forehead.

He heaved a breath and did as she ordered. She snatched the weapon from his waistband at the small of his back, placed it on the ground, and kicked it, sending it spinning across the asphalt.

He heaved a dramatic sigh. "Really?"

Satisfied, she lowered her weapon but didn't holster it. "What the hell do you want?"

He faced her once more, the aviators shielding his eyes. "Your partner, Falco, is making a grave mistake."

Judging by the look of this guy and his cocky attitude, he was part of O'Grady's crew. "Explain."

"The Boothe investigation. It's a touchy situation. Falco needs to tread lightly. Leave the past in the past. There's no need to go back down that road."

Now she was pissed off all over again. "You know what? I am sick and tired of hearing about the past." She narrowed her eyes. "What the hell is it to you?"

"Let's just say I have a stake in how this shakes down. I hate to see Falco pay the price for something he's made amends for many times over."

First Brooks and now this guy? Not to mention, he or one of his friends might have been the one who'd ambushed Luke. "Well, if it's keeping the past in the past you're worried about, you should talk to your LT. He doesn't seem to feel the same way. He's dropping reminders about the past all over the place."

"Politics." Durham chuckled. "You know how the brass play their little games. Just tell Falco to stand down, and it'll all blow over. Tell him Dog has got this."

What was that supposed to mean? "Why would he listen to you?"

Durham shrugged. "Maybe he won't, but no one can say I didn't warn him."

He took the three steps necessary to reach his weapon. "Have a nice day, Detective."

Before driving away, he powered down his window, aimed a finger gun at her, and pretended to fire.

She was beginning to see why Luke wanted nothing to do with the people from his past. Total assholes.

———

University of Alabama Hospital
Sixth Avenue South
Birmingham, 4:00 p.m.

Kerri had parked in the hospital lot when her cell vibrated. Sadie Cross's name flashed on the screen.

"Thanks for getting back to me," Kerri said rather than hello.

"What's going on, Devlin?"

"Detective Douglas Durham," Kerri said. "What can you tell me about him?" He was not the reason she'd left Sadie the message, but he'd placed himself squarely on that list with his little road warrior game.

"Dog. That's the nickname he goes by. Has for years."

"Who is he?" Kerri felt confident he was undercover narcotics, since he hadn't argued with her comment about his LT when she'd mentioned O'Grady. She could also see how well the nickname fit him. The guy was like a guard dog marking what he deemed his territory. Clearly he intended to see that she and Luke stayed away.

"He is not a nice guy," Sadie was saying.

A little boy's voice interrupted, asking for more apple juice. Despite the circumstances, Kerri smiled. Sadie's son, Edward, was a sweetheart, and he kept the edgy private detective on her toes. She'd quit smoking and rarely had so much as a beer. It had been touch and go for a little while, but she'd evolved into a great mom. Tori loved babysitting Edward when Sadie needed her.

"Meaning he's a bad cop?" Kerri asked. "A dirty cop? Both?"

The sound of juice pouring into a glass sounded in the background, followed by a "here you go." Five seconds later, Sadie said, "Dog is very good at what he does. In a manner of speaking, he is a great detective. He believes that justice is what counts in the end. The trouble lies in the getting to that end. He's ruthless. He's dangerous. You want to stay clear of him if possible."

"Not possible. He just pulled a Clint Eastwood, using his vehicle to try and intimidate me. He had a message for Falco—stand down."

"Dog and Falco worked together a million years ago when he was on Paddy's crew. If he's sticking his nose into your case, then the Boothe investigation has something to do with that crew."

Kerri had suspected as much. O'Grady was eyeball deep in this, by God. "Boothe worked for O'Grady until he quit the department about ten months ago. Now his wife and child are dead, and O'Grady is inserting himself into the investigation under the guise that he wants to help."

"I can do some poking around about Boothe and O'Grady for you," Sadie offered. "Just be careful. That world is not the same as yours, Devlin. Those guys operate under a whole other set of rules."

"He started it," Kerri said. It wasn't like she could ignore him. "Whatever went down between Boothe and O'Grady, there's something these guys don't want us to unearth."

"That crew has bodies buried all over Jefferson County. Figuratively and literally."

"One of them ambushed Falco. Beat the crap out of him."

"Damn. He okay?"

"He'll live." Kerri thought of all that Brooks had said. "Did you ever know a Mina Kozlov?"

The pause on the other end of the line lasted until Kerri was through the hospital's main lobby doors.

"Russian chick," Sadie said. "She ended up in the US through the sex slave industry. Managed to break free, but the damage was done. Drugs, prostitution. It was the only life she knew. The story I heard was that Paddy picked her up off the street and helped her get her shit together. In return she became a confidential informant for him. Basically the same thing, just without the sex. He told her what he wanted or needed, and she found a way to produce it."

"Luke worked with her eight years ago. She died." Kerri paused at the bank of elevators and pressed the call button. "O'Grady is trying to use that against him somehow."

"Tell Falco to be careful. O'Grady has a lot of friends who don't know him like Falco and I do. You can't trust him, Devlin. I'll get back to you on O'Grady and Boothe."

"One other thing," Kerri said, catching her before the call ended. "I need a meeting with Clinton Sawyer."

"Okay, Devlin, now you're really asking for trouble. You don't want to rattle that cage."

"Just get the word to one of his people that I have information for him. Information that might come in handy in the near future." They had tried every damned thing else. Why not this?

Sadie laughed. "I gotta tell you, Devlin, you are one ballsy bitch when you want to be. I'll see that he gets your message. Just be ready. You may not like his response."

"I'm always ready." Kerri tucked her cell away as she entered the elevator. She would wait until she and Luke were home and he was resting, and then she would bring him up to speed on her meeting with Brooks and her run-in with his old friend.

When she reached the ER, the nurse at the desk waved her on. The double doors opened, and Kerri walked directly to the room where she'd left her partner.

"It's about time," he said as he slid off the exam table, his agility a little under par. "I thought maybe you got lost."

He'd pulled on the clothes he'd been wearing when he was brought to the ER. Blood on the shirt made her cringe.

"I know, right?" he said, following her gaze. "This is my favorite shirt too."

She wanted to laugh or at least to smile, but she couldn't work up the necessary motivation. "You have your discharge papers?"

He waved the pages clutched in his right hand. "Jeff, from the tow service we used when your Wagoneer crapped out on you, brought my Charger to your place."

"Did your car get damaged too?" He hadn't mentioned that part.

"Don't think so, but I can't drive for a few days, and I figured a tow would be the easiest way to get it home."

Made sense. She nodded. "Let's go."

On the way down the corridor every nurse they encountered called out to him, wishing him a speedy recovery. Her partner could charm most anyone. It wasn't something he did on purpose. It was just his way.

"I swear," he muttered as they crossed the lot to her Wagoneer, "I can't keep the ladies off me. They love me."

He grinned at her, and she had to smile back. It was impossible not to. "Of course they do, you're Luke Falco."

When they were buckled up and headed home, he asked, "So what did the LT have to say? He hear about someone using me as a punching bag?"

"He doesn't know what happened."

"You didn't tell him? Whoa, I'm rubbing off on you, partner."

"Ha ha," she tossed back dryly. "Apparently, Carla Brown filed a complaint against you."

"No shit?" Luke stared at her, his face wearing the same shock hers no doubt had when Brooks had told her. "You were there. What did I supposedly do?"

"I told him I was there," Kerri confirmed as she braked at a red light, "and that her claim that you were aggressive was false." The light changed, and she set the vehicle in motion again. "The real issue is your former LT. O'Grady paid Brooks a visit, and that compounded the situation. He brought up the past and Mina Kozlov."

Luke blew out a burst of air. "I wondered how long that would take. I guess now the LT is thinking I'm some kind of—"

"I told the LT that O'Grady was not to be trusted. Obviously, the whole Carla Brown thing was a setup."

"That son of a bitch," he growled. "I knew he was up to something."

Kerri figured she might as well give him the rest of the bad news. "I met your old friend Detective Durham." She kept her attention on the street.

"When?"

"This is where the story gets interesting." She explained the chain of events that had occurred after she'd left the BPD and relayed Dog's message.

For several seconds Luke said nothing. She glanced at his profile, which was of stone. The tension radiated off him in tidal waves. He was not happy.

"We'll talk."

The two words were ice cold.

"I think you should stay away from him." Kerri made the turn onto her street. She felt Luke's stare, refused to acknowledge him.

"Trust me," he said in that same icy tone, "I would love to, but they're not leaving me a choice."

He was right. O'Grady had taken that option away.

"What about this guy Durham?"

"Dog used to be a good cop," Luke said, a kind of sadness in his tone now. "A long time ago. He and O'Grady don't play by the rules, Kerri. They make their own. I don't want you anywhere near this . . ." He shook his head. "This is my fault."

Before she could argue with him, her cell vibrated against the console. She didn't recognize the number, but it was local. "Devlin."

"Detective, this is Phileas Crandall. I'm in my kitchen preparing dinner, and I just spotted someone going into the Boothe house. A man, I think. I don't see Jana's car, so I'm certain he shouldn't be there."

"I'm on my way, Mr. Crandall. Stay in your house. Do not confront this man." It could be Durham or some other thug sent by O'Grady. "I need to know you're hearing me, sir."

Crandall promised to do as she ordered.

Kerri executed a U-turn and headed in the other direction.

"Crandall spotted an intruder at the Boothe house," she explained to her partner.

"Only one reason I can think of for someone to bother," Falco said.

He was right. Anything of value had been damaged in the fire. Unless there was something hidden in the house that only mattered to the person covertly searching through the rubble for it.

Kerri pushed the Wagoneer faster.

19

5:40 p.m.

Boothe Residence
Chablis Way
Birmingham

A walk through and around the Boothe home failed to produce any suggestion that an intruder had disturbed or attempted to disturb the property. It was full-on dark now. Flashlights had helped the final few minutes of their search, but in the end, there was nothing to see. Whoever the neighbor had noticed skulking around was gone now. Could have been a reporter or a blogger who had planned a segment on the latest headline tragedy. Or one of those people who just liked to photograph tragedy for sharing on social media. At this point the only crime was trespassing. The crime scene had officially been released.

Kerri glanced toward Crandall's house. He waited on his front porch, the overhead light spotlighting him like the central character in a stage play.

"I guess we should let Crandall know it's all clear," Luke offered.

"Then we should get you home," Kerri grumbled. "You're supposed to be taking it easy."

"I'm good."

She shone her flashlight in his face. "No, you are not, so don't lie."

He held up a hand to shield his eyes. "All right, all right. I feel like I've been hit by a Mack Truck, and my ribs and head are aching something fierce. But this—what we do—can't wait. We both know it."

He was right. Except she could have done this alone. *Should* have done this alone. But that would have entailed taking the time to drop him by the house before responding to the call. Wouldn't have worked.

Kerri shifted the beam of her light to the ground. "After we talk to Crandall, we're going home. You're taking a long, hot bath, and then you're going to bed."

"I can do that," he agreed as they walked toward the neighbor's house. "It would be a lot more fun if I didn't have to do it alone."

"You're on limited physical activity, Detective."

"We can work with that."

She shook her head and moved ahead of him, calling out a hello to Crandall.

"Did you find anything?" Crandall wanted to know as soon as they had climbed the final step to his porch.

"We did not. But thank you for letting us know."

Crandall looked from Kerri to Luke as he arrived at her side. The older man's face scrunched with surprise. "What happened to you?"

"I wish I could say you should see the other guy," Luke confessed.

Crandall rubbed his cheek as if he could imagine how much the swollen eye and bruised jaw hurt. "Being a cop is more dangerous than ever," he commented. "I'm sure people like me don't tell you often enough how much we appreciate all you do."

"Thank you," Kerri said, before redirecting. "Did you get a close enough look at the intruder to give us any details?"

He braced his hands on his hips and wagged his head. "Unfortunately not. He had on one of those dark hooded shirts and dark trousers. Maybe jeans. I'm assuming it was a man, since he was fairly tall." He nodded to Luke. "Like your partner here."

"Can you describe the vehicle he was driving?"

"I never saw a vehicle, which I found quite fishy. I suppose he parked somewhere down the street and sneaked this way." He sighed. "It seems I'm not a lot of help."

"Better that you called than not," Kerri assured him. She was here; she might as well move to the next item on her list of follow-ups. "Mr. Crandall, how well do you know Rebecca Boothe, Logan's mother?"

"I guess I'd call her an acquaintance. I've spent very little time with her." His brow furrowed. "Long ago I formed the impression that she and Allison didn't get along, which probably explains why Mrs. Boothe wasn't around much."

"When I interviewed her," Kerri said, "she spoke as if she knew you quite well."

"We've run into each other at the market." He gave a slight shrug. "At Leah's birthday party some years ago. But honestly, I don't think we've ever had an actual conversation."

"Did Allison ever speak to you about her relationship with Mrs. Boothe?" Crandall had previously stated that he and Allison were close, but then Scott had told Kerri that her daughter was very private about her personal life. Kerri was definitely interested in what Crandall had to say. A more objective response than the mother's or the mother-in-law's.

The older man rubbed at his chin and mulled over the question. "As I say, the two didn't get along. I tried not to get involved in any sort of family issues. I was happy to lend an ear, but I mostly kept any conclusions and advice to myself."

"But she shared personal concerns with you," Luke said, recognizing what Kerri had been looking for.

"Oh, certainly. Allison and I talked many times," Crandall asserted. "We were quite close."

"And Jana," Kerri said, pressing along that same vein, "has she ever spoken to you about any issues with Mrs. Boothe? Or her private concerns about her daughter?"

Crandall looked from Kerri to Luke and back. "Do you consider Mrs. Boothe a suspect?"

"She's part of the family," Luke pointed out. "We're investigating everyone in the family and anyone close to the family. She's no more a suspect than Mrs. Scott, but she is a person of interest."

"I can see how we're all persons of interest." Crandall nodded. "As to your question, I don't have any sort of relationship with Mrs. Boothe. I can say that both Allison and Jana do not care for her. Knowing these two women quite well, I am unconditionally certain there is good reason."

"You watch the Boothe home." Kerri phrased this as a statement, not a question, based on the facts that he'd been the first to notice the fire on Sunday night and tonight he'd spotted an alleged intruder. "Have you over the past few months noticed anything odd or that made you feel concerned happening at the Boothe home? Besides the fire, obviously."

"I'm a good neighbor, Detective Devlin. Allison is—was—like family to me. Jana and I have known each other for quite some time. I consider her a dear, dear friend. I do watch the house, yes. When they first moved in next door, Jana asked me to watch out for her daughter and granddaughter."

"Did she have reason to be concerned about Allison's safety with Logan?" Luke asked.

Kerri gave her partner a mental high five for cutting straight to the heart of the matter.

"Well, I suppose . . ." Crandall shook his head. "Good heavens. Please sit down. I can't believe we've been standing all this time. I didn't offer you a seat. Or something to drink."

"Thank you, but we only have a few minutes more, Mr. Crandall," Kerri offered, then repeated the question Luke had asked. "Did Jana have reason to worry about Allison's safety? Or Leah's safety, for that matter?"

Crandall exhaled a burdened breath. "I really don't like to discuss such things, and I certainly don't want to break Jana's confidence. Or Allison's, no matter that she's no longer with us. I pride myself on being an honorable person, Detective. There were times when we spoke of private matters. Like any family, there were issues occasionally."

"I'm certain you are an honorable man and that you want to stand by your promises," Kerri agreed. "We would never ask these questions unless the answers were critical for solving how and why the lives of two people were taken on Sunday night."

After a moment's hesitation, Crandall started with, "Logan often drank too much. He worked undercover, as you know. He'd come home, driving wildly and then staggering to the door. Once he had sideswiped another vehicle. Considering all that, yes, Jana asked me to keep an eye on things and let her know if anything ever got out of hand. She didn't want to intrude the wrong way in their lives. But she worried about her daughter and granddaughter."

"You believe Logan Boothe to be capable of violence?" Luke asked.

"I hate to say such a thing, but yes. There is just something about him. A coldness. I've thought over and over about that night and the night before, and I suddenly remembered that on Saturday night I heard Logan yelling. He'd arrived home around ten thirty or so. I was sitting on the porch having a beer. The next thing I knew, he was shouting. I couldn't understand what he was saying, but he was fired up for sure."

"Did you hear Allison during any of this?" Kerri asked, wondering why this man had previously stated the Boothes hadn't had loud arguments.

"I didn't. No. She was never loud that way."

"Then you can't be sure," Luke interjected, "that he was arguing with Allison."

"I suppose not," he admitted.

"Did you speak with Allison at any time on Sunday?" Kerri decided Crandall liked to talk about these things more than he'd let on. She was also beginning to think his memory wasn't as good as she'd first thought or that maybe he wasn't as completely forthcoming without the right prompts.

"I didn't. I wish I had. I truly, truly do."

"You stated before that the Boothes didn't have loud arguments," she reminded him.

"They don't." He shook his head. "I mean, they didn't generally. With all that happened, I completely forgot about Saturday night. It wasn't the norm."

All the more reason he should have remembered.

"Thank you, Mr. Crandall." Kerri flashed him a smile. "The more pieces of this puzzle we can put together, the more likely we are to be successful at finding the truth."

"I'm so sorry I didn't mention that disagreement the first time we talked. Frankly, I'm certain I was in shock. I still am, really. This has been a nightmare, and I've worried so that I should have done more to help Allison and her husband. I can't help wondering if something could have been done to head off this tragedy."

"You kept her mom informed," Luke said. "That was more than most neighbors would have done."

Crandall ducked his head. "I did what I could. As I said, Jana is a dear friend."

"Thanks again," Kerri said. "We'll let you get back to your evening."

"You know . . . ," Crandall said, waylaying their departure.

Kerri caught Luke's gaze as she turned back to Mr. Crandall. He looked beyond exhausted. She needed to get him home.

"I've been going over and over that night," Crandall said.

"Did you remember something more?" Luke asked.

"I think I know what woke me up."

"Not a car door closing?" Kerri said, reminding him of what he'd stated previously.

"I believe it was glass breaking."

Kerri shared a look with her partner. "Like a window?"

Crandall nodded. "Jana mentioned that Logan's legs were broken, which explains why he kept stumbling when he ran into the house. I'm thinking maybe he jumped out a window. The glass breaking is what I heard, I'm sure of it. That would explain his broken legs and why he was on the ground outside."

It made complete sense *if* he'd been the one to set the fire.

Kerri reminded Crandall to let them know if he recalled anything else and then ushered her partner toward her Wagoneer. Once they were backing out of the Boothe driveway, she said, "You think he watches a lot of crime TV?"

"I do," Luke said. "He's come up with scenarios for a lot of things."

"The same ones we come up with," Kerri pointed out.

Luke scrolled on his phone as he grunted an agreement, then said, "That's what I thought. It was unusually cold on Saturday night—forty degrees." He turned to Kerri. "I remember this because I left that new Switch game in the car and I had to go outside for it."

"You did," Kerri teased. "You said you had to get some practice in before Tori comes back home."

"My point is," he tossed back, ignoring her remark, "why was Crandall sitting on his porch that night when it was so cold? Having a beer, no less?" He said the last in that yeah-right voice.

Kerri nodded. Good point. "Was he lying about the whole incident, or was he eavesdropping? He could be using one to explain the other."

"I'm thinking he was eavesdropping," Luke said. "Mrs. Boothe might have been right when she said Crandall watched everything and reported to Allison's mom."

Kerri thought of her own daughter and wondered what she would do if Tori married someone who Kerri suspected abused her in some way. She shuddered, couldn't even consider it.

"Maybe Jana Scott had a reason for asking Crandall to keep an eye on things." She had two very good reasons, in Kerri's opinion. Her daughter and her granddaughter.

"Definitely looks that way," Luke agreed.

Kerri took the left into her driveway, immensely grateful to be home at last. They needed some quiet time. Luke should have been resting already.

He reached for his cell as they walked toward the door. "Hey, Shelly, what's up?"

Kerri suffered a twinge of worry. She hoped everything was okay with Liam. She reached her key toward the knob but stopped shy of inserting it. She blinked rapidly in an effort to force her eyes to focus. What the hell was on her door?

"Are you shitting me?" Luke growled in response to whatever Shelly said. "Don't worry. I'll get this under control."

Kerri glanced at him, then back at her door. Someone had—

"Son of a bitch," he muttered, following Kerri's gaze. "I'll call you back, Shelly."

Luke gently set Kerri aside.

Someone had spray-painted a black *X* on her door.

"They did the same thing to Shelly's door," he said, his gaze fixed on the symbol.

"They're sending us a warning." For the first time, Kerri was really, really glad Tori was in New York. Maybe Sadie had been right. Maybe Detective Durham was dangerous. Kerri didn't doubt one bit that O'Grady was. Then again, maybe she shouldn't have sent that message to Sawyer.

"No."

Kerri looked up at Luke.

"They're sending *me* a warning."

20

7:00 p.m.

University of Alabama Hospital
Sixth Avenue South
Birmingham

Luke burst from the elevator. He grimaced, cursed himself for not waiting for Kerri to exit first.

He was beyond pissed.

At the door to Boothe's room, he had the presence of mind to stop and allow her to go in first. Besides, he didn't want the uniform stationed just outside the door to be able to say he'd witnessed Luke charging into the room.

This had gone too far.

Kerri hesitated before entering the room and assessed him a moment. "You're good, right?"

If by "good" she meant ready to jerk Boothe out of the damned bed and kick his injured ass, yeah, he was better than good.

"I'm great." He forced a smile she would see through in a heartbeat, but it was the best he could do.

"Whatever you say. Just remember your actions reflect on both of us." She pushed through the door and left him feeling like he'd just kicked a dog.

He would never kick a dog.

But he might kick this guy's ass. Verbally, anyway.

And that was her point. To remind him that he was under extra scrutiny right now.

Kerri stopped on the right side of the bed; Luke moved to the other side. He wanted the dumbass to feel surrounded. He'd lost his wife and kid; wasn't that enough? Did he want other people's lives screwed up too? At the moment, Luke had no sympathy for the man.

Whoever Boothe was protecting, it damned sure couldn't be worth the price he'd already paid.

Thankfully, his momma was nowhere to be seen. Jesus. Luke hadn't even considered he definitely didn't need the woman witnessing what he wanted to say to this dumb shit.

"Boothe, we have a dilemma," Kerri announced, getting the ball rolling.

Boothe cut her a look. Didn't open his mouth.

Luke gritted his teeth. Resisted the urge to give him a little physical therapy on those banged-up legs. A new rush of outrage blasted him. What kind of asshole protected his wife and kid's killer?

Assuming it wasn't the asshole who killed them.

"Your wife and your daughter were marked, as you've been told," Kerri went on. "Did this have anything to do with the five thousand dollars you sent to someone on PayPal?"

He closed his eyes as if the move could block the conversation and their presence. Luke's anger inched higher up the Richter scale.

"Someone—someone we believe you know—has marked my house and the house of persons close to Detective Falco," Kerri tried again. "We need you to give us a name. If you paid someone to do something and it went wrong, just tell us. Time is running out, Boothe."

Not one word. The bastard didn't even crack an eye open. Luke shifted his weight to the other foot. This was getting them nowhere.

"I need," Luke said, "a moment alone with him."

Kerri swung her attention to him, a hell-no look clear in her eyes.

Before she could make some excuse about why his request wasn't a good idea, he added, "Trust me. I know how to handle this."

One second turned to five. He urged her with his eyes to please trust him.

"I'll be right outside the door chatting with the detail officer." She looked from Luke to Boothe and back to assure both she would be listening. She would give Luke her trust, but she was not doing so blindly.

Fair enough.

Boothe's eyes popped open then as if he'd just realized he might be in trouble.

Good.

The door closed behind Kerri.

Luke chuckled. "Just you and me now, buddy."

Boothe stared at the ceiling.

"I used to be like you."

Boothe glanced at him, then quickly returned his interest to the ceiling, which wasn't interesting at all.

"I did my job. Better than most, in my opinion. Stayed between the lines. No breaking the *big* rules, just a little bending here and there as needed." He shrugged. "You know the deal."

"I don't need to hear your life story," Boothe muttered.

"What you need," Luke said as he leaned forward and braced his hands on the bed rail, gripping it hard enough to whiten his knuckles, "is completely irrelevant to me, Boothe. This is about what *I* need. And I need you to tell me who did this—assuming it wasn't you, of course."

The guy's face contorted with anger. "I've already given my statement. I did this. You should arrest me and stop fucking around."

"Say it," Luke hissed the words at him. "Say. *It.*"

Boothe glared at him. "I did it. You got that, *buddy*? I. Did. It."

Luke moved his head side to side. "No, man. Say *it*. Say what you did."

"I fucking set the fire," Boothe snarled, tears welling in his eyes.

Luke shook his head again. "Say what you did, you fucking coward. It should be easy. *I* . . ." He enunciated the words slowly, drawing them out. *"Killed . . ."* Luke made a rolling motion with his hand. *"My . . . wife . . . and . . . my . . . little . . . girl."*

"Go to hell. I don't have to say anything to you, asshole."

"*I* . . . ," Luke repeated, "killed Allison—the woman I loved."

"Fuck you!"

"I killed," Luke said, more loudly this time, "my sweet baby girl."

The machine monitoring Boothe's vitals displayed his accelerated heart rate and climbing BP. Good. Luke's tactic was working.

"I did it!" Boothe screamed.

"Did what?" Luke yelled back at him.

"I killed them!"

"Who?" Luke demanded.

"My wife." Boothe's voice broke. "I killed my wife."

Luke gave him a look that said *and?*

"My daughter," he cried. "I killed my little girl."

The door burst open. Luke straightened away from the bed. A nurse rushed into the room. Kerri glanced in but stayed in the hall.

"What's going on here?" the nurse demanded.

Boothe sobbed like a baby.

Luke shrugged. "He's upset. He lost his wife and kid in the fire."

The nurse's eyes narrowed with skepticism. She shifted her attention to her patient.

"You're okay, aren't you, Boothe?" Luke prodded.

He glared at Luke before gazing up at the nurse. "I just need more pain meds."

"Let me check your chart." She sent a pointed glance to Luke. "I'd better not hear any more shouting, Detective."

"Yes, ma'am."

When the nurse left the room, Luke leaned close again. "You dumb fucker, I know you didn't kill your wife and kid. Do I look that stupid?"

Boothe pressed his quivering lips together to hold back anything he might say in his current condition. Luke had rattled him.

Idiot. "If you don't give me something to work with, more people are going to die. People I care about. If *you* let that happen, *I* will make you regret it."

"Kill me," Boothe pleaded, his lips twisting with the words. "Do it now. Please."

Luke rolled his eyes and straightened away from the bastard. "You want the easy way out? Not happening."

He'd wasted enough time.

Luke walked around the foot of the bed and headed for the door.

"Falco."

He hesitated and looked back at Boothe.

"If you're smart, you'll arrest me and close the case."

The nurse appeared at the door with the pain meds. Luke sidestepped out of her way, then left the room. To the uni on duty, Falco said, "Make sure this door stays open from now on. I don't want this guy taking himself out."

The uniform nodded. "You got it, Detective."

On the way to the elevators, Kerri asked, "You get anything from him?"

"I did." He pressed the call button and turned to her. "Whatever it is they're holding over his head, it's powerful. He won't budge, just keeps repeating his confession."

"It's possible he fears for his mother's safety," Kerri pointed out.

They loaded into the elevator car and headed down to the lobby. "I'd definitely put her at the top of the list."

Kerri watched him. He tried to keep his face clean of tells as he leaned against the wall, but exhaustion nagged at him. The pain in his side was worse now. His head throbbed like a son of a bitch. And all he wanted to do was lie down somewhere.

With her, preferably.

The ghost of a smile tugged at his lips. He was too exhausted for the real thing, but he could deal with some nice cuddling.

And a heart-to-heart. There was more he needed to share with her.

Boothe was the perfect example of what it cost to keep secrets.

———

Devlin Residence
Twenty-First Avenue South
Birmingham, 8:35 p.m.

Luke immediately recognized the car parked at the street in front of Kerri's house.

O'Grady.

His timing couldn't have been worse. Luke was beat. And yet his timing was perfect. Luke had questions for him.

Kerri parked in the driveway, and they climbed out. O'Grady waited at the front door.

"Whoa, what happened to you?" O'Grady said as they approached.

"You didn't hear?" Luke growled. He wasn't playing games with this bastard.

Kerri unlocked the door. "Let's take this inside."

O'Grady laughed. "Sounds like you've lost your sense of humor, Falco."

The urge to commit a violent act roared through him as he followed his former LT inside. How had he ever looked up to this guy? He had been a fool. No question.

"Beer?" Kerri asked as she tossed her keys aside and shouldered out of her jacket.

"I'll take one," Luke said. "O'Grady isn't staying."

The other man's own sense of humor seemed to fade. His jaw tightened.

"Your LT," O'Grady said, "Brooks. He called me about you. He seems to think you're having a little trouble with your temper. You know, the way you did back in the day. He said he was planning to talk to your partner about it. Is she the one who punched you? Sometimes people get upset when they find out something they weren't expecting."

There were so many things Luke wanted to say to this man—his former mentor and tormentor. But he wouldn't waste his breath.

"Are you purposely attempting to muddy the waters of this case?" Luke asked the son of a bitch. "I mean, Boothe ain't talking, and let's face it, this thing kind of has your style written all over it. An elaborate cover-up, complete with the patsy to take the fall. A neat little box all tied up with a bow."

O'Grady chuckled, but the sound held no humor whatsoever. "Are you accusing me of something, pretty boy?" He glanced at Kerri as she joined them. "Did he tell you that's what I used to call him? All the female marks and CIs loved him so much. He was young and handsome. He could wrap any of them around his little finger. Isn't that right, Falco? You were a real lady-*killer*."

The one thing that kept Luke from diving at him at that very instant was Kerri. He could no longer keep his ugly past from her. But he would not show her the man he used to be. He never wanted her to see that side of him.

"He didn't have to tell me." Kerri passed the beer to Luke. "I picked up on the charm the day we met."

"You be careful, Detective Devlin." O'Grady reached for the door. "You never really know a person who lies to himself."

Luke smiled. "I learned from the best. Speaking of which, I have a feeling you know exactly what went down Sunday night at the Boothe home. Why don't you tell us now and save the taxpayers a few dollars?"

Fury blazed from O'Grady's eyes.

"Boothe was part of your crew. There's no way you're in the dark about this." Luke moved his head side to side. "No way."

"You know," O'Grady said, "I wish you were right. I do. I wish I knew who did this. But I don't. So do your job, Falco," O'Grady warned. "Boothe confessed. Make the arrest and move on. Don't go falling down that same rabbit hole you dropped into last time."

With that final advice, he left. Luke shoved the door shut behind him.

"He lied about Brooks," Kerri said, her own anger tingeing her voice. "Brooks said O'Grady came to him. I don't believe for a second that Brooks went to him. Doesn't matter anyway; Brooks knows me. He'll take my word over O'Grady's."

Luke set his beer on the table next to her keys and reached for her hands. She moved closer to him.

"You don't have to protect me, Kerri. I'm stronger than I look."

She laughed. "I know how strong you are. I'm not protecting you, I'm backing you up. You're my partner. I trust you. I believe in you."

"You can't possibly know what that means to me."

"Right now," Kerri said as she pulled him toward the stairs, "what I know is that you're taking that bath we talked about, and then I'm tucking you in for the night."

"I like the sound of that."

She led him up the stairs and to the bathroom. "Strip," she said as she sat down on the edge of the tub.

While he peeled off his clothes, she started the water running and adjusted the temperature. As the tub filled, she pulled the ponytail holder from her hair and massaged her scalp.

He loved her hair. Loved everything about her.

She turned off the water and stood. "In the tub, *pretty boy*."

He'd never hear the end of that one.

Luke climbed into the warm water, sat down with a groan. He hadn't been this sore in a damned long time.

She knelt beside the tub, bar of soap and washcloth in hand.

"You're not climbing in with me?" He had really hoped she would.

She doused the washcloth in the water and rubbed it over the bar of soap. "Not tonight." She washed his face, gently. "You need to heal."

He relaxed against the end of the tub and closed his eyes. This was nice too. He could be happy with having her hands moving over his skin. *All* over his skin.

Her soft hands moved to his chest. "O'Grady just scooted to the top of my suspect list," she said. "I've had my doubts about him, but at this point, he's gone way too far."

Luke opened his eyes. "Whatever happened," he said, "O'Grady knows. He likes knowing and watching others dance around trying to find the right rhythm. He gets some sort of twisted glee out of it."

He'd watched him do it a hundred times.

At least.

"We need to beat him at his own game," Kerri suggested. Her hands moved over his arms, sliding the cotton cloth up and down and around, easing his tension like nothing else could. "All we have to do is find his motive, and we'll understand how this is all supposed to end. Then we'll get him."

Luke gasped when her hands moved lower. "We still have Sawyer to figure in." He groaned. "If," he squeaked, "Boothe was working with him, he may have screwed up in some way. Or his going to the dark side could be the reason O'Grady decided to teach him a lesson."

Her right hand settled on him in just the right spot, and his breath caught. "Would O'Grady go so far as to have ordered a hit on his family?"

Luke forced himself to focus on the question. If her hand moved, he was going to explode. "I want to say hell no, he'd never go so far as to murder innocent people. But I can't be sure. He was ruthless eight years ago. Who knows now?"

That cold, hard truth made him feel sick inside. Was he any better?

170

"Then the answer is," Kerri offered, "anything is possible." Her hand shifted to his right leg.

"No question." He forced his eyes closed again. Allowed her touch to crush the haunting doubts.

"You're so tense."

No kidding. "A little," he admitted.

"We just have to treat O'Grady like any other suspect. Make him sweat."

Oh yeah. He could do that. He frowned, turned to look at her. "I need details on how you plan to do that."

"I've already started. O'Grady hooked us up with this Carla Brown character, who I'm guessing was nothing more than a setup. She claimed Boothe was working for Clinton Sawyer. I decided to reach out to him in a way he couldn't ignore."

Luke went stone still. "We've put out feelers on Sawyer and gotten nothing. We've been to his house." He had a bad, bad feeling about this.

"I talked to Sadie. She said she'd look into the Boothe-O'Grady backstory. I also asked her to send Sawyer a message. She has the kind of contacts he won't ignore."

Oh hell. "Well, that should get a reaction." He thought of the *X* on her door as well as Shelly's. "Or maybe it already has."

"Yeah, I thought of that. But I only mentioned my name. There wouldn't be a reason for Sawyer to post a warning to Shelly. Relax," she urged. "We can handle this."

He eased back against the tub and closed his eyes. She was right. They could handle anything. Maybe.

Her hands started moving on him again.

As long as she didn't stop what she was doing.

He trusted her completely. She would never let him down the way he'd let down the people who'd counted on him.

21

Eight Years Ago

December 3

9:20 a.m.

I crack my eyes open and wince.

The crashing of cymbals in my skull has me snapping them shut.

If I dare move, I'm pretty sure I will puke.

Maybe if I just lie really still, this hellacious hangover will settle down. Expecting it to pass is probably wishful thinking.

I close my eyes again and will away the pounding there. My mouth is dry. Damn, we should never have had those tequila shots after all that bourbon. I know better, but last night I was in a bad place.

If I didn't feel like death warmed over, I would laugh at how stupid I am.

Somehow, I manage to sit up. The room spins for a bit. Man, I can't ever remember having a hangover this bad.

When the room stops circling, I push to my feet. Stagger drunkenly. Chances are, if I had a blood alcohol test, I would still be considered legally drunk. Maybe way beyond that. Shit.

I lumber to the bathroom and piss like a racehorse. At the sink I wash my hands and face in hopes the water will make me feel more human. Doesn't help. My reflection in the mirror over the sink tells the story loud and clear. I'm a piece of shit. I do things I shouldn't . . . for the greater good, of course. Ha ha.

The whites of my eyes look like road maps. They feel dry and gritty. The stubble on my chin is far too long to be called stubble anymore. I've lost weight. I look like a junkie. A piece-of-shit, living-on-the-street druggie.

I'm a cop. One of the good guys. But I don't feel good. I don't feel anything.

I'm numb.

To my life, to everything.

The memory of Mina shouting at me echoes in my ears. We had sex. Got drunker. Fought like hell. Had more sex. And then I must have blacked out. I don't remember anything after that last sex session.

A scream explodes in my head. A memory . . . a dream. Not real.

I grip the porcelain sink and stare into the mirror. Someone screamed at some point during the night. I try to recall the events leading to that moment, but they won't rise above the fog in my head.

I dry my hands and wander back to the bed.

Mina is still sleeping, covers pulled over her. I should get going. I have shit to do. I pull on my boxers and jeans, fasten them. Search for my boots and socks. I find my shirt half-tucked under the bed.

Should I leave her sleeping or wake her up for a goodbye? Probably should apologize for being an asshole last night.

I must have been pretty rough on her. Flashes of her crying keep flickering through my head. I stand at the door a moment, debating myself.

I swore I'd never be like my father. I would never hurt a woman. Never. I would never be a dirty cop. I became a cop to make up for the shit he did in his life.

And I've turned out no better than him.

My gut roiling, I turn around and walk back to the bed. She lies on her side, hair across her face, bare shoulder peeking from beneath the covers. I sit down next to her. I won't be like him, I swear to myself. I will apologize. I won't let it happen again.

"Mina, I have to go."

I should have been out of here two hours ago.

She doesn't rouse, so I put my hand on her shoulder and give her a shake. "Mina."

Her skin is cold. Rigid.

"Mina." This time I turn her over.

Her body is too still.

Hand trembling, I reach out and move her hair away from her face. Her eyes are open, staring at the ceiling.

"Mina."

I shake her, harder. The stiff, rubbery texture of her body sends fear searing through my veins.

She's dead.

"No. No. No!" I feel for a pulse. "Mina, wake up."

There is no pulse.

This can't be.

I stare at her face. Glassy eyes . . . mouth wide open and contorted in a silent scream.

Fuck! Did she OD on something?

Then my gaze slides down farther. Her naked skin is too white, a sharp contrast to the dark portion along her right side. Livor mortis. Bile rises hot and bitter in my throat. I swallow it back.

That's when I see the marks on her throat.

Bruises.

I've seen them before on homicide vics. *Strangled* homicide vics.

No way. I couldn't have . . .

Vomit rushes into my throat. I hit the floor on all fours and puke.

"Shit!" I rear back on my knees and try to think. No. I couldn't have done this.

I turn my head far enough to see her. *Mina* . . . lying there . . . dead.

I stare at my hands.

"Jesus Christ," I mutter.

What the hell have I done?

I feel in my hip pocket for my cell phone. I stare at the screen. I should call it in. But I don't. I call the only person in the world who can help me.

Paddy.

While I wait for him to answer, I reach for the half-empty bottle of tequila lying on the floor. Down the rest of it.

The call goes to voice mail, and I throw the phone across the room. No. No. No. What I need is my weapon.

Then it will all go away.

22

Thursday, November 25

9:00 a.m.

Devlin Residence
Twenty-First Avenue South
Birmingham

Kerri ended the call with Tori and stared at the sweet face of her daughter, which served as her phone's wallpaper. With teenagers, sometimes it felt like a break would be so nice. A little time away from the bickering and the growing pains.

A week was far too long.

Kerri missed her daughter like crazy.

"She sounds like she's having a good time," Luke pointed out.

The call had been on speaker because, of course, Tori had wanted to speak with Luke too. She adored him. It was their relationship that made his and Kerri's all the more special. It was difficult capturing the right balance in a new relationship when you were a single mom.

"She does," Kerri admitted. Her ex and his new wife had a baby of their own. He'd wasted no time starting his second family. It had taken a very long time for Kerri to get past the idea that he'd cheated on her.

Worse, he'd cheated on Tori. That was the part Kerri found the most difficult to bear. But she had to give her ex credit; he'd come to his senses and somehow managed to blend his relationship with Tori into his new life. Kerri was grateful.

"She still loves you more," Luke said softly. "You're her momma. Nothing and no one can change that."

Kerri hugged him. How selfish of her to be pining over her daughter's visit to see her dad when Luke's son wouldn't even speak to him right now.

"Did you call?" she asked as she drew back to look into his eyes.

He nodded. "Shelly said he still won't talk about me."

"He'll come around," Kerri promised. "You'll see. Coming to terms with life-changing news just takes time."

"I get it."

As much as she didn't want to add to his burden of unhappiness this morning, she couldn't pretend last night hadn't happened. "Luke, you had those nightmares again last night."

He turned to the island and braced his forearms on the counter. "I'm sorry. Pieces of my life from before keep nagging at me. The worst part is it's the ones that are still foggy, and I can't quite bring them into focus. I know whatever is there, it's bad. The only question is how bad."

Kerri wished she knew the right things to say to encourage or comfort him somehow. "Have you considered going to counseling to get help with pulling it all together?"

He shrugged. "I tried a couple of times, but I just couldn't keep going back. I needed to go forward. To put it behind me."

"The woman who died," she ventured, "do you feel somehow responsible?"

He nodded. "But I can't be sure what happened. I only know that something happened while we were together, and she died. O'Grady took care of it. Sometimes I think I should be grateful he protected me. Other times I just feel like he turned me into something I never wanted to be." Luke shrugged. "In the end, whatever happened, I was responsible."

"We'll figure it out." She gave a nod of finality. "Whatever happened, we'll work with it. That's all we can do."

Sometimes the figuring-it-out part required taking risks. She thought of the black *X* spray-painted on her door. Maybe Sadie was right and reaching out to Sawyer was too dangerous. Whatever the case, it had to be done. Sawyer was just one more hazy potential scenario in this case. Not following that lead was out of the question.

"You know"—she swiped her hands on her hips—"I think I'll dig out some white paint I have somewhere in the garage and paint the front door. Otherwise, the neighbors will be freaking out."

"I'll help."

Kerri held up a hand. "You're on light duty, Detective. I've got this. You make the fruit salad. Diana will be thrilled. She likes yours way better than mine."

"I will make one hell of a fruit salad." He gave her a salute and headed for the kitchen.

Finding the paint took no time. It was getting the can open that took forever. Finally, with the paint opened and stirred, she walked out the garage overhead door and went around to the porch. The garage was so full of stuff it wasn't possible to park inside. Maybe one day she would get a wild hair and throw half the junk away.

But not today.

Covering the black thoroughly would likely require primer, which she did not have. Multiple coats of what she had would have to do.

A middle-aged man wearing a jogging suit, his dog trotting ahead of him, threw up a hand and called good morning as he walked past on the sidewalk.

Kerri smiled and did the same. Maybe they should get a dog. She'd thought about it plenty of times. She'd always talked herself out of the notion, since she was never home and Tori was so little. Things were different now. Tori was older and very reliable. Luke would help.

Maybe, she decided.

She had just turned back to the door when the dog rushed up her driveway and disappeared behind her house. The guy in the jogging suit followed, shouting the dog's name.

Kerri placed her brush down on the lid of the can and headed that way. Her backyard was fenced, but she rarely closed the gate. Catching the dog once he was inside the fence shouldn't be a problem.

She rounded the corner of the house and drew up short.

The muzzle of a handgun stared her in the face. Her hands automatically went up, and her senses soared to high alert.

"All we have to do," he said, "is stay calm, and we'll get through this just fine, Detective Devlin."

"You are . . . ?" she asked, feeling at a distinct disadvantage. Adrenaline charged into her veins. The man knew her name, and he had a gun.

A good thing? Not likely.

"I'm your escort to the meeting you requested."

Luke appeared behind the man, who abruptly stiffened at the feel of a weapon nudged into his skull. Kerri relaxed marginally.

"I'm her partner," Luke said, "and I don't like being left out."

A third male voice piped up. "Let's take a ride."

The new arrival to the party was a man in a black suit. He hovered behind Luke.

Where the hell had he come from?

Her backyard, obviously.

From the corner of her eye she spotted a black car pulling into her driveway.

"Let's go," the jogging suit guy said with a flick of his gun barrel.

Kerri did an about-face and headed for the car, which was not just a car. A limo. The rear passenger door was open, and she and Luke climbed inside along with the man in the jogging suit. The one in the black suit slid into the front passenger seat. A third man was behind the steering wheel.

The man waiting in the passenger compartment of the limo wore dark glasses. He appeared to be between thirty-five and forty and dressed the part of someone who rode around in a limo with his own personal driver and security. High-end designer suit, perfect hair. Probably hand-made shoes. He looked vaguely familiar.

The limo rolled out of the driveway and onto the street. Kerri's pulse rate picked up. Beside her, tension radiated from Luke. The man in the black suit had taken his weapon. At least he'd had one. Kerri had been caught completely off guard.

"Detective Devlin." The man with the dark glasses shifted his attention from Kerri to Luke, then back to her. "I understand you have a message for me."

Clinton Sawyer. It seemed he'd gotten word she was looking for him. He was younger than she'd expected. Tall, broad shouldered. He looked more like a businessman than a thug. The transformation as people like Sawyer climbed up the food chain could be startling.

Didn't matter how expensive his suit or his car—he was still a thug.

"Logan Boothe," she said. "I heard a rumor that he works for you. Or worked for you. Can you verify?"

The limo turned at the intersection. Kerri hoped a simple cruise around the block was the plan.

Sawyer made a sound, a sort of low, dry chuckle. "That's not a message, Detective. That's a question."

"I know. Sorry. But his family was murdered, and we—my partner and I—are working the case."

He eyed her from behind those dark glasses for a stretch of time that felt entirely too long. "This Logan Boothe has never worked for me. Whoever gave you this information lied."

No surprise there. Before Kerri could say more, Luke said, "This rumor has some legs, Sawyer, considering Boothe's wife and daughter were marked with *X*s on their foreheads. The word on the street is you've been known to use that symbol for canceling issues."

"You think I'm the only one who can use this symbol?" Sawyer retorted, his tone oddly calm . . . almost patronizing.

Kerri hastened to say, "No," before Luke could toss back some smart-ass remark. "I was thinking this was someone who wanted to make it look as if you were responsible. Maybe the same someone who tossed your name around."

To Kerri's relief, the limo pulled back into her driveway and came to a stop.

"That would be my guess as well, Detective." Sawyer nodded to his cohort, who opened the door and climbed out, leaving the door open for their exit. "For the record," Sawyer said before dismissing them, "I don't murder children and wives." He looked out the car window. "Have a nice Thanksgiving, Detectives."

They exited the limo, and the jogger guy climbed back in. She and Luke watched the limo disappear down the street.

"You believe him?" Kerri asked, feeling strangely dirty after sitting in the car with the guy.

Luke shrugged. "I guess we'll know soon enough. If our sources lied about him, I expect there will be a reaction. Sawyer doesn't strike me as the type who tolerates having his name used as a cover."

"We should pay another visit to Ms. Brown," Kerri suggested. "This time you should stay in the car."

Luke grunted what might have been an agreement.

Two hours later they had found no sign of Carla Brown. One of her neighbors said she'd left on Tuesday night and hadn't been back. On a hunch, Luke tried contacting Josh Carr. No answer, and his voice mail box was full. He, too, seemed to have disappeared.

As much as Kerri would have liked to call O'Grady and demand to know if he'd heard from Brown, she didn't care to go there. If Brown's body showed up, O'Grady would no doubt attempt to pin that on Luke as well.

Not happening on Kerri's watch.

Swanner Residence
Twenty-Third Avenue South
Birmingham, 12:30 p.m.

Kerri's sister, Diana, knew how to pull off a family get-together like nobody's business. Diana and her husband, Robby, as well as the twins, Ryan and River, had gone all out with the festivities, complete with harvest decorations. Jennifer Whitten, Diana's lifelong best friend—more like another sister, in Kerri's opinion—had arrived with home-made pecan pies. Her mother's recipe. Since her mother had passed, Jen had declared that Kerri, Diana, and her crew were the only family Jen had left.

Truth was, Jen had always been like family to them.

The whole clan had gone on and on about Luke's banged-up face. But the biggest surprise of the day was that Diana had invited Sadie Cross and her little boy, Edward. The twins were having a blast teaching him the ropes of their favorite video game.

"Edward is growing like a weed," Diana said as she placed the dinner plates around the dining table.

"And he's so cute," Jen said, following behind Diana with the silverware.

Kerri tucked a napkin next to each plate. "He looks more like you every day."

Sadie positioned a glass next to each place setting. "He's the love of my life."

Kerri and Diana exchanged a grin. "Kids change everything," Diana pointed out.

"I hope to have at least one someday," Jen announced.

Kerri and the others stopped in their tracks and stared at Jen.

She waved them off. "No, he hasn't popped the question yet, but I'm expecting him to by Christmas."

Jen had finally found a man who adored her completely. He was a couple of years older than her, the president of a bank, and he was a widower with no children. He showered her with expensive gifts and catered to her every whim.

He was all that Jen had dreamed of. After all she'd been through with the men in her life and her mother, God rest her soul, she deserved to finally find real happiness.

"He'd better," she added. "My eggs aren't getting any younger."

They all laughed, and for a moment Kerri let go of the murder and mayhem that filled her life as a cop. Today was about family and giving thanks.

The men swaggered into the room.

"What'd we miss?" Robby, Diana's husband, asked.

"It's a girl thing," Diana said.

Robby made a face. "In that case, we definitely do not want to know." He turned to Luke. "You ready for another beer?"

"Always ready," Luke tossed back.

"I'll take one," Jen called out.

"Anyone else?" Robby said from the fridge.

"Not me." Sadie held up a hand stop sign fashion. "I'm driving."

Kerri bit her lip to hide her grin. Sadie was taking motherhood very seriously. She'd totally turned her life around. Still a damned good PI, she was an even better mother. Equally important, she was immensely happy. The pain she had survived was finally behind her. Like Luke, she'd been taken by her years of undercover work to very dark places. She'd spent months as a prisoner and then had been separated from her child for years before she'd learned he was still alive. Kerri's gaze settled on Luke. She desperately hoped he would find that same peace about his past. Soon.

"I'm saving myself for wine," Diana said as she stepped back and studied the table.

For the first time since her tragic and untimely death, Amelia was not the primary topic of conversation at family gatherings. It was more an unspoken knowing these days. Amelia had been Diana and Robby's amazing daughter. At eighteen she'd been murdered. Her case was the first one Kerri and Luke had worked together.

The ache deep in her chest was still present when Kerri thought of Amelia. She imagined it always would be. She couldn't even conceive of the strength it took for Diana and Robby to go on with their lives. The twins likely had a tremendous amount to do with their ability to hold their lives together.

After the whole lot of them had indulged in true southern comfort food until they were stuffed, they divided into squads to get the cleanup done. The twins had brought out all their old Lego sets and were building what looked like a small city with Edward.

Kerri washed dishes while Sadie rinsed and Luke dried.

"I picked up some chatter about Boothe," Sadie said as she passed a plate to Luke.

"We could certainly use a break with that guy," Kerri said. "By the way, Sawyer dropped by my house this morning."

Sadie stalled, stared at her. "Seriously?"

"Seriously," Luke answered.

Kerri gave her the details. "He said Boothe has never worked for him."

"What can I say?" Sadie continued with her work. "I'm good. Like a magician."

"Yes, you are," Kerri agreed.

"Maybe you can use your magic to get Boothe to talk. He keeps repeating his confession," Luke said. "But whatever happened, O'Grady is eyeball deep in it. I know it."

Sadie rolled her eyes. "I don't doubt that. I swear, one of these days that hard-ass is going to get his."

"It amazes me," Kerri said, her frustration showing, "the BPD doesn't recognize him for what he is."

Sadie reached for another plate. "Unfortunately, sometimes it takes his kind to get certain things done."

"Only because it makes things easier for the higher-ups," Luke argued. "The work gets done, and they don't get their hands dirty and still look good."

Sadie shrugged. "Maybe so."

"You said you heard something related to Boothe," Kerri said.

"A couple of contacts mentioned that he seemed to be conducting an investigation into his former LT. Word is, he wanted to take the guy down."

"Dog said O'Grady rode Boothe hard," Luke said, "which is most likely a major part of the reason he walked away from his career."

"Makes sense that he probably blames O'Grady for ruining his career at the worst possible time," Kerri offered. "Just before his daughter was diagnosed with leukemia."

"Maybe"—Sadie took the ball and ran with it—"O'Grady marked his wife and kid to show him who's boss."

"Would he go that far?" Kerri asked Luke. "Cold-blooded murder?" She'd asked Luke this before, and he'd said the man was ruthless. But there was ruthless, and then there was pure evil. This was pure evil. She thought of the woman, Mina Kozlov, who had ended up dead. Her gut clenched.

"There was a time when I wouldn't have thought he would go that far across the line," Luke said, sounding distant, as if he were in a different place and time. "But now I don't know. A lot of things don't add up anymore. Maybe they never did."

Kerri thought of the time when her niece had been missing and how far she had skirted over that invisible line between good and bad. Sometimes a person stumbled over the line without realizing just how far down that unconscious decision would take them and how very difficult it would be to claw their way back.

Maybe O'Grady had done that and found himself in that no-way-back place.

How far would he go to protect himself?

23

4:00 p.m.

Devlin Residence
Twenty-First Avenue South
Birmingham

Kerri had just turned into her driveway when her cell vibrated against the console.

Blocked call.

She almost didn't answer but decided not to risk missing a potential lead. If the caller didn't want his number known, he likely wouldn't leave a message.

"Devlin." This was her standard greeting.

"Detective Devlin, this is Sheree Bledsoe from Dr. Wilson's office."

Kerri put the vehicle in park and shut off the engine. She turned to Luke as she said, "Hey, Sheree, I'm glad you called."

Luke raised his eyebrows in surprise. They hadn't expected to hear from the oncologist's office. If they were lucky, Dr. Wilson had decided to allow an interview. The more they understood about Leah's condition and the frame of mind of her parents, the better. The really surprising part was the timing.

"I know it's Thanksgiving, and I'm sorry to bother you."

"No problem," Kerri assured her.

"I've been thinking . . . maybe the fact that it's Thanksgiving and I've spent the day with my family has made me realize what I need to do."

For a moment she said nothing more. Kerri found herself holding her breath. Hoping. They needed a break.

"There are things I want to tell you, but I could lose my job."

"I understand," Kerri assured her. "If you're not comfortable talking to us about Leah and her family—"

"I'll only talk to you," she interrupted. "Can we meet somewhere? Now? I want to do this before I lose the courage, but I can't do it on the phone."

"Tell me where you are; I'll come to you."

Another lift of eyebrows from Luke.

She gave Kerri the address, and they agreed to meet in half an hour. The sooner, the better in Kerri's opinion.

"You're going alone?" Luke asked when she'd put her phone away.

"She'll only talk to me. Just relax, and I'll be back before you know it."

He shook his head. "No can do. I'll wait in the car. Duck down out of sight. Whatever. But I'm going with you."

She couldn't argue with that.

———

Taylor Cemetery
Sweeney Hollow Road
Birmingham, 4:35 p.m.

Taylor Cemetery wasn't exactly the place Kerri had anticipated meeting with a potential source, but she wasn't going to complain. If the lady was willing to talk, Kerri would come and listen wherever she wanted to meet.

Since Sheree Bledsoe was already at the cemetery and seated on a bench beyond the towering entrance, she hopefully didn't notice Luke in the passenger seat of Kerri's Wagoneer. It was almost dark as Kerri walked through the entrance and deeper into the cemetery.

"Thanks for coming," Sheree said as Kerri approached. "I come here every Thanksgiving to see my grandmother." She glanced at the headstone a few feet away. "She raised me after my mother died. Really, I was so young when it happened she was the only mother I ever knew."

Kerri sat down beside her. "I didn't mind coming. I appreciate you calling." She restrained the urge to launch into a barrage of questions. The woman was nervous; that was obvious in the way her hands were tightly clasped in her lap and twisting together. Better to allow her to do this in her own time.

"One of the things my grandmother taught me was to always do the right thing, even if it was hard."

Kerri nodded, allowed the silence to linger until the other woman was ready to say more.

"The trouble started when Dr. Wilson recommended a bone marrow transplant for Leah. Logan, Allison, and Mrs. Scott were all anxious to be tested to see if one of them could be the donor."

A sinking feeling tugged at Kerri's stomach. In light of what she already knew about the problems between Boothe and his wife, it was easy to anticipate where this was going.

"Thankfully, Allison was a match, so Dr. Wilson set up a date for the procedure. Leah had a bout with a virus, so we had to reschedule." Sheree shivered, pulled her sweater more closely around her. "When I saw the family again, everything had changed. Logan didn't come to the appointment. Allison and her mother were evasive when I asked if he had to work. It seemed like a reasonable question. He had come to every visit up to that point. He'd been very excited about how the transplant might help his daughter. I couldn't imagine him not making time for the appointment. Anyway, later I mentioned something about it to the nurse, and she explained that Logan's test showed he was not Leah's biological father."

This news wasn't as much of a shock as it might have been had she not known the couple had issues, but it did add to Boothe's motive for wanting his wife, maybe even his child, out of his life. Still, Kerri remained unconvinced. "You're certain about the results?"

"Yes. I looked at the report myself. Those of us who interacted with the family noticed the change in Allison and her mother. They were both clearly devastated by the news." Her expression underscored her puzzled tone. "We were all wondering how Allison could not know. I suppose it's possible, depending on the circumstances. But she just didn't seem like the sort to cheat on her husband or to lie to him about something so important. I don't mean to be judgy, but Allison was a very devoted mother and wife. Anyone can make a mistake, but Allison was smart. Very smart. Surely if she'd had even a remote idea her husband might not be the father, she wouldn't have been so gung ho for him to be tested."

Kerri didn't point out that if Allison had had an affair while remaining sexually active with her husband, it was possible she hadn't known. Still, Sheree's point was valid. Why wouldn't she be worried how the test would turn out?

"Did Allison or her mother suggest this was a total surprise or say anything at all about Logan's reaction?"

"Not a word. But the nurse said Dr. Wilson mentioned something about the shock on all their faces when he gave the news. We were all convinced Allison didn't have a clue this was going to happen."

The real question in Kerri's mind now was, Why hadn't Scott said anything? Why would she hide a motive this compelling? She'd been a cop's wife for most of her life. She had to understand the implications.

"I feel terrible telling you this." Sheree closed her eyes and took a breath. "It was the hardest thing to decide and break the rules. But it just felt like it might matter. It felt like the right thing to do."

Kerri was completely confident that it mattered a great deal. "Thank you, Sheree. We are so grateful for the information. Anything we can learn might make the difference in solving our case. This was the right thing to do."

As badly as Kerri wanted to rush away and demand answers from Allison's mother, she restrained the urge and waited for the other woman to make the first move. A couple of minutes later they walked out of the cemetery together. Kerri thanked Sheree again and watched her drive away.

As Kerri drove away from the cemetery, she filled Luke in.

"Game changer," he agreed. "Gives Boothe serious motive. And we've got Scott keeping relevant facts about an explosive motive from us. Who the hell is *she* protecting?"

"We're going to find out," Kerri agreed. "I'm guessing this is why Rebecca Boothe presented the idea that Allison had an affair in the past." Why the hell hadn't she just told Kerri the whole story?

"It's possible they kept this from her," Luke countered.

"I don't really see how. Either way," she said, deciding, "before we confront Boothe or Jana Scott, I'd like to talk to Candace Oden. If she and Allison were friends, she had to have known about the test results— assuming they shared personal details. Most friends do. Which may explain why she believes Logan blamed Allison. It's possible he feels the sperm donor was the one to pass down the predisposition for leukemia."

"Could have come from Allison's side of the family," Luke pointed out. "But as a guy, I can see how Logan might jump to that conclusion."

"All the more reason to be fully armed with facts before we hit him with this."

Luke nodded. "If he was really pissed when he got the test results, the question is, What did he do with that anger?"

"Exactly," Kerri agreed.

Oden Residence
Chablis Way
Birmingham, 5:50 p.m.

Three rings of the doorbell were required before Candace Oden opened her door.

"Sorry, Detective, I was on the phone with my mother. It's Thanksgiving."

"I apologize for the intrusion." Kerri mustered up a smile. "I have a couple more questions for you, if you don't mind."

Oden glanced back into the house as if to check on her child. She hadn't invited Kerri in or even opened the door fully. She clearly did not want to talk to Kerri, maybe to the police in general. Good thing Luke had waited in the car again.

But Oden hadn't seemed to mind the other day.

"Sure. I have a minute." She stepped onto the porch and closed her door behind her.

Didn't really matter to Kerri whether they talked inside or out, but it certainly seemed odd unless Oden had company or was concerned her daughter might overhear more bad news.

"Were you aware of the tests done for finding a bone marrow donor for Leah and the impact the results had on Allison's marriage?"

Oden blinked. "Allison mentioned something about Logan not being a match." She shrugged. "But that happens sometimes."

"Is that all she said?"

Oden's face blanked. "That's all I recall."

She was lying. She'd schooled her expression, and her gaze was all over the place—anywhere but on Kerri's.

"Did she ever mention to you the possibility that Logan might not be the father of her child?"

There it was. The deer-caught-in-the-headlights look.

Oden seemed to draw back. Fear or uncertainty flickered in her eyes. "What?"

"Leah was not Logan Boothe's biological child. Were you aware that was a possibility?"

Rapid head shaking. "No. Of course not. Why would I know something like that?"

"You and Allison were friends. You said Logan blamed Allison for Leah's illness. There must have been a reason. And now we know there was."

"I'm sorry, Detective, I have to see about my daughter."

"Candace," Kerri said, before she could open the door and disappear inside, "I need your help. If you know anything that might aid our investigation, you need to tell me now. Every minute we waste—"

"I don't know anything." She hurried inside and closed the door.

Kerri resisted the impulse to pound on the door and demand the truth.

Whatever Oden was hiding, she didn't just not want to talk about it. She was afraid to talk about it. Her fear had been palpable.

Kerri climbed into her Wagoneer.

"Anything?" Luke asked.

"She's not talking, but she knows something. My instinct is she's afraid to tell whatever it is."

"Who is she afraid of?" Luke asked as Kerri pulled away from the curb. "Boothe?"

Kerri shrugged as she navigated through the neighborhood. "I'm having a tough time coming up with another name."

"If we're headed to Scott's house, I'm going in this time. I want to hear how she explains this one." Luke tapped his fingers against the console. "The woman was a cop's wife. She knows better than to omit any facts. There's something going on here, Kerri. Something they're all in on."

He was right. Scott, Boothe, his mother, maybe even Oden. They were all hiding something relevant.

Kerri didn't call to see if Jana Scott was home. She didn't want her preparing for the visit. She wanted straightforward answers. Nothing planned or overly thought out.

"Man," Luke said, "that's some view."

He was right. The view over the lake even on a cold November evening was gorgeous. Kerri could see why Mrs. Scott and her husband had wanted to build here for their retirement years.

A single ring of the bell, and the door opened. Jana Scott looked from Kerri to Luke and back, blinked, then drew in a sharp breath.

"Do you have news?" she asked.

Now Kerri felt bad for not warning her. As certain as she was that the woman was holding back, seeing the pain on her face made sticking to her guns difficult. "No, ma'am. I'm afraid not. But we do have a couple of questions for you. I know it's Thanksgiving, but we really need to speak to you now."

"Of course. Come in."

They followed her inside. Kerri was grateful to be out of the crisp air.

"Would you like coffee or hot chocolate?" Scott gestured to the sofa.

"No, thank you." Kerri perched on the edge of the sofa.

Luke declined the offer as well and sat next to Kerri.

When Scott settled into her preferred chair, her posture remained a little straighter than necessary. Tension radiated from her. Grief showed on her face.

"We're having the memorial service on Sunday afternoon," she said. She clasped her hands in her lap. "I intended to wait until Logan was released from the hospital, but Rebecca insisted he didn't want us to wait. So . . . I made the arrangements." Her breath hitched. "It's better not to wait, I think."

Kerri bit the bullet and asked the question. "Mrs. Scott, why didn't you tell us about the results from the bone marrow tests? This is the sort of issue that could translate to motive."

Tears spilled over the older woman's lashes and slid down her cheeks. "Detective, I am very much aware how this looks. But it wasn't something I wanted to be a part of the investigation. There had to be a mistake. Allison was never unfaithful to Logan. Never. I refused to have my daughter's name dragged through the mud."

Kerri gave her a moment to compose herself. "Was the test repeated?"

She shook her head. "Logan refused. He was so angry. Allison tried to tell him it wasn't possible, but he was too hurt. Too outraged."

"Angry enough to hurt Allison?"

Scott dabbed at her eyes with the sleeve of her blouse. "I don't know. I honestly don't. There was so much tension, so much hurt between them those last few weeks. I don't want to think so, but I'm not sure of anything anymore."

"I have a daughter," Kerri said. She smiled. "She's almost fifteen, and suddenly I know nothing, and she knows everything."

Mrs. Scott laughed, the sound rusty. "I remember those days."

"I love my daughter so much. I trust her and I know she's a good person. Can I ever know her every thought and action? No. None of us can. You must realize it's possible Allison kept this from you. It may have been a mistake, and she was embarrassed."

Scott leaned forward, hands pressed together in front of her face as if she intended to pray. "I am telling you the truth. She never cheated on her husband. If she had, she certainly wouldn't have insisted she hadn't when test results showed a different story."

"Are you saying she lied?"

"No." She pressed her forehead to her fingertips, then straightened and stared directly into Kerri's eyes. "I am telling you the test had to be wrong."

What she was suggesting was not impossible. Just highly improbable.

More tears gushed from Scott's eyes. "I just wish Allison hadn't been at home that night. I wish Leah had been with me. Anywhere but in that house."

"Remind us again," Luke said. "When did you last speak with your daughter?"

"I called her that afternoon. Around three, I think. We talked about Leah's appointments coming up. I assured her again we would figure out the money." She swiped at her wet cheeks. "That was about it."

"Was she in an upbeat mood? Depressed?" Previously Scott had said her daughter was in good spirits.

"She was as upbeat as you can expect under the circumstances. Her child was very, very ill. She and Logan were okay by then. Working things out, she said. Working on ways to help themselves financially. They had a plan. She didn't elaborate, and I didn't have the presence of mind to ask that day." She sighed. "I wish I had."

"Did you see or speak to Logan that day?"

She shook her head. "He was running errands, Allison said. He had a meeting with someone about a job, but again, she didn't give any additional details. She seemed excited about the meeting. Maybe a little apprehensive."

This part was new. Something else to ask Boothe about.

Boothe had a hell of a lot of explaining to do.

24

7:00 p.m.

Scott Residence
River Woods Road
Hoover

The moment the detectives were gone, Jana called Rebecca. Rebecca preferred that Jana wait until after nine, when visiting hours ended, so that she could step away from the room and take a short walk in the crisp night air to do her talking. She didn't like leaving Logan alone during visiting hours when someone might bother him. Jana was no fool. Rebecca didn't want to be away from the room in the event the police came to interview her son. Any mother would do the same.

Jana still found it difficult to empathize with Rebecca. Too much water under the bridge. Too many hurtful words tossed about. In truth, Jana had never liked her. Still didn't. How could she?

But now was not the time to opine on their petty differences.

Her heart twisted so tight she could scarcely breathe.

They needed each other. The police knew their secret. Jana had been married to a cop for forty-odd years. She shouldn't be surprised. Birmingham had plenty of good cops. Detective Devlin and her partner were very good.

"Hello." Rebecca sounded breathless, as if she'd hurried out of the room.

Jana took a breath and said what had to be passed along. "Detective Devlin found out about the DNA issue."

She refused to call it anything but an issue. It certainly was not because her daughter had cheated on her husband. Fury gripped her by the throat. Never. Allison had been a wonderful daughter, a loving wife and mother. This was not her fault.

They would all know in the end. But first, there were certain steps that had to be taken. Steps that would ensure justice. No matter how badly Jana wanted to scream the truth, she understood all too well how these things worked. Raymond had told her often enough.

There would be no justice unless she and Rebecca saw this through to the end.

She ordered herself to relax. The silence on the other end of the line told Jana that Rebecca was taking a moment to choose her words. She'd said plenty when they'd first found out. She'd called Allison a whore. She'd said all sorts of horrible things. Had accused Jana's sweet daughter of lying and allowing them to fall in love with Leah when she wasn't even Logan's child.

But that had been before.

Before they'd known.

Before Allison and Leah had been murdered.

The fracture in her heart widened. God, how she missed her precious girls.

"I suppose they're trying to use it as a motive for Logan having done this awful thing," Rebecca said, her voice weary now.

Logan was her child. Of course her first thought was to protect him. Allison had loved him, believed in him. How could Jana not believe in him?

But she had learned what had really happened. As had Rebecca. And they understood what they had to do.

"You know they will," Jana confirmed. "It's standard operating procedure." She lowered into a chair, her knees suddenly too weak to hold her weight.

"Even knowing what we know, I can just imagine what you're thinking," Rebecca said with something like disgust. "You're asking yourself, Did her son want to raise another man's sick child? Or maybe he had decided Allison had cheated on him and wanted to be done with both of them!"

A sob tore from Jana's throat. "I didn't say any of that."

"But you thought it, didn't you? I know you think you're better than us. That Logan was never good enough for Allison. I'm not stupid."

"Rebecca, please, let's not rehash that ugly history. What we have before us is far too important to be drawn into something so utterly irrelevant."

"Yes," she agreed, "you're right." She cleared her throat, seemed to steady herself. "Isn't it strange how protecting their own doesn't apply to all equally?"

Jana closed her eyes, struggled to maintain her composure. "It's wrong. Either way, it's just wrong." She opened her eyes and dredged up her courage. "But we will make it right, and then everyone will understand."

If it killed her, Jana would see to it that this was finished.

"I did what you told me to do," Rebecca said. "I mentioned my concern that Allison had an affair. It wasn't easy, considering the bad light it would cast on Logan . . . but I did it."

"Good." Jana understood how these investigations worked. She needed Devlin and Falco considering all the necessary possibilities. Logical, methodical steps. There could be no mistakes. No holes in the story.

"Just remember this," Rebecca warned. "If Leah had been with you on Sunday night like she was supposed to be, at least she would still be alive."

The call ended. Of course Rebecca had to get in one more dig.

As Jana's heart fell to pieces inside her, the phone slipped from her limp hand.

The truth was, Rebecca was right.

Leah should have been with Jana that night.

25

7:20 p.m.

Devlin Residence
Twenty-First Avenue South
Birmingham

They had barely gotten into the house when the doorbell sounded.

"I'll get it," Luke said, already moving toward the front door. He was ready for this day to be over. He'd enjoyed the short break with Kerri's family and their friends. But it hadn't been the same without Tori.

Kerri tossed her keys on the counter and followed the path he'd taken. "I'm afraid to wonder what now."

Luke sent her a look. "Don't even go there."

They had made the decision to wait until morning to confront Boothe and his mother with this new information. Luke checked out the window. Surprised, he glanced at Kerri. "Brooks."

She looked as confused as he felt. "Brooks?"

Luke shrugged and unlocked and opened the door. He considered the possibility that O'Grady might have taken another stab at him. For whatever reason, he'd decided to set Luke up. No surprise. O'Grady covered his own ass at the expense of others all the time. Eight years likely hadn't changed his habits.

Luke just hated that the bastard's games were messing with the new life he'd built.

"I apologize for showing up unannounced," Brooks said. "Especially on Thanksgiving, but I felt this couldn't wait."

"No problem." Luke pulled the door open wider. "The day is about giving thanks."

"It is indeed." Brooks looked exactly like he always did. Suit, tie. All crisp and professional. Maybe he'd decided it was time to speak directly to the source about his accusations. As he stepped inside, he nodded to Kerri. "Devlin."

"Lieutenant."

She was still fired up at the guy. Luke couldn't help feeling elated by her loyalty. He liked that she was ready to fight for him. He hoped she wouldn't regret it.

"Have a seat," Luke offered. "You want a beer, sir?"

"No, thank you. This won't take long. I have a family dinner at eight."

Luke closed the door. Maybe he was about to be put on suspension. That would suck big time. Mostly he hated that it would look bad on Kerri. Damn it. Not to mention he figured she would go off on the LT, and that wouldn't be great for her career either.

"I came by to apologize."

Luke did a double take. "Apologize?"

Kerri looked as stunned as he was at the announcement.

"Yes, but first . . ." Brooks frowned. "What happened to your face?"

Luke shrugged. "I had a little run-in with a guy who didn't want me nosing around in certain business."

Brooks winced. "Looks painful."

"It is."

"Anyway," Brooks went on. "I'm sure Devlin has told you that I called her in and made a number of accusations regarding your work history."

Luke shrugged. "She mentioned it, yeah."

"I wanted to apologize for not speaking directly with you regarding these accusations and, basically, for the entire fiasco."

Fiasco? That was something Luke definitely hadn't expected to hear.

"What's going on, LT?" Kerri asked.

"Did Carla Brown withdraw her complaint?" Luke asked before Brooks could respond to Kerri.

"Unfortunately no, but she does seem to have disappeared." Brooks pushed the lapels of his jacket aside and set his hands on his hips. "Falco, when you first transferred to MID, I'll admit I was a little skeptical. You had a bit of a shady record. You looked more like a criminal than a cop."

"What you see is what you get," Luke admitted.

Kerri flashed him a smile. She knew this better than anyone.

Brooks nodded. "This is true. At any rate, as I told Devlin, the department takes complaints of harassment very seriously. With the high-profile police-brutality issues of late, we have to be very careful."

"I understand, sir. You're only doing your job." Luke did understand. Mostly.

"Well, in this case I was wrong." He turned to Kerri. "What's going on, Devlin, is that another detective has come forward on Falco's behalf. If I have anything to do with it, Lieutenant O'Grady will be thoroughly investigated if even half the statement the detective made is true. He claims to have evidence, and honestly, I believe him."

"It's about time," Kerri said.

Luke wanted to be happy about this too. No one deserved to get theirs more than Patrick O'Grady. But there were things O'Grady knew about Luke that frankly scared the hell out of him.

"For now," Brooks explained, "this investigation is to be kept quiet. Internal Affairs will be briefed tomorrow."

So this was really going down. Luke nodded. "Let me know if I can help in any way."

He would like to know who the detective who'd come forward was. Maybe it was Boothe. Maybe O'Grady was somehow involved in what had happened to his family, and Boothe had been waiting for an opportunity to spill what he knew. His confession could have been part of some delay tactic. Didn't make a whole lot of sense, in Luke's opinion, but the guy was messed up emotionally right now.

Brooks extended his hand. "We will talk about this again soon."

"Yes, sir." Luke shook his hand.

Kerri did the same.

Luke closed the door behind Brooks and watched from the window as he drove away. His ribs hurt with the deep breath he dragged in. He should be worried. But it was too late for that. Whatever he'd done, there was no taking it back now. It would all come out in the coming investigation.

It was time.

Nothing stayed buried forever. And you couldn't go back for do-overs. Not when someone had died because of your mistake.

He would give anything to make it right.

26

Eight Years Ago

December 3

"Stop, you're hurting me."

I hear her, but I can't see her.

Mina?

What's happening?

Can't open my eyes. Can't move. Am I dreaming?

"That's the point."

Wait. Did I say something? My mouth isn't moving. It's dry like sand. Can't swallow. Can't open my eyes.

Crying.

Who's crying?

"Mina?"

Was that me calling out to her?

I feel my lips move. Hear the croaky sound of a male voice.

I try again to force my eyes open. Won't work.

Then I'm gone.

———

"Falco, wake the fuck up."

My eyes open a narrow slit.

Light screams in my skull, and I squeeze them shut again.

"Come on, man, we gotta get out of here."

"Dog?" I lick my lips. Grimace at the shitty taste in my mouth. My head is throbbing like it might pop any second.

What the hell?

I feel myself moving upward. I jerk free of the hands tugging at me. Almost fall.

"We don't have time for this shit," Dog snarls. "Get up!"

My eyes open again. I blink through the pain.

I'm in a room. Dog is standing over me, pulling at me.

"What're you doing?" I demand. My voice sounds like a rusty can being twisted.

His face is suddenly close to mine. "We gotta go, asshole. Now move."

I stagger to my feet with his help. Glance around. Tousled bed. Dumpy room.

I must have stayed the night at Mina's place. Passed out, I guess. I have one mother of a hangover.

"Wait, wait, wait." I pull loose from him. "What the hell you doing here?" I glance around the room again. Where is Mina?

"We gotta go, Falco. We're burning this shithole down."

"What the hell you talking about?" He reaches for me, but I sway out of his way. The son of a bitch has lost his mind.

Dog grabs me by the shoulders and shakes me. Pain screams through my head, and I shut my mouth tight to keep from spewing vomit in his face.

"Listen to me," he growls. "Bad shit went down here last night. Maybe you remember, maybe you don't. Doesn't matter. We have to get out of here *now*."

He's moving again, lugging me with him.

"Why are we burning the place down? Mina's gonna be pissed, I can tell you that."

"Too much evidence. Your DNA is probably all over the place."

We're outside now. He drags me toward my car. Pushes me into the front passenger seat. I collapse with a grunt. Damn, I feel like hell. Can't keep my eyes open. The light hurts like a mofo.

Dog slams the door and hustles around the front of the car. I stare at the room that was once a garage. The house it's attached to is small and divided up into four dinky rooms, which are also rented out.

As the car starts moving, backing out of the driveway, I see a flicker in the window. I lean forward and stare.

Hell yeah. There's a fire in the room we just . . .

"Hey. Shit. We have to call this in. The place is on fire."

"I told you we had to burn it down." Dog rolls onto the street and guns the accelerator.

"Wait." I shake my head. Wince. God damn this headache. "What the hell is going on, man?"

He glances at me, his face all grim and shit. "Mina is dead."

"What? No way. She was with me last night."

Evidently Dog has lost his mind.

"Yeah," he agrees, "that's the problem."

I lick my lips. Try to swallow. "Look, I don't know what the fuck is going on, but I need you to take me back. Something ain't right."

"You're damn straight it ain't right," Dog shouts.

Another blast of pain has me holding my head.

"Trust me, bro. You'll thank me in the end."

"What the hell are you talking about?" I demand. "Just . . . forget all this shit and let me call Mina. She'll explain everything."

He slams on the brakes.

I bump against the dash 'cause I don't have my seat belt on.

"Mina is fucking dead, dipshit," he shouts in my face. "You killed her. Now shut the fuck up and let me finish saving your ass."

27

Friday, November 26

7:30 a.m.

Devlin Residence
Twenty-First Avenue South
Birmingham

"You ready?" Kerri was beyond ready to get out there and find some reasonable explanations for all the scattered pieces of this damned puzzle.

She'd barely slept last night, going over and over the seemingly unconnected details of the case. Particularly the part about Leah not being Boothe's biological child. She still did not get why Scott hadn't told them. The woman knew better than to hold back. Of all people in this mess, Jana Scott understood how an investigation worked.

There was something more she wasn't sharing.

The question was, Could it be the one detail they needed to close this case?

Luke dragged on his jacket. "As ready as I'll ever be."

His face looked worse this morning. The bruising had gone to an all-new level of purplish black. Judging by his frequent grimaces, the pain from the other injuries was nagging at him.

He was the other reason she'd barely slept.

"Seems like you're not ready."

Kerri blinked and refocused on him. "I'm sorry. What?"

"You zoned out on me there for a minute. You sure you don't want me to drive?"

"No way. Doctor's orders, remember?"

"Damn." He made a face. "It was the nightmares again, huh?"

She shrugged. Hated to make him feel worse. "Did you remember anything else?" He'd said some of the memories were foggy.

He rubbed his hands over his face and through his hair. "The nightmares are driving me crazy for sure. It's like reliving over and over the worst moments of those last few weeks working in O'Grady's crew. I don't want to recall those days, but I know I have to because there are things that are unclear."

"Your memories are hazy, right?" Tension swirled inside her. The CI, Mina, had died. O'Grady had told Brooks that Luke was responsible. Kerri refused to believe the bastard. There had to be more to this story.

Luke nodded. "Some parts I can't remember at all. Last night I dreamed that Dog was there . . . when Mina died." He shrugged. "I need to talk to him about it. Feel him out about this secret investigation into O'Grady's activities. I keep wondering if he's the detective who went to Brooks."

Kerri had considered the idea. "Until you can locate Dog for a meet, we need to talk to Boothe again. See how he reacts to the news that we know about the test results."

Luke reached out, took her hand in his. "I'm sorry if any part of this ends up hurting you. Sorrier than you'll ever know. The last thing in this world I want to do is hurt you. I swear I will find my way through this."

She gave him a reassuring smile. "We'll get through this *together*."

In her pocket, her cell vibrated. She let go of his hand and reached for it as she headed out the door. The alert was an email.

While Luke locked up, she read the message. A surge of adrenaline fired through her. "We've got something on that burner phone Boothe called on Sunday evening."

"A name and address?"

"Only the address." She headed for her Wagoneer. "Apparently the dumbass reloaded minutes and is using the phone again."

"Thank the good Lord for dumbasses," Luke said, climbing into the passenger seat.

———

Play It Again Games
East Avenue
Birmingham, 8:50 a.m.

"The place doesn't open until nine," Luke said. He looked from his phone to the shop with the bars on the windows. "Someone should be showing up soon."

Since they'd had some time, Kerri had made a stop at her favorite drive-through for frothy, sweet coffee. She usually went for just plain old black, but sometimes the extra flavor—and sugar—were necessary.

"Only three employees," Luke went on. "One, Damon Patterson, is the manager. According to some of the comments and tags on Facebook, the other two are Rexie Walker and Caleb Stover. Walker is a high schooler, but I can't see much on Stover's page. It's private."

A beat-up Chevy that puffed smoke for a couple of seconds after it was turned off parked a few slots away, and a tall, skinny white guy who looked about twelve climbed out and strode to the shop entrance. Chains bounced against his thighs. Jeans looked about three sizes too large and at least a few years older than him. Tie-dyed tee.

"That's Patterson, the manager."

"He looks like a kid." Kerri frowned. When had she gotten so old that a store manager looked younger than her daughter?

"Twenty-one," Luke confirmed.

Another car arrived, this one a vintage Ford sedan painted a wild lime green with massive tires. The whole car seemed to shudder with the music blasting from its speakers. The driver emerged. Big guy. Broad shoulders. Long dark hair. He glanced around the lot before going toward the shop entrance.

"That is Mr. Stover."

"He looks more like the manager," Kerri pointed out. "Forty at least." She watched him enter the shop. "You're the gamer. You go first and do the talking. I'll wander in and make the call."

"You got it."

Luke jumped out damned fast for a guy with cracked ribs and strolled up to the store entrance. When he'd gone inside, Kerri got out. She walked more slowly, giving Luke time to distract the employees. She entered the digits on her cell but didn't hit call until she stepped inside.

The bell over the door jingled.

Two seconds later, the older guy, who was showing something to Luke, reached into his right front pants pockets. When he withdrew his phone and glanced at the screen, Kerri ended the call.

Gotcha.

As if he'd read her mind, the guy looked up. She showed her badge. "Caleb Stover, my name is Detective Kerri Devlin, and I have a few questions for you."

He flew over the counter with only one hand balancing him, like a gymnast on a pommel horse.

For a big guy, Stover was fast.

Kerri sidestepped to block his path toward the door.

He slammed into her, and they both crashed to the floor. Her flat on her back. Him facedown on top of her. The breath whooshed out of her lungs, and her brain felt as if it had bounced a little in her skull.

When Stover would have scrambled up, Luke said, "Get up slowly, dipshit."

Straddling Kerri, Stover managed to push himself into a standing position. Luke put his gun in the taller man's face. "Now, the detective said she had a few questions for you. Are you going to answer here or downtown?"

"I ain't saying shit, asshole."

Kerri was on her feet again, cuffs in her hand. "Guess it's downtown, then." She cuffed the jerk and gave him a push toward the door.

As they left the shop, Luke glanced at her. "You okay?"

"Other than feeling like I was hit by a lineman from the Crimson Tide football team, I'm great."

———

Birmingham Police Department
First Avenue North
Major Investigations Division, 10:35 a.m.

They'd spent the first half hour after cuffing Stover waiting at the game shop for a cruiser to pick him up. Luke had questioned the shop owner while Kerri had kept an eye on their uncooperative person of interest. The shop owner had insisted he knew nothing of Stover's activities outside the shop. Once they were back at the office waiting for Stover to be processed and placed in an interview room, Kerri had started pacing. She'd considered dozens of scenarios, and none felt exactly right. But one stood out above all the rest.

Had Boothe paid someone to burn down his house with his family inside?

"Here we go," Luke announced, tapping his computer screen. "We just got ourselves some more leverage."

Kerri moved to his desk and peered at the social media screen he'd opened.

"Stover is selling services on Facebook's Marketplace."

"What kind of services?" All manner of cretinous misdeeds fluttered through her head.

Luke grunted. "Car detailing. House painting."

"Yeah, right. Can we see a client list?"

"Nope, but according to Boothe's PayPal account, he paid Stover five K to paint his house."

"You got into his PayPal account?" Kerri was impressed. So far the company had not been forthcoming with the account information. A warrant was in the works.

Luke cleared his throat. "Sadie's friend—you know, the computer geek—he got in. Gave me the password."

So that was who he'd been texting while Kerri had been pacing.

"We won't be able to use the information as evidence," she pointed out, when what she wanted to say was that she should have thought of that option already.

A uniform poked his head into their cubicle. "Your guy Stover is ready. He's in two."

Kerri thanked him. Stover had been sequestered to interview room two.

"Let's see what the house painter has to say," she suggested.

"I say his prices are too high," Luke pointed out.

"He must be a very good painter," Kerri agreed.

Inside, Stover sat at the table, his hands cuffed behind his back. He had attacked Kerri even after she'd identified herself. A very serious lapse in judgment.

"Mr. Stover, have you decided if you want to have an attorney present?" Kerri asked as she settled at the opposite side of the table. Luke preferred his position against the wall, looking down on the man seated at the table.

"I don't need an attorney," Stover growled.

Great. She loved it when that nuisance could be set aside. "Let me remind you again of your rights." She made the necessary statement. "Do you understand the rights I've just explained to you?"

He glared at her.

Kerri smiled. "I've got all day, Mr. Stover."

"I fucking understand."

"He understands," Luke echoed.

"Great. Let's get on with it, then. Mr. Stover, you and Mr. Logan Boothe entered into an agreement on November eighteenth for the sum of five thousand dollars. Will you confirm the services you were contracted to render?"

He stared at Kerri. Said zilch.

"Did you get that, Devlin?" Luke pushed off the wall, leaned forward, and braced his hands on the table. "Boothe hired Stover here to kill his wife and kid."

Kerri opened her notepad and picked up her pen. "I did, yes."

"That's a lie!" Stover screamed.

She and Luke exchanged a glance. "I believe you misheard," Kerri said. "He was hired to set the house on fire with the wife and child inside. There's a slight difference there."

"You're fucking liars," Stover snarled. "The wife and kid were never part of the deal."

Luke drew back, planting himself against the wall once more.

"I see," Kerri said, feeling triumphant. "You were contracted to burn the house. You had no idea the wife and child would be inside."

"I didn't do it," he said, quieter now. Resigned or perhaps desperate after realizing what he'd confessed.

"But you did," Luke said. "You were smart too. Only used the accelerant downstairs. Let the smoke do the rest."

Fury sparked in the man's eyes. "I did not set the fire."

"You just said," Kerri countered, "you were paid five thousand dollars to burn his house."

"I was paid five K up front. Once the house was *painted*," he said with a sneer, "and the insurance collected, I would get five K more."

Kerri relaxed into her chair. So it was about insurance. Just not life insurance. "How much you think a house like that—older, not such a hot neighborhood—goes for? One fifty? Two hundred thousand? And you were only getting ten K for taking all the risks? Doesn't sound fair to me." She glanced back at her partner. "Sound fair to you, Falco?"

"Man." Luke shook his head. "You got screwed."

"I told you, I didn't fucking do it."

"Because you realized you were getting screwed?"

He glared at Luke this time. "The price was set because I felt sorry for the family. The kid was sick. I was trying to help out. But then I got fucked."

"What do you mean?" Kerri asked. "How did you get fucked?"

"Boothe called me Sunday night and said we had to talk. I told him to fuck off. I didn't care who he was. The time for talking was done. Then, when we showed up in the neighborhood to do the job, the stupid bastard was waiting. Headed us off at the corner before we turned onto his block. He cried like a little girl. Begged me not to do it. Told me I could keep the five K. Said there had been a mistake."

Kerri's pulse was racing now. "This must have been frustrating for you."

He shrugged. "Not really. I got my five K. It was my painters who were pissed. You see, they do the painting and split the final payment. You think I'll be able to hire more painters if shit like this gets out?" He looked from Kerri to Luke and back. "I don't know who burned down that house, but it sure as hell wasn't me. I run a contracting service for painting and shit like that. I don't do arson. I sure as hell don't do murder."

"What about your 'painters'?" Luke asked. "Did they paint the house anyway just to teach him a lesson?"

"No way. They left with me, but first they beat the shit out of him." He sat back in his chair. "I ain't saying nothing else. I didn't do this shit. You give me immunity, and I'll be a witness for you about my business transaction to paint that house. That's all I got to offer."

Kerri pushed her notepad across the table, then the pen. "I'll have the handcuffs removed. I need you to write down exactly what you just told us. Then we'll talk about what happens next."

In the corridor Luke gave the instructions to the waiting uniform. Kerri walked a few yards away from the interview room and leaned against the wall.

"What do you think?" he asked her.

"I think he's telling the truth, sort of."

"Me too. Sort of. He was hired to provide a service."

In all honesty, Kerri was still suffering a little whiplash. "Boothe and maybe his wife, apparently, decide they need the extra cash and hire Stover to burn the house. For the insurance payout."

"Maybe it was to prevent her mother from having to mortgage her house the way his mother did," Luke offered.

"But then they back out," Kerri went on. "It was Allison's childhood home, so maybe she decided it would be too painful to her mother."

"Boothe tries to call it off and gets the shit kicked out of him. While he's down for the count, someone—not Stover or his people, according to him—burns the house. The perp may or may not have known the wife and kid were inside."

Kerri shook her head. "You realize this takes us all the way back to square one."

Not one single piece of this puzzle would fall into place. Damn it.

"Unless," Luke said as he leaned his shoulder against the wall next to her, "Boothe is telling the truth and he did it himself." He gave her an eye roll. "Except we both know he didn't do it."

"Hold that thought." Kerri pushed away from the wall. She strode back to the interview room, where the officer was overseeing Stover's statement.

The officer and Stover looked up when the door opened. "Two questions," she said. "What time did this incident with Boothe take place?"

Stover mulled over the question a moment. "Hold on." He pulled out his cell phone. "Wait, wrong one." Then he pulled out another.

Kerri rolled her eyes.

He checked the screen. "Ten thirty on Sunday night."

Kerri nodded. "And where exactly did this happen?"

"At the corner of the block. There's an empty house there."

Kerri knew the one. "When you and your painters left, where did you go?"

Stover shrugged. "We drove to a friend's house for a party. Stopped at the Quick Stop on Thirty-First, near Lorna Road. Got beer."

She gave him a nod, started to go, then hesitated. "One more question. What was Boothe's condition when you left?"

Stover looked bemused. "He was fucked up."

"Yeah, yeah, but was he conscious? Alert?"

Stover shook his head. "He was out. Down for the count."

"In your statement, we need to know the exact date and how Logan Boothe contacted you."

Stover made a face. "I already told you. Sunday night. He called that once, and then he was waiting for us."

"No. I mean when he contacted you about 'painting' his house," she clarified.

"Look." Stover stared at her as if she were a few cards shy of a full deck. "I was contacted only once about the house-painting job prior to my conversation with the guy who got the shit beat out of him. But he was not the one who contacted me or hired me to paint the house."

Kerri hesitated a moment, then asked, "If Logan Boothe didn't hire you, who did?"

Stover crossed his arms over his chest. "Like I said, I ain't saying nothing else without an immunity deal. I think I want to call my lawyer now."

Kerri walked out of the room and returned to where Luke waited. "So," she began, "Boothe couldn't have set the fire. At ten thirty that night he was unconscious, badly injured, and more than half a block away."

Luke scoffed. "I knew Boothe was lying. So that leaves—"

"There's something else you should know," Kerri interrupted. "Stover says it wasn't Boothe who contracted him to 'paint' the house."

"The wife?" Luke offered.

Kerri shrugged. "He won't say unless he gets immunity, and he wants his lawyer."

Luke rolled his eyes. "Holy shit."

"There's no point hanging around here. He could be waiting for his lawyer for hours. We should move on to the next most likely possibility."

"We can't question the wife," Luke griped. "She's dead. That leaves us with the grandmothers."

"I think we can safely scratch Scott from the list."

Luke made a check mark in the air. "Done."

"I have a hard time seeing Rebecca Boothe risking her grandchild's life. She says Jana Scott and her husband considered their daughter above Logan. Clearly, she feels victimized to some degree by the Scott family. But I still can't get right with her hurting her grandchild, even if they weren't related by blood."

"Agreed."

"Next up is O'Grady," Kerri said, moving on. "He has inserted himself into this case repeatedly. Openly pushing us to take the easy way out and name Boothe as the killer. His own crew said he and Boothe had issues. He's tried to make you look bad from the beginning. As much as I would love to put this at O'Grady's door, that leaves us with the same questions we've had all along. Would he murder a woman and child? More importantly, why? He's a respected detective with a stellar career. At least until recently. But is he a cold-blooded killer? And if he wanted to silence Boothe, why not just kill him?"

The scenario just didn't work for her. Not completely.

"He's ruthless for sure." Luke considered the idea for a bit. "Based on what I know about him, if it came down to protecting himself and his crew, he would do whatever necessary. But I'm completely with you on this point: If Boothe was the trouble, why not just eliminate him? Why risk leaving him alive after killing his family? Makes no sense."

"Exactly," Kerri agreed. "What we need is to find the way Boothe and O'Grady connect in all this," she suggested. "There has to be something. Otherwise, why all the fanfare? What would O'Grady have to gain by any of this? What is he protecting? His crew? Himself?"

A potential answer bloomed in her mind. "What if O'Grady is the one working with Sawyer? I can see him having enough politician in his blood to deflect his own misdeeds onto someone else."

"Let's back up here," Luke said. "Scott said her daughter and Boothe were working on some plan they wouldn't talk about. What if Allison is the one who hired Stover and Scott talked her out of it? Maybe that's the thing Scott is hiding. She feels guilty about it but doesn't want to tarnish her daughter's name or make Boothe look any more guilty."

"You're right," Kerri agreed. "She was definitely holding back something. I'm guessing she's not going to break on that one. Having us find out about the DNA issue was painful enough. We should ask Boothe." There was that one sticking point Kerri could not get right with. "As logically as all this appears to fall into place, there's still the question of why Boothe would protect the person who killed his wife and kid."

"We should ask him," Luke concluded. "There's just one problem. While we're questioning Boothe, how are we going to distract his mother?"

Kerri couldn't see an easy way around the woman.

"Before we go to the hospital," she said, "let's drop by that Quick Stop. See if they have security cameras."

Anytime they could confirm a witness's statement, it was worth the extra legwork.

—————

University of Alabama Hospital
Sixth Avenue South
Birmingham, 1:55 p.m.

"You've got maybe fifteen minutes," the uniform on security detail outside Boothe's room said. "I persuaded the charge nurse into telling the mother it was bath time for the patient."

"Appreciate it, Johnston," Luke said. He gave the guy a fist bump.

Kerri had to hand it to her partner. The plan for getting Boothe alone was genius.

Their stop at the convenience store on Thirty-First had confirmed Stover's statement. He and his friends had rolled into the parking lot in that big-ass lime-green sedan at 11:20 p.m. on Sunday night, a mere fifty minutes after the meet with Boothe at ten thirty. Since the drive to the Quick Stop took twenty minutes, that left only half an hour for the exchange and the thorough beating. No way could they have started the fire.

It was well past time Boothe started giving some straight answers.

Their patient-suspect looked slightly better today. His bed was raised a little higher, putting him in a more upright position. As they entered the room, he ignored them, stared at the muted television. The game show on the screen suggested his mother had selected the channel.

"Afternoon, Boothe," Luke said as he leaned against the wall next to the man's bed.

He glanced at Luke but said nothing.

"You're looking stronger," Kerri commented. She took up a position on the opposite side of his bed.

In true Boothe form, he said nothing. He had apparently said all he intended to during his and Luke's rather loud exchange the last time they'd been here.

"Why didn't you tell us about the test that revealed Leah wasn't your biological child?"

Boothe continued to stare at the television, but Kerri spotted the slightest flinch. The subject was a touchy one for him. A logical reaction.

"It would have been nice to hear it from you," Kerri nudged.

"It's none of your business," he said, his voice not so rusty today.

"What it is"—Luke moved away from the wall and closer to the bed—"is motive."

Boothe spared Luke a fleeting glance. "I already told you I did it. I guess now you have your motive to tie it all up in a nice, neat little bow."

Kerri made the next move. "Why did you and Allison change your mind about going for the insurance on the house?"

Boothe sent a sharp glance in Kerri's direction. She'd hit a nerve.

"Is that why you argued so loudly on Saturday night?"

"I don't know what you're talking about. We had movie night Saturday. Pizza, popcorn, the works." His voice trembled. "Movie night was Leah's favorite."

Kerri gave a somber nod. "I imagine it was a poignant evening, considering you knew it would be the last one."

He blinked repeatedly. Said nothing.

"The guy you hired," Luke contended. "Stover. He's already come forward. Told us everything."

"I did it," he repeated. "You should've already arrested me."

The guy was stubborn. Kerri would give him that. "He also told us how his friends worked you over for backing out. I would think having all those injuries and being unconscious would make splashing gasoline around in your house and then lighting a match a little difficult."

"I said I did it." He leveled a long look on Kerri. "What kind of detective are you?"

"A good enough one to know when a suspect is lying."

His attention returned to the television.

She and Luke shared a look. Kerri gave him a nod.

"The sooner you cooperate with us," Kerri urged, "the sooner we can get to the truth." Why the hell was he so determined to fight them every step of the way? He was a detective! He understood full well what he was doing.

He said nothing.

"I get it now," Luke said. "The whole insurance-fraud scheme was Allison's idea. You're protecting her."

"You have no idea what you're talking about," Boothe said tightly, his gaze straight ahead as the game winner jumped up and down on the screen.

"What's all this?"

Rebecca Boothe strolled into the room, her eyes shifting from Kerri to Luke and back, then narrowing with suspicion.

"I'm glad you're back," Kerri said with a bright smile. "Detective Falco and I have a few questions for you."

The look of fear on Logan Boothe's face at that moment spoke volumes.

He understood they were getting closer.

To further amp up the man's uncertainty, they took their conversation with his mother to a private waiting room down the hall. People so often made telling the truth harder than it needed to be.

Rebecca poured herself a cup of coffee from the machine in the room. Judging by the strong smell, the pot had been simmering for a good long while. The thought made Kerri's teeth ache. Scorched coffee was worse than no coffee. Then again, the woman had spent the whole week at the hospital. Maybe her taste buds had adapted.

Rebecca settled into a chair and looked expectantly at Kerri.

"When did you learn," Kerri asked, "that Leah wasn't your son's biological child?"

"The same time he did." She stared into the cup, made a face, then set it on the table next to her chair. "About a month ago. It was rocky for a while, but things were calming down."

"Were Logan and Allison fighting more than usual because of this news?" Of course they would be. This was marriage-wrecking information.

"What did *she* say?" Rebecca demanded, her voice tight with indignation. "I suppose Jana's the one who told you. She would do anything to make my boy look guilty."

Kerri didn't bother explaining that her son was doing plenty all on his own toward that effort. "Mrs. Scott was not the source of this information."

"Well, surely you understand," she groused, "that he was devastated. As was I. Oh, but Allison insisted she had never been unfaithful." She rolled her eyes. "I guess Leah came about by way of a divine miracle. Why do you think I mentioned an affair? There had to be one."

Kerri moved into more sensitive territory. "How did this change your relationship with Leah?"

An eyebrow shot up the woman's forehead. "Are you accusing me of something, Detective?" Emotion shimmered in her eyes. "Let me tell you, I loved that child more than life itself. Nothing could have made me stop. Nothing."

"I have no doubt," Kerri assured her. "You're aware we have to ask these things."

Luke went next. "Did the news change Logan's relationship with Leah?"

Rebecca stared at the ceiling and shook her head. "As God is my witness, he could not have loved that child more. The only thing this news did was make him upset with his wife. It tore him apart."

"Enough to make him want to hurt her?" Luke pressed.

"No. No. No! He would never have hurt Allison. They fought about it. Who wouldn't have? But they worked it out. I've never seen them stand together more strongly than in the last few weeks."

"Were you with him on Sunday evening?" Luke asked.

"No, but I know my son. He would never, ever do such a thing."

"He has motive," Kerri said, "and he was there. A neighbor saw him."

Fury roared out of the woman. "My son is innocent."

"If he's innocent," Luke asked, "what was all the yelling about on Saturday evening?"

"I don't know what you're talking about."

"Mrs. Boothe," Kerri said, "we know Logan and Allison hired a man to burn the house for the insurance money. Is that what they were arguing about on Saturday night? Is that," Kerri pushed, "why Logan told the man they had changed their minds?"

Rebecca blinked. Stared at Kerri for a long moment as if she didn't know what to say. "Saturdays are movie night."

"Just because Logan was at home with his family doesn't mean they didn't argue," Kerri said.

"They wouldn't have ruined the evening for Leah." She squeezed her eyes shut, dropped her head.

"Mrs. Boothe," Luke said, drawing her attention to him, "we've interviewed the man they hired to do the job."

"They were desperate," she murmured, lips trembling, her voice low. "I'd already mortgaged my house, but Allison didn't want her mother to do the same. She decided maybe they could get enough from the insurance on their own house. With coverage for contents, it might just be enough. But Logan worried about the neighbors and what if someone else got hurt. There was too much risk. He said he'd found a different plan." Her gaze lifted back to Kerri's. "Don't you see? Allison is the one responsible for all this. My son and I have always gotten the short end of the stick."

"Tell us about this plan Logan came up with," Luke prodded.

"That's all I know. A new plan of some kind."

"To get the money they needed?" Kerri suggested.

She nodded. "I think so. You have to believe me, Logan didn't hurt anyone." Renewed anger sparked in her eyes. "If you want to know why Leah is dead, why not ask Jana? Leah was supposed to spend the night with her on Sunday night. She always spent the night with Jana on Sundays. But not this time, and now she's dead. While you're at it, you might ask that neighbor who saw my son where he was at earlier that evening."

With that, the woman stood and stormed out of the room.

"I'm wondering"—Kerri turned to her partner—"why Crandall would lie about the argument—assuming these two are telling the truth."

Luke shook his head. "No kidding. Is there anyone in this family or close to this family who can just tell the truth? Just say whatever it is they mean instead of alluding to something without really coming out and saying it?"

"Doesn't look that way." Kerri pushed up from her chair.

"Maybe he heard someone else arguing," Luke offered as he got up. "Or he just wants to stay relevant to the investigation. This is probably the most excitement he's had in ages."

Her partner was right. Families were like that sometimes. Kerri knew this firsthand. No one really wanted to hurt the others . . . unless there was no other choice. Everyone wanted to be in the know . . . a part of whatever was going on. Frankly, it was often the people who loved each other the most who could levy the broadest damage.

Any minute now Kerri expected the whole bunch to start popping up, knives out.

"I'm thinking," Luke said as they walked toward the elevators, "this new plan maybe had something to do with Leah's biological father."

Kerri paused at the elevator and pressed the call button. "In what way?" His own son learning the truth of his biology lingered on the fringes of her mind. No doubt Luke was thinking of Liam and their situation as well.

"What if the bio father is some rich guy they decided to blackmail?" Luke raised his eyebrows at her as they stepped into the elevator. "The guy might be willing to pay to keep his indiscretions quiet."

"Definitely a possibility worth looking into." Kerri selected the lobby level. "Maybe this whole thing is about protecting secrets."

Luke dropped his head against the elevator wall, then grimaced. "That still leaves us with the big, glaring question: Why would Logan Boothe protect his wife and child's killer? Why would any of them?"

"Right."

Back to square one.

28

2:30 p.m.

Scott Residence
River Woods Road
Hoover

The wind rushing across the lake made the afternoon cool despite the inordinately bright sun. Kerri suppressed a shiver. If only that light would penetrate the veil of secrecy this family had pulled firmly into place.

Allison and Leah were dead. Whoever or whatever the survivors were protecting was not going to bring them back. It would only allow a murderer to get away with what he'd done. It didn't make sense.

Luke pressed the doorbell again, then lifted the collar of his jacket. "Breezy today."

Kerri searched his bruised face, his eyes, which were red from restless sleep. She wished this case weren't taking such a personal toll on him . . . on both of them. "Winter is almost here."

Even in the south, winters could be cold and gray.

The front door opened, and Scott looked from one to the other. Uncertainty flashed across her face.

"We have a few more questions for you, ma'am," Kerri said, keeping her tone light. As much as she resented all the secrets everyone seemed to be keeping, this woman had been through enough without Kerri giving her unnecessary grief.

"Come in." She opened the door wider, then closed it behind them.

"Sorry for the unexpected visit," Luke offered. "I'm sure your husband told you how things can suddenly crop up during an investigation."

Like finding out about the DNA test from someone outside the family. This was the one sticking point with Scott for Kerri. Why not advise them of the situation right from the beginning? Understandably she wanted to protect her daughter, but her daughter was dead—murdered. Finding her killer was far more important than protecting her reputation.

Scott nodded. "I am familiar with the routine." She organized her lips into a smile that wasn't a smile at all. "We should sit."

Kerri and Luke followed her into the family room with its gorgeous view of the lake. Kerri could stare at that view for hours.

"Are these more questions about the DNA test?" The quiver in Scott's voice and the shimmer in her eyes warned she was struggling to maintain her composure.

"Ma'am, did you recall anything else from your conversation with Allison on Sunday that might help us with our investigation?" Kerri asked. If what Rebecca Boothe had said about Leah spending Sunday nights with Scott was true, why hadn't she mentioned that detail? The realization had surely crossed her mind.

Scott appeared to consider the question a moment, then shook her head. "No. I haven't recalled anything else." She smoothed a hand over her thigh as if ironing out a nonexistent wrinkle in her trousers. Her lips tried to smile but couldn't quite make the stretch. "I've tried to remember every word. I hope I told her how much I loved her."

Kerri remembered being desperate to recall what she'd last said to her niece. "I'm sure you did."

Silence hung in the air for half a minute.

"You have a beautiful home, Mrs. Scott," Luke said as he glanced around. "I'll bet Leah loved that lake. Did she spend the night with you on occasion?"

A true smile spread across the woman's lips this time. "She adored the lake. My husband used to take her out on the boat all the time. It was her favorite thing to do on Sunday evenings. She spends—spent— the night every Sunday. It was sort of Allison and Logan's couple time."

"But she didn't stay this past Sunday night," Kerri noted.

The happiness drained from Scott's face as if the plug had been pulled on a tub of water. "No." She drew in a ragged breath. "She did not."

"Is there a particular reason she didn't?" Kerri pushed. "Was she not feeling well? Or maybe you weren't well enough for a visit?"

The older woman's hands knotted in her lap, and she cast her gaze about the room as if searching for something that needed doing to avoid the question. Summoning her courage or her determination, she finally settled her attention on Kerri. "Actually, I had a rare evening out myself."

Her voice trembled, and Kerri regretted the necessity of this line of questioning. "We all need one now and again."

Luke stood and walked over to the fireplace. He studied the framed photos displayed across the mantel. "You can see how much she loved her time here."

The older woman's lips quivered. "She did." A tear slid down her cheek.

Kerri felt like a total shit, but this woman wasn't being completely forthcoming. They needed answers. "You went out on Sunday night. With friends?"

"Yes." She swiped the tear away. "It was Phil's birthday." She squared her shoulders. "Phil Crandall," she clarified. "He has been a friend of the family for quite a long time. Like me, he's alone, and with all the support he'd given Allison and Leah over the years, I wanted to ensure he had a nice birthday."

"He seems like a great neighbor," Luke said as he joined Kerri on the sofa once more. "It must have been nice to know Allison had someone close by to call on if the need arose."

"He has always been there for us," she agreed. "He and Raymond were good friends. Once we moved to the lake, Phil made sure they didn't lose that connection. As long as weather permitted, they were on the water fishing every chance they got."

"It was very nice of you to make sure he wasn't alone," Kerri agreed.

Scott gave a single nod and appeared to have trouble keeping her smile in place. "Before . . . when Raymond was still alive, he and I always took Phil to dinner on his birthday. He has no children or close relatives."

More of that heavy silence filled the room once more before she spoke again.

"I wish I had stayed home," she finally said, shadows clouding her eyes. "I would give anything if Leah had been with me that night like she was supposed to be."

"Looking back after a tragedy," Kerri said gently, "we always see the things we could have done differently. But we can't go back in time. We can only do what we believe is right during any given moment."

"I'll bet if your husband was still here," Luke pointed out, "he would have been the first to suggest taking Phil to dinner. It was tradition, right?"

Scott nodded, but it was obvious she was having trouble maintaining her composure. Once the first sob broke loose, she fell apart completely.

"I am so sorry," Kerri said. "It wasn't our intent to upset you."

Luke crossed the room and grabbed a box of tissues and brought them to the poor woman. She accepted the box and yanked out several to stanch the flow of tears.

When at last she was able to resume the conversation, she said, "I did what I thought was the right thing. But it turned out to be a miserable evening, and by the time I was going home, it was already past Leah's bedtime. I will never forgive myself."

"None of this was your fault, Mrs. Scott," Luke assured her.

"Do you mind sharing why it was such a miserable evening?" Kerri asked. "Did something happen that upset you?"

She couldn't help wondering if Scott had maybe known about the plan to burn the house and if maybe she had spoken to her daughter that day. Kerri wished like hell they had ordered the grandmothers' phone records that first day the way they had Logan Boothe's.

"By the time we finished our meal, Phil's behavior had become quite disturbing."

Kerri and Luke shared a look. This was certainly not what Kerri had expected to hear.

"How so?" Luke asked.

"Phil is a wonderful friend, and he really has been more like family all these years," she explained. "But that night he seemed to feel we were on a date of some sort. He tried holding my hand and suggested we go back to my house for some quiet time together. It was so very strange. I'd never looked at him as anything other than a friend—a dear friend. But I quickly realized he hoped for more. Or at least it felt that way. It was just . . . unsettling."

"Was there a disagreement or maybe harsh words exchanged?" Kerri couldn't deny being surprised. Crandall didn't give off that sort of vibe. Perhaps the mistake was an honest one. They were both alone. Had a solid connection. Why not explore other options?

"No, I pretended to have a migraine, and he brought me home. I didn't want to hurt his feelings. It was easier that way. With all that's happened, he hasn't mentioned those awkward moments, and neither have I." She closed her eyes for a moment. "I'm sure it's the last thing on his mind, as it is for me."

"I'm certain he understands," Kerri offered. "You've known Mr. Crandall a long time. I can't imagine he would ever do anything to hurt you or to jeopardize his relationship with Allison and Leah."

"Oh no," Scott assured her. "He adored them both. So many times he said watching Leah grow up was like having a child of his own. I've certainly always told him how Allison and Leah are my top priority. I really believed he felt the same way, especially after Raymond passed away."

"Just one more question, Mrs. Scott," Luke said. Scott shifted her attention to him. "Were you aware your daughter and her husband hired someone to burn their house for the insurance money?"

Shock invaded her expression. "What on earth are you talking about? Allison would never do such a thing! Who told you this horrible lie?"

"There was a plan to burn the house," Kerri explained. "If you knew anything about it, you should tell us now."

Scott squared her shoulders. "I don't know where this asinine idea came from, but rest assured I will be calling Chief Dubose. This is unacceptable, Detectives. I am appalled that you would even ask such a thing."

Kerri and Luke exchanged a glance. This was the first time Scott had pulled the chief card. Her horror certainly appeared real. But wasn't finding the truth the goal here? "Ma'am, as we've said before, we have a duty—"

"Don't you dare spout duty to me," she snapped. "I know what your duties are."

"The man hired to do the job," Luke explained, "is in holding as we speak. Logan Boothe paid him five thousand dollars up front to do the job."

Shock, fear—a collage of emotions claimed her face. "I don't believe you." Her voice shook. Her hands trembled.

The woman had had no idea. "Mrs. Scott," Kerri said gently, "are you sure Allison never explained the plan they had for coming up with the money they needed? You mentioned Allison seemed to be excited about it."

"Had they learned the identity of Leah's biological father?" Luke asked. "Maybe they asked for money from him."

"I'm afraid I'm not feeling well." She rose from her chair, swayed slightly. "I'd like you to go, please."

"Thank you for your time, Mrs. Scott," Kerri said.

When they had exited the house, the door locked sharply behind them.

"I'm thinking she didn't have a clue about the proposed insurance fraud," Luke said.

"But she didn't seem surprised at the idea they'd learned the identity of the biological father."

"No, she did not." When they'd loaded into her Wagoneer, Luke added, "She didn't tell us about Leah and their Sunday-night routine either."

"Or her odd evening with Crandall." Kerri started the engine. "Maybe we shouldn't have given our eager witness a pass."

"Maybe not," Luke agreed. "Maybe he's keeping some secrets too."

Birmingham Police Department
First Avenue North
Major Investigations Division, 5:50 p.m.

Kerri tossed her cell onto her desk. "Sadie will let us know if she uncovers anything about Crandall beyond what we've found."

Luke had turned his computer monitor so they could both see the screen as they dug into Phileas Crandall's background.

"The one oddity I see," Luke said, "is that his wife, Lisa, died twenty-some years ago, and he never remarried. Which isn't unheard of, I guess. Did his libido suddenly wake up, and he decided he wanted to do the dirty with Jana Scott?"

Kerri rolled her eyes. "Maybe he never met anyone he wanted to pursue, and Scott was taken—at least until last year. He may have recently come to the conclusion that they're good friends, both alone, so why not?"

Luke scoffed. "More likely he discovered the power of those little blue pills."

Kerri ignored the remark. "Did you find cause of death on the wife?"

"Car accident." He clicked a few keys, then pointed to the screen, where a badly damaged sedan was the eye-catching shot for the "Holiday Tragedy" headline from a San Antonio newspaper. "She wasn't wearing her seat belt. Crandall, who was wearing his, survived. He sustained a head injury and was found unconscious but alive in the car. The wife was pretty much sprawled on the hood and not breathing."

"Jesus." Kerri made a face. "That's a hell of a way to go."

"Whoa, whoa, whoa." Luke leaned forward to peer more closely at the screen. "Lookee, lookee what I found."

"The wife's obit?" Kerri leaned closer as well.

"The deceased was survived by a *daughter*." He made a knowing sound. "That's interesting, don't you think?"

"Definitely. Scott said Crandall had no children."

"Hold on, maybe he doesn't." Luke tapped the screen. "The daughter wasn't a Crandall. So I guess she was a stepdaughter."

Kerri stared at the damaged vehicle in the newspaper photo. "We should track her down and ask a few questions. See if there's anything we should know about our Good Samaritan neighbor."

"Cover all the bases," Luke agreed.

"Wait." Kerri replayed her conversations with Crandall. "Maybe I misunderstood, but I got the impression his wife died more recently." She tried to think of something specific he had said. "Something about him still struggling with living alone."

"I don't remember him mentioning a date or time frame, but you're right—he did give the impression it hadn't been all that long," Luke said. "Definitely not two decades."

"I'll double-check my interview notes." Kerri fished out her notepad and started flipping through pages while Luke focused on locating a phone number or address for the long-lost stepdaughter, Lorna Collette.

An alert that she'd received a text message had Kerri checking her screen. *Tori.* She smiled.

Can't wait to see you on Sunday!

Me too! she typed back.

The heart emoji that followed made Kerri smile.

She really hoped this trip had been a good one. Tori needed the bonding time with her father. Though she adored Luke, Nick was her father, and they needed to maintain that connection.

Brooks stuck his head into their cubicle. He glanced at Luke, who was on a call, then motioned for Kerri to step outside.

"The chief wanted me to check in and see how the case is going. He's got one of those crazy viruses and is stuck at home for a few days."

Kerri had wondered why he hadn't been blowing up her phone. "We're still digging, making some amount of headway. Boothe stands by his confession, but we're reasonably confident he's covering for someone. Hopefully we'll have something more concrete soon." She briefed him on Stover and the new look at Crandall.

"Sounds good. Let me hear from you if there's anything new."

"Yes, sir."

Kerri watched the LT go. He was a good man. A good cop and leader. The fact that he had the humility to say when he was wrong made her all the more grateful to be a part of his team.

She stepped back into their cubicle. "Did you reach the stepdaughter?"

Luke slid his phone into his pocket. "I left a voice mail."

"Brooks was checking in for the chief. Chief's home with that virus."

"I was wondering why he wasn't nagging us about the case."

"The concept you mentioned about the bio father," Kerri said, "I'm thinking there's something to that. Scott cut off our interview right after you mentioned the idea."

Luke grabbed his jacket. "It's possible the fire wasn't about insurance fraud. It may have been about blackmail."

Kerri pulled on her jacket. "If Candace Oden really was a friend of Allison's, wouldn't she know what was going on? Her reaction when we told her about Leah not being Boothe's bio daughter was obvious. She already knew. If she knew that, it's possible she knew way more."

"Let's pay her a visit."

"After," Kerri offered. "We should have food delivered for dinner."

"Or dig into some of those leftovers. That dressing Diana made was the bomb."

Her sister would be pleased by his compliment. "Leftovers it is, then."

It was the Friday after Thanksgiving, and most everyone was already gone for the day. Didn't mean they weren't working, just that they weren't hanging around the office. Even when a detective had a day off, the case lingered on the fringes of whatever else they did.

"I think there's some of that pecan pie in the fridge too," Luke said as they entered the stairwell.

"The pecan pie is mine," Kerri warned.

"I see how it is," he teased.

"Be nice and I might share."

He scoffed. "I'm always nice."

He was. Her partner was a really good guy. No matter what had occurred in the past, he was a nice guy, and she was grateful to have him as a partner.

She glanced up at him as they pushed out into the cold night air.

He made her happy.

Very happy.

29

8:00 p.m.

Devlin Residence
Twenty-First Avenue South
Birmingham

"Wasn't that way better than takeout?" Luke closed the dishwasher. He was still feeling bad about that tumble Kerri had taken at the game shop. If he'd been on his toes, he could have stopped Stover.

"It was. I'm stuffed. I'll grab a couple of beers."

"You okay so far with me being here?" He shrugged. "Like this, I mean."

She passed a beer to him. "I'm better than okay with it." She headed for the dining table, where their working files were spread out. "I like it."

She liked it. He grinned. All right. He liked the sound of that. "I'm glad."

They sat across the table from each other. "I was thinking," she said, "when Tori is back, we can discuss a more permanent arrangement—the three of us, I mean."

Now *that* had his heart thumping. "More permanent is good." Just saying the words made him a little giddy.

"Okay." She drew in a big breath. "I'm still annoyed that we couldn't catch Oden at home."

"She's probably gone for the holiday weekend. We'll catch up with her." Unless she'd disappeared. Carla Brown and Josh Carr damned sure had. This case was way twisted. Just as soon as they discovered the end of one thread, another one frayed.

Kerri surveyed their notes. "I'm thinking we can rule out both grandmothers. Rebecca Boothe is pushy and judgmental, but I don't believe for a second she killed her granddaughter. Whether she was her biological grandchild or not."

"I'm with you on both. The biggest thing these two are guilty of is keeping secrets. Who the hell knows why?"

Secrets were something he knew way too much about. Regret gnawed at his gut.

"Boothe is doing the same thing," Kerri noted. "O'Grady as well, for that matter. On top of that we have your old pal Dog and then the neighbor Candace Oden. They all appear determined to avoid full disclosure. It's making me crazy."

"Which is preventing us from solving the case." Luke braced his forearms on the table. "I've been trying to reach Dog off and on all day. He's dodging my calls."

"You said in your latest round of nightmares, you remembered him being there. You think he'll tell you what he knows?"

"I hope so. I also believe he's the detective Brooks was talking about."

"You really think he would rat out O'Grady? I got the impression he's like O'Grady's right-hand man."

"Maybe I'm wrong," Luke admitted. "All I know is that once I bumped into him again, suddenly there's a detective spilling on O'Grady. I think we can safely say it's not Boothe."

"Wait a minute." Kerri tapped her fingers against her lips. "You remember the day he went all *Fast and Furious* on me?"

Luke nodded. How could he forget? He still wanted to kick the
guy's ass just for that.

"He said something about leaving the past alone, and I told him he
should talk to his LT, because he was the one bringing up the past. I was
angry about all the stuff O'Grady said to Brooks. Maybe Dog decided
if O'Grady could turn on you, he might turn on him next. Why not
beat him to the punch?"

"You might be on to something." Luke sat up straighter. "Let's just
throw it all on the table. My money's on O'Grady. I can't get past the
idea that he is involved in this somehow." The possibility that he might
have been involved with what had happened to Mina tore at his gut. If
he learned . . . but he couldn't go there right now.

"His interference doesn't really make sense otherwise," Kerri agreed.
"You mentioned before that if push came to shove, O'Grady would do
whatever necessary to handle the situation."

"In all fairness," he felt compelled to throw out there, "I'm nowhere
near objective on the subject. I don't want my issues with O'Grady to
mess with your cop instincts or to lead this investigation in the wrong
direction."

"It's possible," Kerri confessed, "I may not be as objective as I
should be either. On some level I understand he's part of the past that
haunts you. The idea makes me dislike him."

Luke's chest tightened. That was the thing about Kerri. She was
totally loyal. She cared about him and couldn't ignore how the damage
O'Grady had done affected him. God, how had he gotten lucky enough
to find her? He asked himself that every day.

"There's more I should tell you." Fear thickened in his throat. The
way she looked at him right now—as if he were some amazing person—
was the way he selfishly wanted her to look at him until he drew his last
breath. He was terrified that would change.

"I know who you are, Luke Falco," she said when he hesitated.
"I know you had an abusive father who tortured both you and your

238

mother. I know you've spent a good deal of your life trying to prove that you're better than him." She reached across the table and squeezed his hand. "Trust me, you are."

His heart swelled to the point of threatening to bust wide open. "Hearing you say those words—feeling how much you trust me and care about me—is like a gift I never expected to receive." He looked down, shook his head. "I know I don't deserve it." He met her gaze once more. "But I damned sure don't want to lose it."

"Whatever happened in the past is in the *past*. You've said many times you were a different person then. How could I hold that against you now?"

He held up a hand. "Before you say more, I want to make sure you understand all of it—at least all that I can remember."

"All right." She reached for his hand, gave it a squeeze. "I'm listening."

"I worked under deep cover with O'Grady for the better part of five years. He was the reason I was fast-tracked to detective." He shrugged. "In the beginning, I admired him. Hell, everyone around him did . . . in the beginning. He turned us into this sharp crew who could get anything done. But things slowly began to change. I think he became addicted to the power."

He took a moment to steel himself. She sat stone still, waiting for him to continue.

"He became more and more obsessed with getting deeper, doing what no one else had done. He pushed us to meld with our targets. To become like them. To be whatever necessary to sink deep into their worlds." He paused to force in a breath. "I was particularly good at it. I had no issue with doing whatever drug was put in front of me. I was one of the lucky ones. I could do it for months and walk away without a backward glance. Still, it took a toll. I started to hate myself—the way I hated my father. I just kept falling deeper and deeper into this hole, and I couldn't find my way back."

He thought of the days and nights he barely recalled. The things he'd missed. The things he'd ignored. Like his wife and, eventually, his kid.

"I can't imagine anyone working in that world without suffering a heavy toll," Kerri offered. "It's a tremendous sacrifice."

He nodded, then went on before he lost his nerve. "The better I got, the more O'Grady pushed me. I was like his own personal pet project. His golden boy who was going to make him a star."

He closed his eyes and struggled to keep his voice steady. How had he allowed himself to be manipulated so completely?

"I could blame it all on O'Grady," he allowed, "but I got caught up in the thrill too. It was powerful. A better high than any drug. I could make anyone believe whatever I wanted them to believe. I was a master of deception."

Sometimes it didn't seem possible that he'd been that naive and stupid.

But it was real, all right. Too damned real.

"On our final op together, we were this close"—he held his thumb and forefinger about half an inch apart—"to getting deep into our target's world. I had him right where we wanted him. I was tight with someone very close to him. She . . ." He swallowed at the tightness in his throat. "She trusted me. I guess she was infatuated with me. O'Grady was certain she would do anything I asked."

"Mina."

Hearing her name made it hard to breathe. He nodded. "She was the CI O'Grady had developed. She fell hard for me. Trusted me, and I let her down."

He slugged down half his beer. Wished he could wash away the memories, but they weren't going away. "We were rocking along just fine, and then O'Grady picked up some chatter about her. He was certain she intended to double-cross me. I didn't believe him, but he kept insisting I had to be careful. I had to watch her closer. I had to . . ."

Bastard. He'd driven Luke nuts with the idea that Mina was turning on him.

"As you know, shit rolls downhill, so I started giving her a hard time. She kept trying to prove to me that she was loyal. It got all crazy. Shelly was on me about the baby coming. He was due any day, and she needed me. Suddenly the drugs were the only thing that gave me any relief. I couldn't get through the day or the night without them. That had never happened before."

Kerri sipped her beer. Her movements quiet, careful.

"This one night things got out of hand, and we—Mina and me— had a fight. A bad one. I don't know what happened. I just know the next morning I woke up with the worst hangover of my life. Dog was yanking me out of bed, saying we had to get out." He drew in a deep breath. "I was confused as hell. I didn't understand what he was talking about. Then he told me Mina was dead." Luke's throat closed completely for a moment. "I didn't believe him, but it was true. He said we had to get out and burn the place down—the room she rented. I thought he'd lost it, but he said we had to because my DNA was probably all over the place. I didn't understand what difference it made, and then he said . . ."

He couldn't bear to look at Kerri as he said the words. "He said I killed her."

Silence.

The thumping in his chest pounded in his brain.

"But you can't be sure," Kerri countered. "You don't recall what happened. Drugs were involved."

"It was only the two of us there that night." He considered the vague memory of hearing a man's voice. Probably just wishful thinking.

"How did Dog know where to find you?"

"I didn't report in that morning. In my dream, I called him. O'Grady, I mean. Either way, he sent Dog to find me. When he discovered the situation, he called O'Grady and did what he was ordered to do."

"What about Mina?"

"According to the investigation that followed, she died in a house fire. Dog was careful about the fire. He made it look like an accident. She was a smoker. We'd been drinking, so there was alcohol. It was too easy. It was always too easy."

There. He'd told her the kind of man he really was.

He'd expected her to yell at him for keeping this from her all this time. He'd expected her to order him out of her house.

But she said nothing.

Which was way worse.

Finally, he lifted his gaze to hers and looked for the disgust and hatred he'd anticipated.

Instead, she watched him, her face showing no hint of judgment. "Seventeen months ago I killed a man." She shrugged. "He was trying to kill me at the time, so I suppose you could call it self-defense. Except I know better."

No. No way. "It's not the same, Kerri." He couldn't allow her to compare herself to him. She was a saint compared to him. The bastard had killed her niece, and he would have killed Kerri too.

"It's exactly the same. I put myself and this man in a position that resulted in his death. Then I covered it up. You know. Sadie knows. But I kept it from my daughter, my sister, and my lieutenant. And I wasn't drinking. I wasn't on any drug. I was stone-cold sober. Top that, partner. At least you're not completely certain you killed anyone. I know what I did."

Kerri Devlin did not cry often, but a tear slipped down her cheek then, and it ripped his heart from his chest.

He was on his knees at her side before the next tear fell. "You aren't like me, baby. I was a bad person. I did so many bad things. I can't even remember them all. You . . . you are not like me at all."

"Shut up."

He closed his mouth. Blinked at the burn in his eyes.

She placed her hands on either side of his face. "I don't care what you did. I would still go through any door with you, Detective Luke Falco."

He pulled her into his arms and held her tight against him. Ignored his aching ribs. She was all that mattered.

This—what they had—was all that mattered.

30

9:00 p.m.

There were those who only learned the hard way.

Through life's tragedies and pain.

Pain cleared the clouds of uncertainty from the mind.

Finally the path was wide open. No more obstacles.

Moving forward.

The past was behind him now.

Time to stake a claim.

But first it was necessary to watch. And wait. Years of doing exactly that had been all the preparation needed.

The door had closed, but a window had opened.

The time was now. He understood this finally.

He had done everything precisely as planned. He had not missed a single detail.

There was only the finale.

31

Saturday, November 27

10:00 a.m.

Devlin Residence
Twenty-First Avenue South
Birmingham

Luke watched Kerri rushing around the living room, then the kitchen.

"Whatcha looking for?" He had to press his sore lips together to prevent his grinning.

"I can't find my cell phone." She moved the notes from their working file aside. "I had it last night."

Last night. Luke barely resisted the urge to sigh. Last night had been amazing. They'd made love and talked and made love again. She'd made him understand whatever had happened that night eight years ago had been outside his control. She wanted to talk to Cross about helping figure out the truth about that night. Maybe Dog would help. Luke had reached out, and Dog had finally responded with an agreement to meet. Whether he would help or not, Luke would have to see.

It was a good plan. And way past time he cleared up that black cloud hanging over his head. Running from the past wasn't going to change the facts. Better to learn what those facts were and go from there.

"Your phone is under the table." He gestured to the floor. "I vaguely remember it hitting the floor during a certain move we made."

"Thanks." She snatched it up, her cheeks pink, maybe from the search or maybe from the memory of what they'd done on that floor. "I have to go pick up the cake I ordered for Tori."

He groaned. "I finally reached Dog. He's coming by at ten thirty. You want to wait so I can go with you?"

"Can't." She reached for her jacket. "Dreamcakes closes at noon on Saturdays. I won't be long." She went up on tiptoe and kissed his bruised jaw. "Stay put until I get back."

"Yeah, yeah. Be careful."

She paused at the door and grinned at him. "I notice you didn't have any bad dreams last night."

He grinned. Winced at the burn. "Slept like a baby."

"Good."

With that, she was gone. He watched from the window as she backed from the driveway and drove away. However hard he tried, he would never deserve that gorgeous woman.

He rinsed their coffee cups and set them on the counter. For the next few minutes he occupied his mind with reviewing their notes. Otherwise he would just walk the floors until Dog showed up. Stover and his attorney were still refusing to give a statement. The only thing they'd gotten from Stover with any measure of certainty was that Logan Boothe was not the person who'd contracted him.

The big question in Luke's mind was, Would Allison actually go to bed—tucking her daughter into her own bed first—knowing Sunday was the night the contract was supposed to be carried out? Even if her husband had promised to stop it, it seemed like a bad idea to Luke. Why hadn't she been walking the floors until her husband got back home? Why take the risk?

The doorbell echoed through the house. He glanced at the digital clock on the stove. Ten thirty.

"Right on time."

His cell vibrated as he walked toward the door. A text from Kerri.

Gonna stop by Oden's house on the way home.

He frowned. Be CAREFUL.

The thumbs-up was her response.

Oden, like the rest of this cast of characters, appeared determined to keep her secrets.

Luke checked the peephole and confirmed Dog was staring back at him before opening the door.

"Thanks for coming by." Luke waited for the man to come inside, then closed the door behind him. "I can't drive until next week." He pointed to his head. "Concussion. One of your boys worked me over but good."

Dog pushed his sunglasses to the top of his head. "You accusing a member of my crew of something?"

"I ain't accusing nobody," Luke corrected. "I'm telling you one of them ambushed me and beat the crap out of me."

Dog growled. "Is that why you been blowing up my phone? You're like my ex. Bugging the shit outa me."

"It would be nice to know why you ordered him to rough me up, but that's not why I've been calling you."

"First"—Dog braced his hands on his hips—"I didn't order anyone to rough you up. Maybe you pissed somebody off showing up at the cabin like that the other night."

"Second?" Luke asked.

Dog glowered at him. "Second what?"

"My partner's really smart, and she says you don't do a first unless you've got a second."

Dog rolled his eyes. "Whatever. Why am I here, Falco?"

Probably no point in asking him to have a seat. "We need to talk about what happened to Mina."

Dog shook his head. "I should have seen this coming." He glared at Luke. "Look, you have got to leave this alone. If you keep digging, you're going to end up burying yourself."

"Why? If I killed her, I want to know. If that means paying the price for what I did, then so be it. But I want the truth."

"Everyone wants the truth," Dog said with an overdose of sarcasm. "What is the truth? Is it what you have to do to get the job done? To bring a perceived state of justice?"

"It's just the truth. I want the truth."

"As cliché as this sounds, man," Dog offered, "the truth will not set you free."

A flare of anger set Luke on edge. "I didn't call you here to philosophize about the perception of truth."

"Just say what you want to say. I got shit to do."

"I remembered something about that night." He had to tread carefully here. "There was someone else in the room, I think, besides Mina and me. A guy, maybe. I remember—or at least I think I do—hearing him say something."

Dog waited for him to go on, his face and eyes clean of tells.

Luke bit the bullet and asked the question driving him crazy. "Was it you?"

Something like outrage flickered in Dog's eyes. "Are you seriously asking me that question?"

"You're the one who dragged me out and burned the place down."

Dog stepped in closer. "You need to let this go."

Luke shook his head. "Can't do it. This has to end now. I know someone besides me was there the night Mina died."

Dog held his gaze for a long moment. "There was a time when you trusted me."

Luke couldn't deny that once he had not only trusted but looked up to him. After what had happened, things were never the same. Luke hadn't trusted anyone . . . until Kerri.

"I need you to trust me now," Dog urged. "Things are about to change. You have my word. But I want to stay alive to see it happen, and I want you to stay alive too. So just back off for a little bit longer."

The idea that Dog was the detective Brooks had been talking about quaked through Luke again. Would he really cross O'Grady?

"All right," Luke said. "I'll back off. For now."

"Okay. Good. I'll be in touch."

When he was gone, Luke pulled out his cell to call Kerri. He wanted her to know about this. But a call came through before he could tap her name.

Cross.

"Yo," he said, answering the call. "What's up, Cross?"

"Your old friend O'Grady, that's what's up."

Luke walked to the nearest window to watch for Kerri's return. "Give me the dirt. I'm salivating already."

"I've been following through on one of the things you said about O'Grady," she explained. "You mentioned that he stayed in tight with the wives when the husbands were under deep cover. I tracked down several wives but only three who were willing to talk. All three said O'Grady came around at least once a week to check on them and their kids, if they had kids."

"Yeah," Luke confirmed. "But trust me, that doesn't make him a nice guy."

"You are so right. It appears he had a deviant motive for all those in-home visits."

"Shit," Luke said, making a face. "Don't tell me he was pimping out the wives."

"You're not far off the mark. I'm thinking he was using them for his own pleasure. One of the wives ended up divorced because while her husband was under deep for three months, she ended up with an STD. This woman swears she did not cheat on her husband."

Sounded like Allison Boothe.

"Another," Sadie went on, "said she had to start being gone on the days O'Grady was supposed to stop by. She'd noticed that after his visits she always felt sick and hungover. Once she started avoiding him, she didn't have the episodes anymore."

Luke thought about how hungover he'd been the morning after Mina's death. He'd never had a hangover like that before or since.

"You think he was drugging them?" he asked.

"That's what it sounds like to me. Wife number three said he always insisted on having a drink with her when he came over. She didn't really like to drink at all, but she wanted to keep her husband's boss happy."

The urge to hunt the son of a bitch down and pound the truth out of him pulsed inside Luke.

"You should ask the ME," Sadie suggested, "if the tox screen on Allison Boothe and her kid included testing for GHB or Rohypnol."

"Thanks, Cross." He barely kept the fury out of his tone. "You find anything else, let me know."

"There is one other odd thing," she said before hanging up.

"What's that?"

"The wives I interviewed said another woman—a cop or a PI; I got different stories when I asked—anyway, she was asking the same questions about O'Grady. This was about two weeks ago."

"There's supposed to be an ongoing investigation into O'Grady's activities," Luke told her. "It could be part of that."

"Yeah, probably."

"This cop or PI was definitely female?"

"Definitely female."

"Thanks, Cross. Let me know if you hear anything else."

After the call ended, Luke considered the other possibilities. Yeah, the female could have been from the department. Someone following up on claims against O'Grady.

Had that investigation started two weeks ago? No. Brooks had said someone had only just come forward.

Had to be someone else two weeks ago. Someone with a different agenda.

He doubted it would have been Allison Boothe. The other wives might have known her. Maybe Jana Scott or Rebecca Boothe? Or Allison's one friend . . . Candace Oden.

The reality of what Sadie had just told him slammed all the way home.

Shelly.

Barely able to see for the haze of anger, he called his ex-wife.

"Hey," she said. "Sorry I haven't called you already, but he's still refusing to talk."

Luke reached for calm. "I understand." He opened his mouth. Closed it, then tried again. "I was calling to ask you a question about before. When we were together."

"Okay." Her voice sounded skeptical.

She had every right to be suspicious of where this was going. "When I was in the field, did O'Grady ever check on you?"

The pause that followed told him he wasn't going to like what he was about to hear.

"He came around. A few times. He said he was checking on me for you. But he always wanted to have a drink. I was embarrassed because you know I don't drink."

She hated the taste of anything with alcohol in it. Luke recalled all too well. She couldn't have been more different from him. "I remember."

"Well, so, I pretended to drink, and before he left, he made, like, passes at me. Then, the last time, he came back inside after I thought he was gone. Scared the hell out of me. He never came back after that."

Thank God. "Why the hell didn't you tell me?"

A long pause, and then, "Do you really have to ask? You thought O'Grady was God. You were never going to believe anything negative I said about him. You would have accused me of trying to come between you and the job."

He wished he could deny the charge, but she was right. "I'm sorry, Shelly. Sorrier than you'll ever know for letting you and Liam down."

"I do know," she offered. "You were a different person then, Luke."

Emotion crowded into his throat, burned his eyes. "Thanks."

"Luke," she said, her voice soft, "we got past all that a long time ago. It's time to let it go."

"Hug Liam for me, will you? Just don't tell him it's from me."

She laughed. "I will."

Shelly was right. It was time to let it go. He would do that just as soon as O'Grady got what was coming to him.

Sick bastard.

32

11:30 a.m.

Oden Residence
Chablis Way
Birmingham

Kerri knocked and pressed the doorbell. Three times, no less.

No answer.

Why pull the disappearing act? Unless she had something to hide?

The answer was simple. Candace Oden did have something to hide, and she was scared. Kerri had spotted the shadow of fear on her face that day. She knew something, and she was afraid to reveal what that something was.

Kerri went back to her Wagoneer and searched for a piece of paper and a pen. She wrote a note asking Oden to call her as soon as possible and tucked it into the door. Before she turned away, she tried the knob.

Locked.

Considering Oden might have known something about the perpetrator who'd set the Boothe fire, Kerri decided she had exigent circumstances and could at least check the windows and doors in the house. It was a stretch, but she'd done a little stretching before.

One by one, she moved from window to window and looked inside where she could. She did the same at the doors.

The house appeared to be clear. No sign of Oden or her daughter. No indication of foul play.

She climbed into her vehicle and backed out of the driveway. She rolled forward slowly, taking in the devastation left behind at the Boothe home. As she moved beyond the house, she spotted Mr. Crandall in his front yard, waving at her.

No, not waving *at* her. Waving her down.

Kerri turned into his driveway and braked to a stop. She shut off the engine and climbed out.

"Everything okay, Mr. Crandall?"

He frowned. "I'm worried about Jana."

"Has something happened?"

"Well, no, not that I know of." He rubbed at his forehead. "I'm just concerned that it's been five days since the horrible tragedy happened, and there's no closure. I'm not sure how long she can hold up under the strain. She's been through so much, you know."

Kerri did know. Mrs. Scott had lost her husband last year. For the past ten months she'd suffered through the nightmare of her granddaughter's illness. Now this. It was more than any one person should have to endure.

"I wish we could make the process move more quickly," Kerri offered, "but these investigations take time. There are numerous layers in a case like this one. We have to take it slow and make sure we don't miss anything."

From the family's perspective it likely looked as if they were doing nothing, when really they were doing all they could.

He exhaled a big breath. "I do know this. I had many, many conversations about cases with Raymond. He reveled in detailing the rigors of police work. I feel as if I could be a detective myself after all those fishing trips listening to him tell his war stories."

"You were friends. I'm sure Mrs. Scott appreciates the shared memories."

"She does. We often talk about all the times together. I was with him, you know, when he passed."

"I didn't know that." Scott hadn't gone into detail about that day.

"I honestly thought he'd just accidentally fallen into the water. He was fiddling around with his rod, hadn't taken his seat. Suddenly he was in the water. I threw down my rod and jumped in to help him. It was like trying to wrestle a greased pig. He squirmed and wiggled. I didn't realize he was having a heart attack. By the time I got him back into the boat and to shore, it was all over."

"It must have been very difficult for you."

"It has been very difficult watching Jana struggle with so much loss. She really needs to be able to move on with her life. It's just so unfair for her to continue to sacrifice her happiness for everyone else."

"We're doing all we can, Mr. Crandall." The more he talked, the more emotional he seemed to grow.

"Jana told me Logan confessed. Why can't you just arrest him and close the case? Isn't that the way it works?"

"It's not always so simple, Mr. Crandall," she said, hoping to allay his concerns or at least to calm him down. "We have to make sure all the pieces fit. The loose ends are tied up. Unfortunately, in this case we haven't reached that place just yet. But we will."

"It's because he was a detective, too, isn't it?" he said with sudden indignation. "It's that blue code or whatever."

"I assure you our handling of the investigation has nothing to do with Boothe being an ex-cop. We take all the same steps no matter the identity of any and all suspects." She tried not to be taken aback by his accusation. Crandall didn't seem to be himself today. Maybe the stress was getting to him.

"I'm sorry." He held up his hands in surrender. "I'm upset. For Jana. I'm certain you and Detective Falco are doing everything within your power."

"We are," she agreed. "It's essential that we make sure we don't miss a step in this, or the wrong person could be arrested, and the actual perpetrator gets away with murder."

"But he confessed." Crandall's exasperation was showing again.

"He did; however, there are holes in his story. A perfect example is, Why did he run back into the house to save his family—risking his life—if he's the one who set the fire? Why work with his wife to solve their financial issues if he was just going to kill her anyway? There was no life insurance. What did he have to gain? We know what he lost. Basically everything." She kept the house-insurance scenario out of the conversation. Crandall had no need to know about it.

He stared at her, blinked. "I hadn't considered all those questions." He chuckled dryly. "I suppose that's why I'm not a detective. Please, Detective Devlin, excuse my meltdown. I am just so worried about Jana. She's in a very precarious place right now, and that Boothe woman is driving her insane."

Kerri hadn't gotten that impression from Scott the last time they'd spoken, but it was possible she was too nice to say something as unkind—true or not—as what Crandall had just announced.

"It's a difficult situation," Kerri agreed.

"Well, I apologize for wasting your time, Detective."

"No trouble. Please feel free to contact me if you think of anything that might affect our investigation."

"I certainly will."

She started to turn away but hesitated. "Have you seen Candace Oden? I've missed her the past couple of times I've come by."

"I haven't seen her in a few days." He studied the house across the street. "She stays to herself a good deal of the time."

"She and Allison were friends," Kerri tossed out.

He nodded. "I think the friendship was on and off. There was some jealousy, I think, over Logan. He was a bit of a flirt with Candace."

"Did you ever see any indication that there might be something more than friendship between Candace and Logan?" The rumor about an affair was still unsubstantiated.

His eyes narrowed. "I saw him going in and out of her house several times. Alone, of course. I wondered if he was looking for a way to start over with a new family. A daughter who's healthy. A wife who isn't so clingy to her mother."

Kerri zeroed in on the last. "Was Allison and Jana's relationship a bone of contention for Allison and Logan?"

"At times. Jana helped them so much I sensed that it made Logan feel inadequate. Some men are like that, you know. Jana was far too good to them all."

"Mothers want to help," Kerri admitted. "We like taking care of our kids. Even when they're grown and have lives of their own."

He nodded. "I just want her to take care of herself. To be happy. That's all I've ever wanted."

Kerri smiled. "I'm sure she appreciates your concern." The newspaper article and obituary she and Luke had read vied for her attention. "Did you tell me you don't have any children, Mr. Crandall?"

Surprise went unchecked in his expression. "If you're asking, I'm sure I must have. Either way, you're correct. I don't have any children. Unfortunately. Allison and Leah were like my own, though."

"It's a shame about the accident that killed your wife." She grimaced. "It must have been a terrible time for you."

"Yes. Terrible." He nodded. "Well, thank you, Detective, for all you do."

Kerri watched as Mr. Crandall strode back to his home. His concern for Jana Scott bordered on obsessive. His worries might be well intended, but he really should back off just a bit. He hadn't missed a beat when she'd asked about his wife. And he'd totally left out the stepdaughter. Evidently, he and the stepdaughter had parted on bad terms.

As Kerri climbed into her Wagoneer, she figured the trouble had involved money. The deceased wife's estate.

Her gaze snagged on his home as she drove away. She just couldn't shake his words. She fished for her cell phone and called Scott. It was possible she would see Kerri's number and hang up. She doubted the woman had forgiven her and Luke for yesterday's exchange.

"Hello?"

The single word warned she expected the worst. "Hey, Mrs. Scott. I just spent some time chatting with Mr. Crandall."

"Is something wrong, Detective Devlin?" She didn't hang up, but her voice was a little stilted.

Kerri was definitely still on her bad side.

"I don't think so, but I did want to ask you about something he said. He mentioned that he was worried about how you're handling the rigors of our ongoing investigation. He feels you're very vulnerable now. Considering how upset you were when we last spoke—"

"I was married to a detective for decades," she said, cutting Kerri off. "I know how these things go. As much as I would love to know how and why this happened and who is responsible, I am painfully aware of how the process works. However quickly you solve this, it won't bring back my daughter and granddaughter. You take your time, Detective, and do this right. I want justice, not a speed walk through the investigative steps. As for our last conversation, my only excuse is that I am human."

Okay, then. Kerri pushed on. "He told me about what happened with your husband."

Scott sighed, the sound weary. "It was a very bad time for me. I married right out of college. I basically grew up with Raymond. Spent my whole life with him. Losing him was a difficult transition."

"Mr. Crandall thinks highly of you," Kerri tossed out. "He seems adamant that he wants you to be able to move on."

"Sadly, this is where he and I disagree. Moving on isn't an option. I will just have to be content living with my memories."

"One last question," Kerri said. "Did Logan at any time suggest that your help with their financial troubles was unwanted?"

"Who in the world said a thing like that? Raymond and I were always happy to help. I firmly believe Logan was grateful." Another weary sigh. "To tell you the truth, Detective, at this point it feels like I no longer have any idea what to believe. But I have always felt my son-in-law appreciated our efforts."

"I'm optimistic that Detective Falco and I will have this sorted out very soon, ma'am."

"I sincerely hope so. I really do."

The call ended, and Kerri couldn't get the idea out of her head that Crandall was just too concerned about his friend. There was always the chance that he was just a little obsessive. Still, they needed to hear back from the stepdaughter. Of course, it had been a very long time since she had known Crandall, but the fact that he pretended she didn't exist said a great deal about how they'd parted.

The fact that he spoke of his wife's passing as if it had only been a short time ago when it had actually been twenty years wasn't over-the-top strange. Particularly with older folks, who oftentimes felt like an event had been only yesterday.

Then again, people were not always who they presented themselves as or even who they saw themselves as. Five people could attend the same event and experience the same moments, and all five would years later recall the event in different ways. Sometimes only days later they would each have a differing degree of recall as to how things had actually played out. This was one of the reasons eyewitnesses weren't as reliable as, say, video footage.

Unlike cameras, humans interpreted what they saw and heard. How it ended up being stored was all in the interpretation.

33

12:40 p.m.

University of Alabama Hospital
Sixth Avenue South
Birmingham

Rebecca's head snapped up. She had dozed off in her chair. She shook herself. She had to stay awake. She could not be late.

It was almost time.

Logan was sleeping. He'd had a bad night last night. The things that detective had said to him had torn him apart. It ripped her heart out to watch him suffer so.

Sweet Jesus, had he not been through enough?

Her cell phone shuddered against her thigh. She stared at the screen. *Jana.*

Moving quietly, she eased out of her chair and slipped out of the room. She smiled at the officer stationed outside the door, even though it infuriated her that he was there. They didn't trust her son. They thought he was guilty.

They would see.

Logan was innocent.

"Hello." She held her breath, hoping Jana had news of the son of a bitch who had something to do with what had happened as surely as Rebecca was standing there in this sterile white corridor.

"Detective Devlin just called me."

"I thought you were making the final arrangements!" They had to get this done. Rebecca didn't know how much longer her son could hold up under this nightmare. If those two detectives kept digging, this could all blow up in their faces.

They knew about Stover.

Dear God . . . she and Jana were so close.

"I have made the arrangements. Everything is on track."

"All right. Good." Rebecca forced herself to calm. "What did Detective Devlin have to say this time?"

"She had a lot of questions about Phil. It sounds as if he was acting very strange. Saying all these odd things."

"Odd how?" The man was always odd. Rebecca couldn't stand him.

"Like how worried he is about me and how he just wants me to be able to move on with my life."

Rebecca shook her head. "I told you he was weird. He's always watching. Logan said the same thing. He is not normal. I don't know how you and your husband were friends with him so long without noticing."

"I suppose we always thought it was just his personality. You know, we all have our ways."

Yes, she knew very well what Jana meant by that statement. Rebecca ignored what was likely a jab at her. "As much as he watches everything, he probably saw what happened Sunday night. He could be a witness."

"If he had seen anything, he would have told me, and certainly he would have told the police."

"Whatever you say. I'll see you in a little while."

"Rebecca?"

"Yes?"

"Do you think we're making a mistake not telling all that we know? What if we're wrong? It could have been someone else."

Rebecca rolled her eyes. "You're the one who was married to the cop for all those years. How do you expect me to know if you can't be sure?"

That was the thing.

They only knew that *one* thing.

But one way or another they were going to find out the rest.

Rebecca stared at the screen of her cell phone long after the call had ended. Her heart ached at the beautiful image of sweet Leah there. The child had been her beloved and only grandchild no matter what that ridiculous test had said.

Their plan had to work. It was the only way to get justice. Jana had said so herself.

For the first time, Rebecca and Jana were united.

They both wanted the same thing.

Justice.

Revenge.

34

12:05 p.m.

Devlin Residence
Twenty-First Avenue South
Birmingham

Luke was getting worried. Kerri should be home by now. Or at least she should have called him with an update.

He called her cell again.

Straight to voice mail.

Had her battery died?

He wasn't waiting any longer. Pulling on his jacket, he headed for the side door. Grabbed his keys from the counter on the way. Maybe he'd run into her on the way to Chablis Way. Kerri would fuss at him for driving. He would remind her that if she'd answered his calls, he wouldn't have had to go looking for her.

Just like an old married couple.

The thought made his chest feel full with something warm.

He needed to tell her about the call from Sadie. He and Kerri were going to take that bastard O'Grady down for what he'd done.

Based on what Shelly had told him and what Sadie had learned, it was a fair assumption that Allison Boothe had been telling the truth.

She hadn't cheated on her husband. She'd likely been drugged and raped.

Fury blazed inside him all over again. Leah Boothe could be O'Grady's biological child. Had the bastard known? Christ. Had Boothe known? Either way, it was motive.

As he backed from the driveway, his cell vibrated. He answered without taking his eyes off the street. "It's about time."

"You been waiting for my call, pretty boy?"

O'Grady.

Fury tightened Luke's jaw. He thought of what this son of a bitch had done to all those wives—to Allison. What he had tried to do to Shelly. Luke forced himself to relax. "What's up, LT?"

Play the game, he told himself. *Just like old times. Lure him in.* When he got his hands on the son of a bitch . . .

Luke stopped himself. As much as he wanted to kill the bastard, he couldn't do that. This had to be done the right way.

"I was thinking we needed to clear the air," O'Grady announced. "You know, put this thing between us to bed once and for all. We've known each other a long time, Falco. Saved each other's asses more than once. We should get this done. Move on."

"You're right." Luke braked to a stop at an intersection. "Name the place and time."

"Why not right now? I can be at the cabin in twenty minutes. We can meet there. I'll call Dog and have him join us. We're all in this together, after all."

"I'll be there." Luke ended the call and tried Kerri again.

"Hey," she said, answering on the first ring. "I was just about to call you back. I left my phone in the car while I was talking to Crandall."

"What'd he have to say?" Luke rolled away from the intersection. The more distance he put behind him before he told her where he was going, the better.

"I'm getting the impression the guy is obsessed with Jana Scott. He went on and on about how it was past time she was able to move on with her life. Wanted to know why we hadn't arrested Boothe. This was more than mere neighborly concern. He seemed annoyed that we hadn't closed the case yet. There was an urgency to his tone. Very strange."

"I'll try the stepdaughter again. Maybe there's something up with this guy."

"I'm leaning in that direction. He may not be the reliable witness we thought he was. He may be hiding important information or using the situation as an opportunity to get closer to Scott. If that's the case, Jana Scott needs to protect herself."

A car sped through the red light, earning a sharp honk from the driver in front of Luke. He winced.

"Where are you?"

"I was coming to check on you, since you hadn't answered my calls."

"I'm on my way home now, so you should turn around and go right back there yourself. Driving is still off limits."

"I'll be back in a few. O'Grady wants to talk. Dog will be there too."

"What're you doing, Falco?"

Falco, not Luke. "I need to do this, Kerri. Remember that trust we talked about. I need you to trust me right now. I've got this."

"Give me the location, and I'll meet you there. Two against one isn't very good odds."

"You're breaking up. I'll call you when this is done. Call Sadie. She has an update on O'Grady you need to know about."

He ended the call. Told himself he'd done the right thing. O'Grady wasn't getting away with what he'd done. Jesus Christ, he could only imagine what Boothe had felt when he'd learned about this, and he must have. Maybe his mother was the woman who'd pretended to be a cop or a PI and interviewed those other wives.

It all fit.

Maybe O'Grady had been the one to contract Stover. He could have had any one of his minions do it. Carla Brown, anyone.

Whatever had happened, both O'Grady and Boothe were eyeball deep in this shit.

Luke intended to find the truth. All of it. About this case and about his past.

Moving on with his life for real was never going to happen until he got this behind him once and for all. He needed to know what had happened that night. He needed to make it right. Mina had a kid. She had parents. They deserved to know the truth about what had happened to her. And how bravely she'd supported the police before her death.

He thought of his own kid, and his gut clenched. He'd screwed up everything he touched for years. It was time to start making things right.

The Cabin
Oak Mountain State Park
Birmingham, 12:40 p.m.

Dog's car was parked in the drive, but there was no sign of O'Grady's. Luke parked and got out. He surveyed the area. Quiet, as always.

The last time he'd shown up here, he'd had the crap kicked out of him.

Not going to happen this time. He was ready.

He rested his right hand on the grip of the weapon at the small of his back and moved toward the door. He didn't have to see O'Grady or his car to know he would be watching—if he was here. Hell, for all Luke knew, he could have hidden his car, or maybe he'd come with Dog. The bastard never took chances. He hadn't survived this long in the underworld without being careful.

Luke rapped on the door and stood to the side.

The door swung inward and Dog appeared. "Come on in."

Luke walked inside, shut the door behind him, keeping his back to the wall. "Where's O'Grady?"

"Haven't seen him yet."

This didn't feel right.

"I'm not feeling good about this," Luke said, surveying the room. "I don't know what he's up to, but it ain't good." It never was.

"He said he was on his way," Dog allowed. "We should give him some time."

Luke assessed his old friend. Was he really a friend? They knew most of each other's secrets. Had covered each other's backs. But that was a different time and place.

They didn't even know each other anymore.

"Do you know what he did to the wives?" Luke asked, hoping like hell the answer was no.

Dog shot him a look over the top of his sporty sunglasses. "What the hell are you talking about?"

"All those times when he was supposedly"—Luke added air quotes to the word—"watching out for the little women for us, he was drugging them and raping them. He tried to do it to Shelly."

Dog's face turned to rock. "You can prove that?"

Luke nodded. "Damn straight." Sadie Cross had statements from several wives.

"I think we've given him enough time," Dog said, his words tight, clipped. "Let's find that motherfucker."

Luke walked out the door, Dog behind him, and stopped in his tracks.

Kerri stood between his Charger and Dog's hot rod, weapon drawn. "Everything good with you two?"

Luke grinned. "It's all good. You might want to put that gun away."

She glanced at Dog, then back to Luke. "Where's O'Grady? I thought he was the host of this party."

"How the hell did you find this place?" Dog demanded. He shot a look at Luke.

Luke shrugged.

"I have my ways." She holstered her weapon. "I brought a friend."

Sadie Cross, tucking her own weapon away, stepped out of the tree line.

"After what she told me about O'Grady," Kerri said, "I thought you two might need some backup."

"Since he didn't show up," Luke explained, "we were about to hunt him down."

"Sounds good to me," Kerri said, letting him know he wasn't getting out of here without her.

Cross moved up beside her. "I'm in."

Dog shot her a look. "Who the hell are you?"

Sadie laughed. "I can be your worst nightmare, Detective Durham, a.k.a. Dog. Or I can be your best friend."

"What the fuck, Falco?" Dog glared at him. "Did you invite anyone else?"

"Don't worry," Luke assured him. "You can trust these two."

Kerri withdrew her cell, checked the screen. She glanced at Luke. "It's Oden."

He followed her to the other side of his Charger, where she took the call, putting it on speaker so he could hear.

"Detective, this is Candace Oden."

"You got my message." Kerri leaned against the passenger-side door.

"I'm sorry I've been avoiding you."

"Are you all right, Candace?"

Kerri was right to ask; the tension was thick in the woman's voice. Luke glanced over at Dog and Sadie. They were still talking, and neither had drawn a weapon. Knowing those two, he was a little surprised.

"I need to tell you the truth."

The comment drew Luke's attention back to the call.

Kerri said, "I'm listening."

"I'm at my mother's. I've only been going by the house for mail and clothes. Since Allison and Leah died, I've waffled between outrage and fear. Outrage because Logan allowed this thing to go too far . . . and fear for my life."

Kerri exchanged a look with Luke.

"I can have you protected, Candace. Giving me the details of what you know is the best way to get the situation under control and to get you protected."

Silence echoed across the line.

"When the news about Leah's DNA came out, Allison and Logan almost fell apart. It took some time for them to get past the shock and hurt." She exhaled a big breath.

"Eventually, Logan thought he had the whole mess figured out. He said he had a good idea who had done this to Allison—to all of them. He . . . he wanted me to help him prove it."

"How did he plan to prove his theory?" Kerri's gaze landed on Luke's once more, and he knew exactly what she was thinking: this was the smoking gun they had been looking for.

Son of a bitch!

"He set up a meeting with the man he suspected at a local pub. I was to go and sit at the bar. Place an order and hang out until he and the man finished their conversation. When they left, it was my job to get the guy's beer glass before the waiter had time to take it from the table. He hoped enough saliva or whatever could be taken from the glass and used for analysis."

"The two of you pulled this off?" Kerri looked impressed.

Luke was as well, though he already knew what was coming.

"We did. I put the glass in a large plastic baggie like Logan asked. We met up afterward, and I turned it over to him. The next week,

Allison thanked me over and over and told me they had the evidence they needed."

"Did she mention a name?"

"She didn't. She said it was better if I didn't know the details from that point forward. All I know is, she said the man drugged and raped her."

Another long look passed between Kerri and Luke. And there it was. They even had an objective witness. Boothe surely had the report, which was solid evidence—at least to the fact that O'Grady had been messing around with the wives.

"Can you describe the man Logan met at the bar?" Kerri asked.

"Tall, broad shouldered. Gray hair. I'm thinking he's in his late fifties. He looked . . . I don't know. Kind of cocky. You know, he had that swagger."

Definitely Patrick O'Grady.

"Thank you, Candace. This information may be crucial to our investigation. You stay put at your mother's, and I'll call you back soon." Kerri ended the call. "We've got him."

"All we have to do is find him." Luke gritted his teeth. The sooner, the better.

35

2:00 p.m.

Irondale Mobile Home Park
Irondale

"I knew from the time Allison was a baby that she was special," the woman said. "She was a miracle. Raymond and I were certain we would never have children. Suddenly, we were expecting, and our precious girl was born."

Paddy blinked, tried to clear his vision. Raymond? Allison? The haze cleared, and he realized it was Jana Scott speaking to him. Assistant Chief Raymond Scott's wife. Shit. *Allison.*

"Allison was always so kind to everyone. She believed the best in all." Scott paused in front of him, and he stared up at her. Couldn't get his bearings. "I was that way to a degree when I was younger," she went on. "But all those years married to a cop forced me to recognize that you couldn't go through life wearing rose-colored glasses." She sighed. "That was my biggest mistake. Not teaching my daughter to be more suspicious and to always look for the worst even the nicest people could keep hidden from view."

What the hell was she doing? Paddy stared down at himself. He was duct-taped to a goddamned chair. The stuff had him wrapped up like a fucking mummy. His torso was secured to the back of the chair. She'd bound his hands to the back legs of the chair. His ankles and shins were secured in the same way, one on each side. He licked his lips, realized his mouth wasn't covered.

"What the hell are you doing?" His voice sounded wonky. Damn. What the hell had they drugged him with?

Wait, wait. Now he remembered. Scott had shown up here to ask about her son-in-law. Dumb fucker. They'd talked and had a beer. They'd even reminisced about Ray and the good old days. Yeah. Yeah. He remembered now.

"Should I tase him? That roofie seems to be wearing off."

Paddy shook his head. Tried to draw the other woman—the woman who'd just spoken—into focus. "Who the hell are you?" he demanded.

What the fuck was happening?

"I don't think that's necessary, Rebecca. We want him conscious and capable of responding."

The other woman nodded. "You're right. We want him to feel the pain."

He drew in a ragged breath. Drool slid from the side of his mouth. "You don't know what you're doing," he said, trying to be calm and to speak in a normal voice. Wasn't possible. His words were slurred and too slow.

"We know exactly what we're doing, Patrick," Scott said. "We know what you did. You do not deserve to carry the badge that was bestowed upon you. Raymond would have called you a real piece of shit."

"I swear to God," he mumbled, licking the spittle from his chin. "I have no idea what you're talking about." He tried to look around, but the two were right in his face. "Where the hell are we?" He stretched his neck to try to see.

"Why, we're in your cheap little tin box of a home. Don't you recognize it?"

These two had gone over the edge for sure. Damn. He shook his head again. He felt like he was in some crazy-ass movie. "I know you're going through hell right now, Jana, but you need to cut me loose so we can work this out. I won't press charges."

The need to vomit rushed into his throat. He swallowed it back, almost gagged.

"You're going to make a statement," she said, "and my friend here is going to record it. If you do exactly as we say and behave yourself, we won't resort to torture. If you resist, you will be sorry. I'm certain you can imagine the sort of measures I have in mind."

He made a choked sound of disbelief. Now he was just pissed. "You cut me loose, and we'll pretend none of this happened." These two were fucking nuts.

The one named Rebecca made a harrumphing sound. "Like that's going to happen." She glowered at him. "We know what you did. My son knows what you did. He confronted you, didn't he?"

Logan Boothe's mother. He should have known.

"You don't know anything!" he snarled. "But I know what your son did. *All* the things he did. He came to me threatening blackmail. Do you understand the seriousness of what I'm saying? *Blackmail.*"

Crazy bitches. They were all the same.

Rebecca laughed. "Oh, we know all the things *you* did to all those wives, *Paddy.*"

"We know," Jana reiterated, "because we tracked them down and bothered to ask. They're all going to testify against you. So, you have two options: do as we say, or suffer the consequences."

Paddy laughed. "If you had any proof, I'd be in an interview room right now being grilled by the chief. You ain't got shit except what that idiot Boothe told you."

"Let me tase him one more time," Rebecca pleaded.

He grunted. Wished he could wipe his mouth. "Jana," he growled, "you understand what kidnapping is. You're aware of the laws you've already broken. Let me go, and we'll forget all about this. Or call it in. If you think I'm such a monster, call it in now."

"No," Rebecca declared. "Jana explained why we have to do things this way. How cops like you sometimes get away with your wrongdoing because other cops protect you. We decided to take care of this ourselves rather than risk you getting off on some technicality. Or by blaming my son."

"I'm afraid she's right," Jana agreed. "There's only one way to ensure true justice, and this is it."

"You don't know who you're fucking with," he warned. When he got loose, he was going to . . . the smiles on their faces derailed his train of thought. He tried to think. To figure out what he'd missed.

Jana explained, "I know exactly who you are. And I know what you are. You give your statement—your whole statement—regarding all that you've done to all those women over the years, including my daughter and granddaughter, and you will live to have that interview with the chief. If not, you're going to have a little accident. The sort men like you make happen when you need to clear an obstacle or cover up a problem."

Rebecca pointed to the stove only a few feet away. His travel trailer's living space was only one small room. There was a tiny bath and a separate sleeping area, but nothing else. He liked it that way. Uncomplicated.

That dumb bastard Boothe had to go and complicate everything. Just because he'd found out his sick kid wasn't biologically his. The fool had gotten what he deserved.

"You see that skillet on the stove?" Rebecca said, drawing his attention back to her. "You were making lunch, and the grease from the bologna you were frying got too hot. The next thing you knew, that hand sanitizer you keep on the counter ignited." She shrugged. "Stuff's like gasoline. You'll be dead from the smoke inhalation before your neighbors even realize there's a fire." She pointed upward then. "You see, we removed the batteries from your smoke detector. Lots of people do that when the batteries get low. No reason anyone should hear a sound. Unless of course you scream, but we've got tape for that."

"A good fire marshal will figure out you were restrained," Jana pointed out, "but the whole incident will be chalked up to your history of taking down all those big drug dealers. Perfectly believable."

They were serious. His heart pounded so hard in his chest he could hardly catch a breath. This had gone way too far. "I did not kill your daughter or your granddaughter," he roared. "Now cut me loose!" He tried rocking the chair, but it wouldn't budge.

"Rebecca was actually the one to think of that," Jana said. "We attached the chair legs to two-by-fours and then screwed those two-by-fours to the floor beneath where you're sitting. The chair won't be moving."

"Enough talk," Rebecca said. "Let's finish this."

"Your son," Paddy shouted at Rebecca, "is the one who attempted blackmail." He laughed. "Who was going to believe him over me? He was pissing in the wind. And so are you. Allison couldn't prove I drugged her. So what if she got pregnant. You got a grandkid out of it, didn't you? As for those other bitches, they're just a bunch of lonely housewives making up shit about their husbands' commander. All I did was take a little something for all my trouble trying to keep them happy. They can't prove any of it. You can't prove one damned thing."

"Did you get that, Rebecca?"

Boothe's mother slipped the cell phone out of her shirt pocket and checked the video. "I did."

Scott smiled. "Text it to me, will you? To that nice Detective Devlin as well."

For the first time, fear coiled in Paddy's gut. "You won't get away with this," he warned. "This was coercion."

Scott laughed. "Did you hear that, Rebecca? He's saying that two little old ladies forced him to confess."

Boothe howled with laughter, then stopped just as abruptly as she'd started. "May you rot in hell."

"Well said," Scott agreed.

Boothe walked to the stove and turned the largest burner to high. Then she placed the large plastic bottle of sanitizer they'd brought in a skillet on top of it. For good measure she added towels all around the stove top. Holy shit. The place would be in flames in no time.

"I didn't kill them," Paddy screamed to their retreating backs. "It wasn't me!"

Scott turned back to him. "What was it Raymond always said? Oh yes: 'They all swear they're innocent. Even when they're guilty as sin.'"

"I swear to you," he cried, "I didn't kill them."

Boothe was suddenly in front of him again with a strip of tape in her hand. He moved his head side to side. Struggled to prevent her from covering his mouth. Still, she managed. He screamed behind the tape. No one would ever hear him.

The acrid smell of smoke instantly filled his lungs.

The two hesitated at the door, and Scott said, "Don't worry, I'm calling the fire department." She smiled. "I hope it's not too late when they get here."

He closed his eyes and tried again to scream past the tape.

36

3:00 p.m.

Irondale Mobile Home Park
Irondale

"His car is here." Kerri glanced around the postage-stamp yard as she parked behind O'Grady's vehicle.

Luke tucked his cell into his pocket. "He's still not answering his phone."

Kerri's phone vibrated with an incoming message. She glanced at the screen. She didn't recognize the number of the sender. The accompanying video started to download.

"Let's go."

Luke's voice dragged her attention back to the moment. She shoved her phone into her hip pocket and climbed out of the vehicle. Durham parked next to Kerri's Wagoneer. He and Sadie got out and joined them in front of the small trailer that was home to O'Grady.

"Take the back," Luke said to Durham.

The other man nodded and headed that way. Sadie hustled around the other end of the trailer. Luke went straight for the front door.

He flattened against the wall next to it, weapon drawn. He banged on the door. "O'Grady, you in there?"

No response.

Kerri took the other side of the door, glanced around. There was a sound. She pressed her ear to the wall of the trailer. Not inside. In the distance. A faint wail. "Is that a siren?"

Luke nodded. "Sounds like it's getting closer." He banged on the door again. Harder this time. "O'Grady!"

The odor of smoke seeped from around the thin metal door. "Luke."

His gaze met hers. His nostrils flared. "Smoke. Shit!"

Luke tried the door. Locked. He drew back and threw his body weight against it. "O'Grady, you in there?"

The siren grew louder and louder. Kerri checked the closest window. Locked.

Luke slammed against the door again. This time it flew inward. He rushed inside. Kerri was right on his heels. Smoke was thick inside. She blinked to see through the haze. Spotted the source of the fire on the stove top.

She needed a fire extinguisher. Didn't see one. Keeping one arm curled around her face, she grabbed for the salt box on the counter. Slung the contents across the flames. Luke was struggling to get O'Grady free.

Sadie was suddenly next to her with a fire extinguisher.

Before Kerri could ask where she'd found it, Durham and Luke were rushing O'Grady out the door. He appeared to be strapped with duct tape to a chair sporting broken legs. The sound of the foam spewing from the fire extinguisher had her turning back to Sadie.

The flames were out, but the place was still filled with smoke. Kerri and Sadie hurried outside. Kerri surveyed the area. No close neighbor to worry about. She coughed so hard she lost her breath. Sadie did the same.

The fire department arrived, and firefighters poured across the yard. Kerri relaxed a fraction and looked for Luke. He and Durham had cut O'Grady loose from the chair.

The shriek of an ambulance pierced the air as the green-and-white emergency vehicle appeared. The brakes squealed as it came to a halt at the curb.

She walked toward Luke as the EMTs moved O'Grady to a stretcher and prepared him for transport.

He was still alive.

Now they knew why he hadn't shown up for his meeting at the cabin.

It appeared O'Grady had finally stepped on the wrong toes. Maybe someone had learned about the IA investigation and had decided he knew too much to risk him cutting a deal.

Which he would probably do. "Bastard." Kerri's phone vibrated, reminding her of the message she had received. She opened the video and hit play.

Patrick O'Grady, bound to the chair, was ranting at someone.

"What the hell?" Kerri held the phone closer to her ear to hear the audio.

Who was going to believe him over me?

She played the video again. It was a confession. O'Grady's confession.

Luke needed to hear this.

University of Alabama Hospital
Sixth Avenue South
Birmingham, 5:00 p.m.

Lieutenant Brooks exited the ER's double doors.

Kerri, Luke, Sadie, and Durham all launched to their feet. They'd been waiting for nearly an hour. Brooks had insisted on taking O'Grady's statement, since he was the only one not personally involved. He'd called in the chief as well.

The video Kerri had received had been taken as evidence. Rebecca Boothe and Jana Scott had known about O'Grady and what he had done to Allison. They were the ones who had questioned the other wives. The two had been working to build an irrefutable case against him, and then the fire that had taken Leah's and Allison's lives had happened. Their quest had taken on a new urgency, ending in a coerced confession.

Units had been dispatched to Rebecca Boothe's and Jana Scott's addresses, but no one was home at either location. There was an APB out for the two. O'Grady had suffered some degree of smoke inhalation, but he'd survived. Scott and Boothe hadn't intended to kill him; otherwise, they wouldn't have called the fire department. The dispatcher confirmed a female had made the call. The two had gotten what they wanted—a confession—and they'd given O'Grady a taste of how it felt to die in a fire. Bastard.

"What did he say?" Luke demanded when Brooks didn't immediately speak.

One way or another they intended to make sure he didn't get away with all he had done.

"He admits to having drugged and raped a number of the wives of his crew members over the years. As for the rest, he says you're lying." Brooks directed this at Durham. "And that the two of you"—he turned to Kerri and Luke—"are just plain crazy."

Kerri rolled her eyes. "Of course he would say that."

Luke muttered a curse. "Please tell me you're not buying this bullshit story."

"I am not buying his story because Internal Affairs has already found two other former members of O'Grady's unit who have given statements. One of the sources claims to have been with him when he murdered Mina Kozlov. It seems she wanted out of the deal she'd made with O'Grady, and he wasn't happy about it. I don't have any other details at this time. I'm only sharing what little I have with you," he said to Luke, "because I'm aware of his past claims regarding her death. I can"—he surveyed the four of them—"say without reservation that O'Grady is going down."

The rush of relief made Kerri's knees weak. "Thank God." She wanted the SOB to spend the rest of his days in prison for all he'd done, including allowing Luke to believe all this time that he'd been involved in Mina's death.

"He's not owning the murders of Allison and Leah Boothe," Luke guessed.

"He insists you have the wrong man on that one."

"He admitted that Boothe had tried to blackmail him," Kerri argued. As much as she wanted him to go down for all of it—including the murders of Allison and Leah—she had begun to have her doubts after interviewing Stover. O'Grady was far too smart to go that route. Unless he'd been trying to set Boothe up. Which was possible.

Damn it.

"He did," Brooks agreed. "But he insists he wasn't worried that anyone would believe Boothe over him. He was confident he could claim Boothe was just a disgruntled former member of his crew. A guy with a vendetta."

"We need to talk to Boothe." Luke met her gaze. "Before he hears about this from his momma."

"If he hasn't already," Kerri said, worried.

"I put a second detail on his room as soon as I heard about O'Grady," Brooks said. "I'm certain she hasn't been able to get to him yet. I want to hear what you learn from him before anyone else." He turned to Sadie and Durham. "The two of you can go for now. I'm sure there will be more questions later."

Brooks headed back into the ER. He and the chief would be monitoring O'Grady for the time being.

"Thanks for backing me up," Luke said to Durham as they headed toward the main lobby.

Durham shrugged. "I should have done it a long time ago. Sometimes loyalty is overrated." He gave Luke a fist bump. "I'm out of here." He glanced at Sadie. "You want a ride home?"

"Sure."

They said their goodbyes, and Kerri and Luke headed for the elevators.

They were both too exhausted and frustrated to talk as they rode the elevator to Boothe's floor.

At his room, the uniforms outside his door confirmed that no one had been near the patient except the nurse on duty.

When Kerri entered the room, Boothe didn't bother glancing her way. He'd likely heard their voices in the corridor. She imagined he had wondered where his mother was all afternoon.

"I thought you'd want to know," Luke said, "your mother is a fugitive."

Boothe's gaze shot to Luke. "What?"

"She coerced a confession out of Lieutenant O'Grady," Kerri explained. "She videoed his confession and left him all tied up at his place."

"Don't forget about the fire," Luke reminded her. To Boothe he said, "She set the place on fire before she left."

Boothe looked from Luke to Kerri, his eyes wide with worry. "What're you talking about?"

Kerri shook her head. "I just don't get it. Why didn't you tell us about the blackmail scheme? That would have put O'Grady at the top of our suspect list."

"I know how you feel, man," Luke allowed. "He tried to do the same thing to my ex. You had every right to go into a psycho rage and do all sorts of stuff. The bastard deserved it."

"Where is my mother?"

"What I don't get," Kerri said to Luke, ignoring Boothe's question, "is why did he protect O'Grady?" She stared directly at Boothe then.

"Why didn't you tell us he did this, and then we could've protected your mother? It should never have gone this far."

He was growing frantic now. "Just tell me she's okay. She didn't mean to hurt anyone."

Luke leaned down, braced his forearms on the bed rail. "I think even a really good lawyer will have trouble convincing a jury of that one, considering that fire. This is looking really bad for her and for you, considering all that Stover told us."

"No." Boothe turned to Kerri, hoping for sympathy. "She didn't understand the kind of person she was dealing with. When she finally told me, I tried to fix it." He closed his eyes. "But Stover wouldn't listen."

Kerri looked from Luke to Boothe. "Your mother hired Stover to paint your house."

"She was angry. She'd done so much for us. When Allison refused to budge about her mother doing the same thing, Mom felt betrayed. Like her home was disposable and Allison's mom's wasn't. I tried to explain, but she wouldn't listen."

"*She* meaning your mom," Kerri stated for clarification.

Boothe nodded. "She didn't tell me what she'd done until Sunday evening. I guess she got worried when I told her Allison and I weren't going out for a date night. By the time she told me, she was frantic. I told her I'd fix it. She gave me this guy Stover's number. I tried to reason with him, but he wouldn't listen. I knew I had to do something, so I told Allison to take Leah and go to Candace's house while I took care of the situation."

"Except Candace wasn't home," Kerri said, feeling sick to her stomach.

Boothe squeezed his eyes shut. A sob burst from him, shook the bed. "I should've made sure—" His voice caught. "Oh God, I should have made sure they left the house. I let this happen."

Kerri didn't see the point in making him suffer more. "After Stover's friends beat the crap out of you, they didn't go to your house, Boothe. They left. Went to party with a friend. We confirmed their alibi. The fire wasn't because your mother hired Stover."

He looked from Kerri to Luke and back, his face damp with his tears. "Then who? Who killed my wife and little girl?"

37

6:00 p.m.

Crandall Residence
Chablis Way
Birmingham

Jana had never been more thankful for Phil. He had been kind enough to give them refuge. The police had already been to his house looking for her and Rebecca. They likely wouldn't be back for a while.

She stared out the window at the home that had been such a happy place for so many years. She and Raymond had raised their sweet Allison there. Allison had been raising her beautiful little Leah there too.

The idea of her granddaughter growing up in the same home as her mother had made Jana tremendously happy.

But it was all gone now.

Raymond. Allison. Leah.

She was all alone.

She had hoped that showing the world what Patrick O'Grady was would give her some sense of relief. But it had not. What she felt was empty. Lost. Alone.

On top of that, now she was a fugitive. She couldn't go back home. She'd managed to take Raymond's old fishing truck from the garage before the APB had been issued. They wouldn't be looking for his truck.

God, how she wished Raymond were here. He would know exactly how to handle this.

But he wasn't.

She'd backed the truck into Candace's driveway to avoid anyone passing by seeing the license plate. It was expired but could still be traced back to her.

"Are you certain I can't make you a nice cup of tea?"

Jana pushed away the worries and turned to their host. With monumental effort she propped a smile into place. "You're right. Tea would be wonderful."

Phil turned to the sofa, where Rebecca sat seemingly in a coma. "Rebecca?"

When she didn't answer or look up, Jana said, "Rebecca, would you like tea?"

The other woman whipped her gaze toward Jana. "What?"

"Tea," Jana repeated. "Would you like tea or coffee?"

Rebecca shot to her feet. "No. No. I'd like to use the restroom."

Phil gave her a nod. "There's one at the top of the stairs." He pointed upward, then down. "One downstairs as well."

Like their own family home, Phil's was a trilevel. It had been perfect for raising a family.

"Thank you." Rebecca bolted toward the stairs and hurried upward.

"Is it something I said?"

Jana turned to Phil. "I'm sure it's not. Rebecca is worried about her son." Jana hugged her arms around herself. "I suppose I'm a bit numb. Not feeling much of anything at this point. I've already lost everything. Rebecca is grieving as well, but she still has her son to worry about in all this."

"We all handle things differently," he offered in that kind way he had. "Come along into the kitchen, and we'll start that tea."

He draped an arm over her shoulders and guided her that way. The move startled her a little, but she pushed the feeling away. Phil was a good friend. Those awkward moments the other night had been the first and only time he'd ever been anything but a dear, dear friend to her and her family.

She should be ashamed of herself for having reacted so badly.

While he filled the kettle and placed it on the stove, Jana was drawn to the window once more. The one over his kitchen sink offered a perfect view into the backyard, where the swing set stood. Memories of Leah's happy laughter whispered through Jana's mind. The girl had loved that swing. It was the same one Allison had had as a child. So many memories.

"I was thinking," Phil said as he moved to her side, "when this painful business is cleared up, we should get away." He looked at her with sad eyes. "You need time to recover, Jana. To heal. I've been so worried about you. You've always put everyone ahead of yourself."

She struggled to keep a semblance of a smile in place. Her mind kept going back to the "we should get away." Her chest tightened, suffocatingly so.

Was she overreacting again?

"You're right," she agreed, her voice a little more brittle than she'd intended. "I should take some time away."

The kettle started to whistle, softly at first and then that high-pitched, shrill sound. He moved back to the stove to attend to the business of making tea.

"I'll find Rebecca and have her join us."

Jana didn't draw a deep breath until she was clear of the kitchen. She glanced around the living room. No Rebecca. Checked the front porch. Not there either. Where on earth was she?

Her gaze shifted upward. Was she stalling in the bathroom to call and check on Logan? Didn't she realize the police would be monitoring his calls?

"Good God," Jana muttered as she hurried up the stairs.

The bathroom was empty.

There were two other doors in the hall. The first was a small, neat bedroom. No Rebecca. Her pulse thumping with equal measures of frustration and anxiety, she moved on to the final door. She glanced back toward the stairs. This was likely Phil's room. She doubted he would appreciate the intrusion.

Dear God, Rebecca was the most inconsiderate, thoughtless person . . .

Jana stood in the doorway, her thought trailing off. Rebecca was in the room, but it wasn't a bedroom. *But it is*, she argued with herself. There was a large four-poster bed. A dresser and night table. But it was more like some sort of shrine.

"What in the world?" The words fumbled out of Jana on a stilted breath.

Rebecca turned to Jana, eyes wide with shock. Her head moved side to side. "I told you he was weird."

Jana wandered deeper into the room. This wasn't just weird . . . this was bizarre.

There were photos of children. A young boy, eight or nine perhaps, and a little girl. Younger than Leah. Jana moved closer, her heart pounding. The little girl was *her*.

"There are dozens of pictures of you," Rebecca said. She gestured to another wall. "It's like he's been watching you and taking pictures you didn't know about for years."

Jana moved to the other wall. Rebecca was right. Dozens upon dozens of candid shots of her working in the yard. Playing with Leah. Staring out over the lake.

"Have a look at this."

Jana's attention settled on the photo Rebecca referred to. It was Raymond on his boat. Fishing. A smile tugged at her lips. He wore that ancient vest that held his favorite lures and looked as if it should have been tossed out ages ago. A large black *X* had been drawn across the photo.

Her heart stalled.

"Sweet Jesus."

Jana looked up at those words to find Rebecca near the corner, staring at the wall.

Her feet and legs moving woodenly, she somehow reached the other woman's side. There were more big black *X*s. One across a photo of Allison and one on a shot of Leah.

The shattered pieces of her already broken heart cried out in misery. No. Please, God, no. This couldn't be possible.

"Did you see the one of us together as kids?"

Rebecca yelped. Jana's voice had deserted her. She faced the man standing in the doorway across the room. "What did you do, Phil?"

"It took me years to find you. Twenty-three to be exact."

He entered the room. She and Rebecca moved closer together.

"This is the photo that led me to you." He tapped a photo and stared at her, as if he expected her to come and have a look.

She moved toward him, her body feeling as if it were unhinged from her brain.

"You were on a local Birmingham morning show," he said proudly. "Back when you were so active in supporting foster children."

Jana stared at the photo, which was actually a screenshot from one of her television appearances. She had been a foster child. She understood the trials and difficulty of that world. She'd spent years working to help others. She still donated heavily to the effort.

"I couldn't believe it when I saw you. The show was picked up by several networks, which is how I saw it in San Antonio. I knew it was you. You looked exactly like her."

Jana blinked the haze of disbelief away. "Like who?"

He grinned. "Our mother, of course. From that moment"—he tapped the photo taped to the wall—"I went through more than you can possibly imagine to get to you." He gave her a nod. "Believe me, it wasn't easy to clear that path. But here we are."

"I'm sorry." She struggled to keep her voice steady. Her mind was whirling madly with questions and fears. What had this man done? "I didn't realize I had any living relatives."

Was he claiming to be her brother?

Her stomach knotted. Bile rose in her throat.

"Hilary—that's your real name. Hilary Blanchett." His lips widened into that hideous grin again. "I'm Hudson. I was six when you were born."

"I was told my name was Jana Dawson." This couldn't be true.

"They lied to you. They lied about everything." Fury flashed in his eyes. "They said I was obsessed with you, that I might hurt you. I would never have hurt you. They were going to send me away."

The ability to breathe failed her. "Who?"

"Our parents." He shook his head adamantly. "They were going to send me away from you, but I took care of the situation. Like I always have." A frown marred his brow. "But I didn't move fast enough, and the state sent me away. They never wanted you to know about me." He searched her face. "Can you imagine? All I wanted was to take care of you, and they stole you from me." He drew in a deep breath. "They kept me in that place until I was twenty-five." His grin returned. "But I found you anyway. That's all that matters."

Too stunned to move, Jana moistened her lips and forced the words from her mouth. "I'm so glad you found me."

"So am I." He hugged her close. "We've missed so much."

Jana tried not to stiffen. Over his shoulder she stared at Rebecca, who stood in that same corner staring at them. Was she in shock?

Before Jana could say anything, Phil drew back. "But we have each other now. There's no one left in the way. The future is ours."

"In the way?" she managed to say as something dark and immensely painful swelled inside her. No. No. No. He couldn't mean . . .

"Taking care of my wife and your husband"—he made a face—"was easy." He pursed his lips and nodded. "Allison and Leah were more complicated. But it was for the best; the poor child had already suffered too much. I knew when she died, poor Allison would be devastated. Why not save her the pain?"

The floor beneath Jana shifted. "The fire." Those were the only two words that would cross her lips. Every fiber of her being screamed in agony.

"Allison told me all about it. She and Leah were supposed to go to Candace's house and stay until it was over, but Candace wasn't home." He smiled. "So they came to me. The timing was perfect. The opportunity too easy to pass up."

Jana closed her eyes for a second to stop the room from spinning. "I don't understand."

"They were taking too big a toll on you, Jana. It was all too painful. What I did was for the best. For everyone, really."

"What did you do?" The deep, guttural sound of her voice made him flinch.

"We had tea," he said, looking taken aback by her tone, or maybe the rage burning her face. "I added a little something to the tea to make them rest. Once they were resting, I carried them one at a time to the house and tucked them into bed. Then I did what those hired thugs were supposed to do." He held up a finger. "But first I added a little touch I thought would be useful. I remember Raymond talking about how these lowlifes like *canceling* each other, so I added the X to make it look as if someone Logan had crossed did the deed. It was really quite simple and painless."

The scream came from deep inside her.

More screaming joined the primal sound.

Jana was certain she would never stop screaming.

38

7:45 p.m.

Chablis Way
Birmingham

Kerri wasn't sure she could go home until they found Jana Scott and Rebecca Boothe. What they had done was wrong, but their motives had been overwhelming. Kerri would have done the same thing. In a heartbeat.

She and Luke had decided to take another swing through the neighborhood. Kerri was certain Crandall would be more than happy to protect Jana. He was probably hiding her right now, despite his claims that he hadn't heard from her.

They parked on the street between Crandall's house and the Boothe home. The house was dark. Dark and silent. It was possible he wasn't home. Frustration zoomed through Kerri. He might have left with them. Hoping to get them out of the city.

One glance toward the Boothe home, and Kerri's gut clenched. They had to find the rest of this story. Stover's people hadn't started the fire. O'Grady swore it wasn't him.

It damned sure hadn't started itself.

"I'll try Crandall's number again," Kerri said, reaching for her cell.

"Hold up." Luke put his hand on her arm. "Let's get a closer look before we give him a heads-up that we're here."

Moving quietly, they exited her Wagoneer and made their way across the yard. Kerri climbed the porch steps while Luke headed around the house to check out the back. Once on the porch, she took a long, slow look around and then from window to window. The house was dark inside. She turned around to survey the front yard once more. Oden's car wasn't in the driveway, but there was an older pickup parked there.

Kerri waited for word from Luke.

She didn't breathe easy until he was on the porch with her once more.

"His car is in the garage. No lights anywhere that I can see in the house."

"I say we knock," Kerri suggested. "If we don't get an answer, we're going in." She thought of the way O'Grady had been bound and his claims of how Jana Scott and Rebecca Boothe had tortured him. "I figure we have exigent circumstances. Maybe Scott and Boothe are holding him hostage too."

"I'm on that same wavelength," Luke agreed. "Those two are probably pretty desperate about now."

More likely Crandall had offered to aid and abet, but it was as good an excuse as any to bust into the place without a warrant.

They took positions on either side of the door. Luke pounded once, twice.

"Mr. Crandall," Kerri shouted, "it's Detective Devlin. Can you open the door, please?"

No answer. She and Luke exchanged a glance. He raised his fist to pound again, but a scream from inside stopped him.

Female.

The hair on the back of Kerri's neck stood on end.

Luke rammed the door with his full body weight. Then again. On the third time it burst inward.

They instinctively spread out in different directions. Weapons drawn. Lights still out for cover.

"Oh God, please help me!"

The desperate plea came from upstairs.

Luke stepped directly in front of Kerri. She knew the move. He wanted to protect her. They lunged quickly but cautiously up the stairs.

Another cry for help.

Farther down the hall. On the left.

Luke pushed through the partially open door.

Kerri slid in right behind him. Something on the floor caused her to stumble.

"Nobody move," Luke ordered. "I'm turning on the light."

The overhead light came on.

Jana Scott stood in the middle of the room, her clothes splattered with blood. Hanging from her right hand was what looked like the upper half of a wooden post from a bed. A quick survey of the bed in the room confirmed a post was missing. Rebecca Boothe was tied to another post on the right side of the headboard. Her clothes, too, were bloodied, but it was difficult to tell if it was her own or someone else's.

On the floor, where Kerri had stumbled, was Phileas Crandall. His head was battered so badly he was hardly recognizable.

Kerri looked to the woman holding the bedpost. "Mrs. Scott," she said quietly, "are you injured?"

She stared at Kerri but said nothing. Kerri eased closer, carefully took the post from her hand, and placed it on the floor.

Luke checked Crandall's pulse. Shook his head.

While he called it in, Kerri ushered Mrs. Scott to the foot of the bed and sat her down. "Are you injured?" she repeated.

Scott looked at Kerri then. Her face was scratched. Wads of hair were nearly pulled loose from her scalp. Skin was torn on her arms. But all that blood hadn't come from her. Kerri glanced from the post on the floor to the body.

Shit.

"He killed my babies," Scott whispered.

"He was going to kill us," Rebecca Boothe cried.

Kerri left Scott and moved to Boothe and began releasing the ropes securing her. "Are you injured, Mrs. Boothe?"

When Boothe's hand was free, she touched her throat. "He was choking me. He was going to kill me. Jana stopped him. Then he went after her. He knocked her down, and she didn't get back up. He . . . he tied me to the bed and started toward her." Sobs made her words nearly indistinguishable.

"But I was able to drag myself up," Scott said, without looking toward Kerri. "I grabbed the bedpost and swung it to stop him."

"You're both okay now," Kerri assured them. "We'll get you to the hospital."

Scott did look at her then. "He set the fire. Killed my babies."

Boothe started to howl in agony. "He killed them. He killed them."

39

9:00 p.m.

University of Alabama Hospital
Sixth Avenue South
Birmingham

Both Jana Scott and Rebecca Boothe were going to be okay. Bruises and scrapes were the extent of their physical injuries. The damage to their psyches was another story. Both had been admitted and were being kept overnight for observation.

Kerri had never felt so exhausted in her life. Luke looked ready to drop himself.

Chief Dubose was with Scott now. Logan Boothe had been notified that his mother was here and okay. Kerri and Luke had taken statements from the women. Her gaze lingered on the door to Scott's room. Boothe's was only a few doors down from where they stood in the sterile white corridor. The usual euphoria that went along with solving a case was oddly missing.

"You ready to go?"

She shifted her attention to her partner. "I guess we're done here."

He nodded. "Yeah."

There was nothing left for them to do.

Even as they moved toward the bank of elevators to go home, her mind kept hanging back . . . going over the detailed and matching statements the women had given.

Crandall had reveled in telling them how he'd used the "cancel" markings to make it appear as if Allison and Leah had been targeted to get at Logan. Crandall had watched and planned everything precisely, taking advantage of any and all opportunities. The photos and notes taped all over the walls of the room in his house confirmed their stories.

The one hitch Sunday night had been when Logan Boothe had come crawling into the yard. Crandall had been the one to knock him unconscious the second time. He'd come up behind him and attempted to finish what Stover's friends had started. And still, somehow, Boothe had survived to try to save his family.

Crandall had admitted this wasn't the first time he'd attempted to clear his path to Jana. He'd killed her husband, Raymond, too.

A true psychopath.

As perfectly as all the facts lined up without leaving a single noteworthy hole, Kerri couldn't get right with the ending. "Something's off."

There, she'd said it. She breathed easier with the burden off her chest.

"Which part?" Luke asked as they paused at the elevators. "The part where Crandall was beaten to a bloody pulp? Or the part where O'Grady says the two tortured him like trained interrogators?"

"All of the above. But the scene at the Crandall house . . ." She shrugged. "It felt staged."

"That's the impression I got too." He made one of those I-dunno faces. "But it's difficult to blame either one of them if they took advantage of the situation somehow."

This was true. "I'm not saying he wasn't planning to hurt them, but he went to a lot of trouble to find and get Scott all to himself just to try and kill her."

"If he went after Boothe, and Scott was trying to protect her, I can see how the situation escalated from there."

"Works for the final report," she agreed. "I'm thinking that since he admitted to marking Allison and Leah, he was the one to post those same *X*s on ours and Shelly's doors to keep the theme going."

"Makes sense."

Kerri bit the bullet and said the rest of what was on her mind. "I can see how a jury will be sympathetic. If Crandall was the killer, then he . . ."

"Got what he deserved?" Luke finished for her.

When had justice started being about getting what one deserved?

Luke abruptly frowned and reached for his cell. "Falco."

Either way, Crandall wouldn't be hurting anyone else.

Kerri hit the call button for the elevator. She suddenly remembered the cake for Tori. Thankfully the weather was cool enough that it should be fine, considering it had been in the Wagoneer for hours. Hopefully, she hadn't slung the box around too much.

The call ended, and Luke slid the phone into his pocket. "Lorna Collette is waiting for us down in the main lobby."

The elevator dinged, and the doors slid open. Kerri frowned. "The stepdaughter?"

"All the way from San Antonio."

"She can't know what's happened." Kerri stepped into the elevator, made the selection for the lobby.

Luke moved up beside her. "I don't think so. When she arrived at the airport, she tried calling me a couple of times. I just noticed the missed calls."

The elevator lurched into downward motion.

They had been a little preoccupied. "She called the department," Kerri guessed.

He nodded. "You got it."

"She came all this way. I'm guessing she has something to say."

Luke hummed his agreement.

The main lobby was empty save for a slender blonde dressed in a dark suit. She sat on the edge of a chair staring at her cell phone.

"I'm Detective Falco. You were asking for me."

She stood, glanced from Luke to Kerri and back. "You called me about Phileas Crandall."

"Why don't we sit?" Kerri suggested.

Collette lowered into her chair once more. Kerri and Luke settled into the others grouped around the small shared table.

"I'm sorry to have to tell you this," Luke said, "but Mr. Crandall is dead."

Collette stared at Luke. Blinked. "Thank God."

Kerri and Luke exchanged a look. Kerri doubted he was any more surprised than she was. This had been that kind of week—that kind of case.

"Let me explain," Collette said. "My mother and Crandall were married for seven years. She was very much in love with him, and all seemed well until the final year, when they started to argue all the time. Mother apparently caught him"—she cleared her throat—"doing his business to a photo of another woman."

Kerri and Luke shared another look. If this were a game show, they would both have the winning answer to this bizarre turn of events.

"I don't recall her name, but I have a copy of the photo and the report from the private investigator I hired after the accident."

"You hired a PI to look into the accident because . . . ?" Luke inquired.

"Because I was certain he killed my mother."

"Did the police find indications that he purposely wrecked the car?" Kerri asked.

"No. He was far too clever for that. My mother wasn't wearing her seat belt, so she was thrown through the windshield when he went off the road, allegedly to avoid an animal, and hit a tree."

Kerri vividly remembered the photo from the article, and she'd read the accident report.

"Mother always wore her seat belt," Collette reiterated. "Always."

"Did the PI find any evidence to support your theory?" Luke asked.

"He did not, and it has eaten at me all this time." She drew in a deep breath. "You see, according to the coroner, my mother lived for nearly an hour after the accident. She would likely have survived if she'd had swift medical attention. But Crandall was supposedly knocked unconscious in the accident and didn't wake up in time to call for help. Imagine how she suffered during that time. The doctor who treated Crandall insisted his head injury was not substantial enough to have rendered him unconscious for that long." She shuddered. "The idea of him sitting there watching her die will always haunt me."

"Why not just get a divorce," Kerri asked, "if your mother felt he was cheating on her?"

"Mother was talking about it," Collette said. "But she died before she could. Crandall walked away with half her estate."

"Would you like to go for coffee?" Kerri asked. "The cafeteria is closed, but there's an all-night shop across the street."

"That's a good idea," Luke agreed. "There are things you should know."

Everyone deserved closure on this one. Kerri's gaze settled on Luke. Like Lorna Collette, he had waited a long time to know the truth about his haunted past.

The euphoria that had been missing tonight was suddenly there.

This had been a tough week, but there was much to look forward to. Tori was coming home tomorrow.

Kerri studied the man who was carefully and considerately explaining a nightmare to a stranger. Luke Falco was a good cop, a good man, and Kerri loved him.

Her heart thumped hard.

She loved him very much.

40

Sunday, November 28

Noon

Devlin Residence
Twenty-First Avenue South
Birmingham

The cake was perfect.

Kerri smiled as she positioned the decadent dessert in the center of the table. Its creamy white frosting covered rich dark chocolate layers. Strawberries lay in a pile on top.

"That's the last of the balloons."

Kerri looked around. Pink and red and white balloons floated all around the room. Two helium canisters had been required to fill them all.

"Perfect." She smiled at Luke. So very grateful for his presence every minute of every day.

They would be heading to the airport in ten minutes. Tori's flight was on time and would be arriving at one. She had no idea about the surprise homecoming party. Possibly they had gone a little overboard.

Kerri surveyed the streamers they had hung and the posters she and Luke had worked into the wee hours of the morning to make.

It would be good to have her daughter home again. Tonight the whole family was coming over for a big spaghetti dinner, since Tori had missed Thanksgiving at home.

"You ready?"

Kerri turned to Luke. "Absolutely."

The drive to the airport would take only half an hour. Her nerves were jumping with excitement as they climbed into the Wagoneer and headed that way.

"By the way, Brooks called a little while ago."

Kerri glanced at him and started to ask how she had missed the call, but then she remembered she had gone upstairs to change clothes three times. Her daughter wouldn't care what she was wearing, but Kerri wanted to look her best . . . for more than one reason.

"He had an update?" She felt confident it was about O'Grady. Her fingers instinctively tightened on the steering wheel.

"O'Grady confessed to the murder of Mina Kozlov and to six counts of sexual assault."

"That's good news." She swerved a little as she shot him another sideways look. "I'm guessing he managed a deal for the confession." The likelihood of a deal was the only downside. He didn't deserve a deal. Guys like O'Grady were the ones who gave cops a bad name. What he'd done to all those women—and likely countless others—was despicable.

"They took the death penalty off the table, but the next time he sets foot outside the prison walls will be for the purpose of being planted."

She could live with that. She took the exit for the airport and found a place to park, then turned to Luke. "No more talk about work."

Last night they had decided to take a few days off. They needed some time to relax and just be.

"Sounds good to me," he agreed. He reached for the door, then hesitated and fished out his cell phone. "Hey, Shelly, everything okay?"

Kerri bit her lip, hoped nothing was wrong.

"Okay," he said.

Kerri searched his face for some clue of what was going on.

"Just let me know for sure. Good. Thank you, Shelly."

The call ended, and he settled his gaze onto Kerri's. "Liam wants to talk to me again. Shelly wanted to know if we could come over for dinner one evening next week."

Relief rushed through Kerri. "Anytime, yes. That's fantastic."

Luke took a deep breath, let it out. "I gotta tell you, Kerri, I was afraid to even hope he'd ever want to see me again."

"Come on." Kerri opened her door. "Let's get Tori and tell her the good news."

The air was crisp as they walked into the terminal. Kerri did something she hadn't done in public before. She reached for Luke's hand, entwined her fingers with his.

His gaze met hers, and the happiness she saw in his eyes made her want to stop right there and hug him.

Why not?

Her feet stopped moving. He turned to her. "Everything okay?"

"It's better than okay." She reached up, hugged him close. "Thank you," she murmured.

He drew back, a bemused expression on his face. "For what?"

"For being you. And for being the guy who showed me I could fall in love again."

He blinked. "Are you saying—?"

"I love you, Luke."

His arms went around her, and he hugged her so hard she couldn't breathe. "I love you, Kerri Devlin. Thank you for giving me my *whole* life back."

Kerri hadn't meant to cry, but she did all the same. She noticed Luke taking a covert swipe at his eyes as well. She would remember this moment for the rest of her life.

Hand in hand, they made their way through the airport, each step buoyed by sheer happiness. She had so much to tell Tori.

At the security checkpoint, they waited while Tori's flight deplaned. Once they picked up her luggage, they could head home and celebrate. She would be so surprised. The whole thing had actually been Luke's idea. Kerri hadn't even thought about having balloons, streamers, and all the rest.

She spotted her daughter, and all other thought vanished.

Her baby was home. Her heart filled to bursting as her eyes drank in the sight of her. She looked so grown up that Kerri wanted to cry. *Again.*

Tori hurried through the security exit and hugged her mom, then Luke.

"Did you have the best time?" Kerri enthused. She really, really hoped so. She had so much to tell Tori.

"I had a good time," Tori agreed. "But I'm glad to be home."

Kerri slung her arm around her daughter's shoulders. Those words were like music to her ears. On the way to the luggage carousel, Kerri gave Tori the good news about Liam. She was thrilled for Luke. Just another indication of how much Tori adored the man. Luke took a position near the carousel and watched for Tori's bags.

"How's your dad?" Kerri asked.

"He's good." Tori grinned. "He asked about you too."

Kerri threw her head back and laughed. "I'm certain he was only being polite."

Tori hugged her mom again. "It really is good to be back."

The words warmed Kerri's heart. In a week or so life would go back to normal, with Tori all snippy and know it all, as teenagers would be. But for a little bit it would be like old times, before hormones and growth spurts.

Luke grabbed Tori's bags, and they headed out of the terminal.

"Dad seems really happy," Tori said.

For the first time, Kerri was glad to hear it. "That's nice."

"*She* is a better mom than I expected her to be," Tori mentioned, her skepticism showing despite her words.

Tori and Kerri had discussed on several occasions how they couldn't see *her*—the new wife—as mom material. They also never called the new wife by her name. It was always *she* or *her*.

"I'm happy to hear it," Kerri said and meant it. "Every kid should have a good mom."

Tori's face scrunched into one of concern. "Dad asked about you more than once. It was kind of weird. Like he was actually worried."

"Really?" Kerri shook her head, couldn't imagine why he would be worried.

"Yeah." She glanced at Luke and lowered her voice. "He wanted to know if you were happy."

Kerri did a mental eye roll. "Did you tell him that I am very happy?"

Tori nodded. "I did. I told him you were getting married."

"What?" Kerri laughed, glanced at Luke. "Why would you tell him that?"

"I'm not blind," she said in that flippant way only teenagers could pull off. "I know it's only a matter of time. I already told Aunt Diana that I get to be the bridesmaid."

Luke grinned. "You two are already planning our wedding?"

The ever-so-slight tremble in his voice had Kerri's chest tightening.

"Of course." Tori rolled her eyes. "The whole family is talking about it."

Kerri smiled up at the incredible guy she and her entire family had fallen in love with. "Sounds like we need to talk."

Luke held her gaze, his eyes filled with the same happiness she felt. "Definitely," he agreed. "I'm ready whenever you are, *partner*."

She went up on tiptoe and kissed him. He dropped the bags he held, wrapped his arms around her, and kissed her back. She didn't care that they were standing in the exit corridor with dozens of people filtering out of the airport around them. She wanted this kiss to go on and on.

"Can we go home now?" Tori whined.

Their kiss dissolved into laughter, and they drew back. The teenager was back.

Life could go back to normal now.

As normal as life for two homicide detectives ever got, anyway.